John Stolze

**The Wage-Workers of America**

and the relation of capital to labor

John Stolze

**The Wage-Workers of America**
*and the relation of capital to labor*

ISBN/EAN: 9783337237868

Printed in Europe, USA, Canada, Australia, Japan

Cover: Foto ©Andreas Hilbeck / pixelio.de

More available books at **www.hansebooks.com**

Yours Truly
John Stolz, M. D.

# THE
# WAGE-WORKERS OF AMERICA

### AND THE RELATION OF

# CAPITAL TO LABOR.

BY

## JOHN STOLZE, M. D.,

AUTHOR OF "SCIENTIFIC LIVING," "CAUSE AND CURE
OF CRIME," "TREATISE ON THE HUMAN FIVE
SENSES," "MENTAL HYGIENE," ETC.

---

" Now to th' instruction of a humble friend,
Who would himself be better taught, attend ;
Though blind your guide, some precepts yet unknown
He may disclose, which you may make your own."

---

READING PA.:
EAGLE BOOK AND JOB PRINT.                1893.

CHICAGO, ILL.:
COLUMBIA PUBLISHING COMPANY.

# DEDICATORIAL!

*" He is next to the gods, whom reason, and not passion, impels."*—CLAUDIAN.

It may be a mere custom for an author to dedicate his book to some one of great accomplishment, or to a personal friend; but in the present instance, the author is actuated by a sense of humble acknowledgment (hereby) of the character, attainments and enduring friendship of the REV. H. W. THOMAS, D. D., of Chicago, whose life has been devoted to the elevation and emancipation of his fellowman; keeping in view social and political equity, promulgating those principles which make of All-of-Us Neighbors and Brothers; this work is respectfully inscribed by the author.

J. S.

# PREFACE.

*" Friends ! Romans ! Countrymen ! Lend me your ear !"*

The lines we have quoted above form the introduction to Mark Antony's speech in defense of Cæsar, which is an acknowledgment of the fact that the orator harangues in vain unless he secures the attention of his audience. So we ask you, kind reader, to lend us your attention, and give careful perusal to the following pages to which you are hereby introduced. The *wage-interest* of the *wage-earners* of this country and the relation of *capital* to *labor* form the text of our dissertation.

The object of writing this volume was prompted mainly by a desire to assist our fellow-citizens in solving the problem of the *troubled labor question*, which we believe to exist principally in a misconception of the true relation of *capital* to *labor*. Civic disturbances, in the form of *riots* and *lockouts*, are signals, or evidences, to the inquiring mind that there is something wrong somewhere in the administration of the government; for it is certain, peradventure, that so long as the *self-evident rights of man* are respected and maintained by the laws of any country, peace and prosperity will reign supreme, for there will be no need for political reform, and, with this object in view, it will be worth any effort we are *capable of* in aiding to bring about such a condition.

The relation of capital to labor is spoken of as an *unsolved problem*. From the fact, then, that the question is profound and intricate, much deep study and extended research is involved ; still we hope our efforts will be rewarded in finding a correct solution. Agitation keeps the subject before the people. Some of the most profound thinkers of the nation are beginning to search for the primary causes of the many undesirable effects, demonstrated in the form of civic disturbances, which have not only cost millions of dollars, but thereby the lives of many citizens have been sacrificed.

All of us are concerned in finding a proper solution of the so-called *labor trouble*, and, with this object in view, we hope this volume will be a great help, for the best that can be done is to *educate*, and to exchange, one with another, our most *matured thoughts* bearing on this question, that in the near future proper means of correction may be attained to stay any further difficulty.

It is said that all the laboring classes of the civilized world have been, and are, as a body poor.   This is an incorrect statement, for the question arises who are the poor and who are the rich?   Poverty and wealth are at best only relative states or conditions.   When the question is viewed philosophically, it is not proper to make a comparison from the standpoint of ownership, or how much wealth one has, but *conditions*.   One may be miserably poor and have plenty of money. Our object, however, is not to champion the cause of the poor with a view of making everybody rich, or to make the rich richer, or to take from them what by right belongs to them ; but what we contend for is *justice*, that all men may have an equal chance under the law of the land to acquire a competency, the same right that nature gives to every man.

The *abolition* of favoritism, trusts, monopolies ; to bring capital on an equal footing with labor, that both may make a legitimate profit, and arrest any further unprofitable means of correcting disputes, *is our aim.*

But little has been written or said by the representatives of the medical profession, and we believe that one who has studied *man*, physically and mentally, and the effects of environment on his health and welfare in general, *is* especially qualified to treat the subject in hand, and thus bring forward the best thoughts from that source.

Personally we have no grievances, neither have we a new and fanciful theory to offer, but shall follow *datas* well-founded in the fundamental elements of good government.   We furnish no special index, for the book should be *read consecutively* in order to be fully appreciated, and by so doing we feel assured that our object will be attained.

     *Respectfully your fellow-citizen,*

                              THE AUTHOR.

# THE WAGE-WORKERS OF AMERICA.

*The Relation of Capital to Labor; Logical Points Regarding the Problem of the Labor Troubles Now More or Less Agitated by the People of the United States; Labor Unions vs. Capital; The Right and Wrong Side; Where the Means of Correction May be Found; The Working Classes and Capital; Happy Homes at Last for All Who Will Study the Subject; The Wise Statesman; The Man Who Has a Head and also a Heart, Etc., Etc.*

If a man *is* in harmony with what surrounds him here,
No power *can* enslave him, no matter what be his sphere.

**The Labor Trouble.** Doubtless there exists at the present time a greater antagonism between capital and labor in this country than was ever known since the Declaration of Independence. The main reason may be assigned to the fact that the people are more wide-awake to their own personal interests; or, perhaps, that the spirit of *money-making* has taken possession of them, and, hence, a greater strife for supremacy has been brought about by various causes. We would mention, first, the rapid growth of the nation—not alone in population, but in wealth, in power, in enterprise, in commerce—so that, notwithstanding its being still a young republic, it is already leading the nations of the earth. This has created a national pride, and every true American citizen feels proud of the country he lives in. Second, the success of American enterprise and commercial supremacy, already being felt in every land, has created such a *potential momentum* in the direction of gaining more and more of the same glory which has been attained in the past (and no one can at this time predict, with a certainty, the limit which may be reached), that, to a very great degree, the individual citizen has caught the same spirit—that is, to accumulate, to gain wealth, to be rich.

**Limits of Right.** Primarily and naturally nations and individuals have a right to use every means, within the limits of *right*, to gain in power and wealth—to get all they can, all they want, and, particularly, all they *need*. But there is a limit; and this limit, both legally and morally speaking, is the great problem to exemplify and plainly outline its safe boundaries, so all peoples can see where to pause and not trespass on nature's reservation.

The idea of right implies a limit or boundary. Personal liberty is a principle based on *inalienable rights* and pursuits, as one's own inclinations or conscience may dictate ; there is a limit in unbounded freedom. The same, however, is true of the restrictions placed upon man in regard to indulgences in partaking of food or drink, or in many other methods or habits of living ; in exercise, labor, rest ; in acquiring possessions, in traffic and many almost innumerable relationships of man's surroundings where nature prescribes certain limitations which circumscribes his liberty.

Physiological and moral limits, however, do not enslave mankind, but, on the other hand, by obedience to these limitations the perfect enjoyment of freedom is the reward. Man is never more free than when his conduct is within the boundaries of right. The moment these boundaries are ignored, either by laws enacted or by individual citizens, ignorantly or wilfully, straightway a condition of slavery is incurred and man is no longer free. Now comes the law of responsibility, which holds a charge against him, and which must be liquidated before perfect freedom can be enjoyed.

This perfect freedom is misunderstood or misinterpreted by many in this country, who take license, or, in plainer words, "take the law into their own hands," and think their natural rights are invaded when they encounter restrictions, which, if they understood their "inalienable rights," as prescribed by the Declaration of Independence of the United States, would make them grateful for the limitations therein. The moment these principles are violated that freedom becomes a state of servility, a charge, a responsibility, and freedom of conduct becomes a subject of legal regulation.

**Inharmony.** The greed and avarice of mankind, individuals and nations, often carried beyond nature's limitation, and infringing on natural rights, has been, and is now, the primeval factor in bringing about strife and discord, which, if not checked, may bring on ruin as the final result.

That there does exist a spirit of antagonism between capital and labor in this country cannot be denied, when the many strikes and revolts, culminating, in some instances, in actual insurrection, have, during the past decade, too fully demonstrated this fact. These are symptoms of a deranged state of the *body politic*, and to find and prescribe some radical cure for this ailment is the sacred *mission work* of the present generation. If not attended to in time absolute destruction will follow, and those who have now the power to avert this catastrophe will bitterly regret their negligence when it is too late to arrest it.

It is not a matter of pleasant contemplation for the people of our great country to entertain the idea that not all is peace and happy harmoniousness in the land.

**The Conflict.** The actual warfare between capital and labor, gradually inaugurated, for obvious reasons is not reconcilable with the plea that we are in advance of other nations, or that we have a republican form of government, with a constitution recognizing the "natural rights" of all men, whatever they may be—rich or poor, wage-worker or capitalist.

The very fact that a conflict *is* waged, by whomsoever it may be, arising from disagreements between the wage-workers and those who control capital, in a country whose fundamental principles of government vouchsafe peace and plenty to every household, suggests an honest and thorough investigation of the *cause* of the grievances ; and, if possible, to find proper means by which to stay any further disturbance.

**Not One-Sided.** The factors which lead to disputes, claims of wrongs, imaginary or real, do not, in fact cannot, arise from *one side* alone. As the saying goes, "there are two sides to a question." Mistakes are, as a rule, easily made, more easily *made* than *corrected*. Doubtless those in control of capital cannot be pronounced free from blame, or, in other words, *faultless*, and charge all the blame to the wage-workers, and, forsooth, *vice versa*.

This now opens the question, and we invite our reader to proceed with us to examine some of the principles relating to *capital* and *labor*, for these are the factors that enter into the main make-up of the "*labor question*," to be settled by the American people in the near future.

**A Co-operative Body.** A short story may be of interest and may help us to reach a correct basis or point of observation, from which to sally forth in search of the truth bearing on the question under consideration.

We were honored not long ago by a visit from our old friend, Dr. Isaac H. Stearns, an old veteran surgeon of the late war, and in conversation on various topics the labor question was broached, and we were pleased with his remarks—though metaphorically spoken—but fully embodying the truth, and that is what we want. The doctor is widely known for good, sound judgment in matters appertaining to statesmanship. To the question we propounded he said : "The natural relation of capital and labor may be likened to the human body. It has a head and it has hands. Then there is a vital system. The head thinks and commands and the hands execute and labor. Work exhausts the body. The head, hands and all parts *wear* more or less by the business of life. The vital system supplies nourish-

ment by digesting food and thus prepares it for the builder's
use in all parts of the body. The hands work and gather
food for the vital system to sustain the head and also give
to the hands a proper quota for subsistence. Through the
sympathetic system of nerves all parts of the entire body
enjoy the *good* in common with the head, and also partake
each its share of suffering." This sympathy of one part
with another he compared to that human nature with which
all human beings are endowed, and which gives birth to the
common law of humanity. The hands then may labor hard
yet come in for their share of enjoyment, when we enjoy
the good things the hands provided for us—a sort of co-
operative *plant*, where the head (*capital*) divides with the
hands (*the wage-worker*). "Thus," he said, "the capital,
which we will call the *head*, cannot, after all, get on very
well without the hands and other expert workers which constitute the body—one grand system of reciprocal operation,
where the slightest inharmoniousness will shock the entire
economy of the whole body." So let us remember that the
head and hands cannot well be separated and continue that
harmony necessary to a perfect existence.

**Push and Enterprise.** It might be profitable to tarry
here a moment longer and say that
the trouble popularly denominated the "*labor trouble*" in
this country largely arises from a simple *misunderstanding*
of the true relation of "*capital to labor*."

Capital *alone* is inoperative without the help of labor.
The same is true, to some degree, of labor. Yet labor *can*
get on somehow without capital. However, in a country
like ours, with as much push and enterprise, which will, in
this particular, give the nineteenth century a place in the
world's history as an epoch of remarkable activity, we cannot well afford to abolish capital and thus clog the wheels
of progress.

**Looking Forward.** Capital is here, labor is here, and
our business is to harmonize the two,
and in some way put and end for all time, in this country,

to any further violence or carnal strife among men, looking
also toward means of a humane way of settling disputes
that may arise between labor and capital in localities or
those of a national bearing.    If, as a civilized and honorable
people, we want to be recognized by the nations of the world,
we cannot afford to have many repetitions of the so-called
"Homestead troubles," recently perpetrated, or the "Idaho
troubles," or the "Coal Creek troubles" of Tennessee, or
the "Pittsburg riots," of some years since, and others, or
many of lesser magnitude, which threatened us with civil
war.    If not the latter, gradually run along until finally the
country fills up with a pauper element, almost as disgraceful to a nation as civil war itself.

**Unwilling to Give Up.**  All this can readily be obviated
by wise statesmanship.   We are
unwilling to give up, and say that it *cannot* be done.    Let
us make this assertion, for the first time in these pages, that
a correct civil government, based on the laws of nature, the
unwritten law of humanity, and the proper and absolute en-
forcement of the laws so framed, will pilot the ship of state
clear of breakers, of riots, insurrections and pauperism.

These are only symptoms of a coming calamity awaiting
our beloved country, and wise heads, and heads *with a heart*,
can *now* so treat the difficulty that in a few years we shall
have passed the danger point altogether.    In this laudable
work labor and capital are equally interested and must co-
operate in order to succeed.

**Capital.**  A man may have a good business, he may have
much money invested in his business, and yet he
is not a capitalist in the strict sense of the term.    Any
amount of money invested is capital—capital stock, goods,
chattels of whatever denomination.    Real estate is capital.
A tradesman represents capital, for his *labor* is his *capital*,
which brings him a profit, and it *should* bring him a profit
every day that his labor is invested, the same as when
*money* is invested.    Money represents labor.    It takes labor
to make money.    The same may be said of money—that it

"takes money to make money." But there *is* money that does not represent labor.

**The Capitalist.** The person who has control of money that does not represent labor is a capitalist. A person who is the owner of a competency, that is, one who is independent, whose income is assured, covering all possible exigencies of want, living at ease, and, if desired, can enjoy the luxuries of life without drawing on his reserved capital ; such may properly be denominated as wealthy or rich. But now if this same person has money besides and has it invested in a manner that it is constantly accumulating, at a greater or lesser per cent., beyond what may be necessary to maintain a reasonable expenditure of living, then such may be called a capitalist.

This kind of capital does not represent labor, and it is on **The Socialist Affirms.** this point the Socialist affirms that all such capital, by the law of right, belongs to the people, and should be divided among them. What is called a dividend in the language of a stock company, which makes an annual *pro rata* division of its profits among those who own the stock, so a dividend should be declared by the capitalists of the whole country for the benefit of the people. Of course, the radical Socialist goes further than this and foolishly thinks, and argues his claims with more energy than wisdom, that no one has a right to be rich, to say nothing of the capitalist—that all men should be equal in their possessions of the things of this world.

What shall we then say regarding the capitalists? The best that can be said, and which our philosophy logically leads us to determine, is that nothing can be taken from a person that by right and law belongs to him.

**What Can be Done?** But this much we say, that the philosophy of good government regulates everything wisely, even the capitalist, so no one can be injured, for the capitalist has his place in society, and in the natural order of things the same as in everything else, and can be as easily reconciled as a part of the whole structure of the *body politic* as a laborer, and the one who has no more than his labor can readily find *his* place and part of the whole.

Who would build our railroads, our bridges, our great works of art if everybody simply made a living and did not in some way accumulate something more, with which they would be enabled to venture into an enterprise where money is needed as well as labor? Some one from the excess of profits, accruing from speculation, builds a beautiful monument, or mausoleum, which at once becomes a pleasing ornament to a city or landscape view in a cemetery. Another has the money to build some grand castle on an elevation overlooking a city. He calls it his residence.

**A Pleasing Effect.** This gives work to the man who wants it and needs it. If everybody built a ten-story house the sameness would destroy the picture ; or, if everyone built a one-story cottage the undesirable effect would be the same. The pleasing effect is the product in the very fact that not all people can have things alike, for want of equal means, equal abilities and the law of variation is obeyed in this as in other matters. If all peoples could accumulate no more of this world's goods than sufficient simply to keep the wolf from the door, who, then, would interest themselves in landscape gardening and build fine mansions, always enjoyable to the passer who has studied art, or whose soul admires the beautiful, in art or in nature?

Equality, therefore, is impossible, since differentiation is a law of nature. If possessions of property, or ownership of much or little, makes a social difference, creates caste, so to speak, then this is an evidence that the culture or education of such people has been wofully neglected, or at least has been misdirected.

**The Monument.** A monument is to be erected in memory of some distinguished person. This is done, not alone in honor of the person who has won great distinction in the service of humanity, but by this public recognition the deed is remembered, and future generations are thereby stimulated to live for some purpose, to do something by which they will be remembered.

The wage-worker alone, or the ordinary laborer, cannot accomplish (in these matters of public art and embellishing our environment) what may be done by the help of the capitalist. A monument costing fifty or a hundred thousand dollars can be built by fifty or a hundred thousand people, but if ten, a hundred, or a thousand capitalists contribute from the profits of money invested (money at work), they did not have to work for, will the man who earns but a few dollars a day object to such an enterprise?

**A Noble Gift.** We will only state one instance in point and allow our readers to draw their own conclusions. A syndicate of Chicago some years ago invested its capital in street railways, which yielded great profit. The capital thus invested became immensely great, but, as we have elsewhere stated in this work, that capital in the hands of a philanthropist need not be feared, for it may be of great help to the progress of science and do many kind and noble deeds that go down into history as an honor to the race.

Recently this same syndicate gave to the Chicago University enough money, conditional, to build the finest, the best and largest telescope in the world. This will be among the wonders of the world. This telescope is to be constructed irrespective of cost. It will cost at a low estimate a round half million dollars. Here we have an exemplification of one of nature's means or ways of making progress in the arts and sciences, which, if a hundred thousand people were called on to contribute each a *pro rata* share to make up the required sum, ninety-nine thousand, nine hundred and ninety-nine would have objected to so foolish an undertaking.

**An Honest Penny.** No, a man has a right to be frugal, economical and wise in the management of his vocation or business, turning an honest penny as often as it is possible. There are philosophic and moral principles which form a natural basis for *honest traffic* and competition in trade, governing the efforts of mankind in acquiring property or wealth. In this all have equal rights. If it were not so law and order would take on the form of discord, and discord is not a law of nature; strife for supremacy would be lowered to brutal force, and civilization again take on the primeval state—the uncivilized.

All combinations of power, or corporations, *using capital* unwarranted by the highest idea of right; all *labor unions*, or orders of whatsoever name or nature, should carefully study the limits of the natural rights of man, that they may *reform, form* and *conform* to the highest principle of *good government*, or discord, revolts, trouble of almost every shade and degree will arise among the people, who otherwise might be happy as one family.

It is given to man to do the best he can within the boundaries of right; license which may carry him beyond this will be contracting a debt, and debt is a mortgage on a man's liberty. In the short run of three score years and ten, or however more it may be, life is too short to go into debt very much; debt enslaves, and we cannot afford to live a life of slavery when freedom can so easily be won, for we are free when we are in harmony with our environment.

### DEFINITION AND CLASSIFICATION.

**Working Classes.** In the ordinary and popular sense the laboring classes are those who perform manual labor. This, however, is not strictly a correct definition, for all people who are not able to live without work are laborers in the strict sense of the term. For convenience we will classify or divide them into *common* labor, *expert* labor, *professional, business* and *commercial* labor. Then, again, labor may simply be performed from physiological necessity, which, properly expressed, comes under the head of exercise, or sport; for labor, when it does not produce a profit, in the sense of earning something, comes under the head of sport, or simply exercise. Then, when labor is productive, when it is performed to conduct and sustain the business of living, all such comes under the head of *work*.

**Work.** However often we may use the word *labor* when we mean work, for either term is commonly understood to mean work; still there is a proper difference and should be so understood generally—that work always *produces*, earns something, while so-called labor does not. When we say *capital works* we do not mean that it labors; or, when a man works we understand that he is earning or producing something, but it is not always so when he labors.

**Work is Honorable.** All work is said to be honorable in America, where the *line* of birth, or blood, or caste, or honor, is not distinguished by possessions or riches, but *is* almost entirely obliterated. Yet we have those among us who are obliged to perform menial labor, servant work, and come under the head of common labor, or *unskilled work*, whether performed as attendants or helpers in our shops, fields or in our kitchens, and this class demands passing notice, for they are here and must receive courteous attention in the study of the "labor question," as much so as those who occupy a higher plane in society.

If the reader belongs to the common working class, and if you do not like your station, our advice to you is to strike out. Study, read books, learn a trade; in some way fit yourself for some particular vocation, like Andrew Johnson, General Grant, Lincoln, Garfield and a thousand others, who rose from the plane you now occupy, and everybody can, who will, rise in grade or degree of work to a more exalted position in the world. But you must not wait until some one lifts you up; you must go to work and lift yourself; you must try and control circumstances. True merit, with "clear grit" to back it up, will soon be in demand for a higher position, and you will think better of yourself and you will have a more exalted opinion of your fellow-man. Those people, as a rule, who occupy a menial station in society, have a very poor opinion of mankind generally,

unless they are too obtuse to be conscious of the plane they
occupy. As an artisan the only way you can rise to a
higher position among the working classes is by skill,
personal accomplishments, a cultured mind, in a word, become master of your business, and capital, as powerful and
arrogant a thing as it is, will make its obeisance to you, and
you are what nature intends you should be, *a free man.*

**A Large Majority.** The working classes include a very
large majority of the population of
this country. There are comparatively few people who do
not, in some way, have to work. The common workers,
performing *manual labor (der Allgemein Tagelœhner)*, are
small in number when compared with the masses of workers who conduct business, *farm work*, and the expert or
skilled workers, all of whom at once rise above servant work
by reason of their vocation, which requires study, experience and training.

This elevates you above the common workman, not in a
social sense, but as compared in skill, and this always has
and always will command better pay. The time it takes to
prepare yourself for the position must be rewarded, and is
by common consent. Of skilled labor we will have occasion
to say more. Also the sociological influence of vocation on
character and the growing depreciation, in more ways than
one, of *skilled labor.*

**The Wage-Workers.** Then all who work for daily
wages, or all who have stipulated
salaries, are properly called *wage-workers*, or *wage-earners*.
This class constitutes a large proportion of the population
of America.

It is a fact that there are over forty-one millions of wage-
earners in this country at the present time, and hence it can
readily be seen that, since there is so large a number of
people in excess of those who do not work for wages, it will
require able statesmanship to regulate by law and to correct
the present status between *capital* and *labor*, so that all people are justly dealt with—that is, that all receive their just

I. HOLDEN STEARNS, M. D.

Plate I—For sketch see page 218.

dues and thus avoid all possible grievances and fulfill the mission of the law. Then there are something over twelve millions of people in this country who belong to the *working class* who do not perform hired labor, but carry on business, or occupations for themselves, and hence are not, properly speaking, *wage-earners.*

**Business Men.** Many of our most substantial business men are those who work (occupation) in connection with their own capital. They invest what money they have and work as well as manage their own business. They may hire what labor they may require, carry on business in a legitimate manner and may be classed with the working classes, but are not *wage-earners.*

A young man learns a trade; for a number of years he is a wage-worker. If he is what every young man should be he will save a little money. In the course of time he contemplates matrimony. He marries, and with his wife they manage to lay aside some of the profits of his labor. Mayhap in a few years a small legacy falls to them. Being a master of his business he starts on his own accord, and not ashamed to work, he manages his own business and labors with his own hands. The wife takes care of the household equally as well and in a few years they possess a competency. These are our most substantial business men. Give them half a chance and they will make life a success.*

In many instances they work harder than any of those they hire. They have to plan and perform great mental work, as well as to work with their own hands. As a rule, when the day's work is done, ordinarily, the wage-earner has no further interest in the business of the man or company for whom he works, more than to put in the day, while those who pay him his hire carry all responsibility, meet all expenses, study the markets, solicit patronage, figure profits and adjust losses. These are the hardest-worked people we have, and the ordinary wage-earner has scarcely an idea,

*This subject is more fully treated in another part of this book under the head of " Competition."

and cares less, about these matters, and many times, according to our own observation, business has been greatly hampered by *labor unions*, who imagine they have been, or are, injured by a slight reduction in wages, when, in fact, the market, and perhaps competition, caused a reduction of profits, so that something had to be done to keep the concern from becoming insolvent. These are matters for the wage-earners to study well and confer with their employer, and the employer should be willing to meet his working people and use every rational means to come to a proper understanding before any rash course is taken by either the employer or the employed, for they are as one after all, and are equally interested in the success of the business of the establishment or factory.

**Adventure Speculators.** Then we have those among us who invest capital merely as a speculation, and who come under the head of *adventurers* in business. This class of business men strain every nerve, stretch their conscience to any extent, to "make their pile," as they say. They care very little for the welfare of their employees, either morally, legally or bodily. They work their people on the *cart-horse* principle, the *chief end* of which is money. It is this class of capitalists who seek for monopoly, to form trusts, pools, and never stop to inquire into the question of right. The people are at their mercy. These institutions make money in two ways. One is by controlling prices—controlling the market. Another way they have is to reduce and keep down the wages of their employees at all hazards, right or wrong, and it is through the instigation of concerns of this order that trouble comes; strikes, disagreements, just grievances, which at once become a matter for legal arbitration and legal regulation, in order that justice is done to the general public, as well as the wage-earners, who come under the lash of capital operated by a spirit of imperialism—which has no respect for humanity other than to fill their own coffers at the expense of all who have any dealings with them.

This kind of corporations or business concerns are often short-lived, for there is but one other way by which they can make *big money*, and this is to go into a state of liquidation at the first opportunity, when it will pay to *wind up* on a basis of *low assets* and large indebtedness.

It is our intention, as far as practical, to make research into the cause of the so-called *labor trouble*, to the end that the management of the same may be entirely under our control. We hope, also, to be fully able, as we progress in our investigations, to elucidate and give good **reasons** for a state of society as described, in one sentence, **by a** representative of New York. He says:

" Within the last decade we have seen tremendous strikes and lock-outs among the railroad men, the miners, the iron-workers, the telegraph operators, the dock laborers, the building trades, etc., all indicating to the student of social relations the growing unrest of the working masses in this country, all emphasizing the fact that our *free political* institutions—if free they are—have not as yet secured to the toiling millions that happiness, the pursuit of which is guaranteed to them as a sacred and inalienable right."

DISCOVERIES ; NECESSITIES ; DEMAND FOR CAPITAL ; FOR TRADESMEN ; FOR SKILLED LABOR ; RUSH OF BUSINESS ; AN AGE OF ELECTRIC COMMERCE, ETC., ETC.

**Discovery.** Progress is the spirit of the age. Improvement is the order of the day. No sooner is a new discovery made than straightway some one makes an improvement and leads off. Discovery, called inventions,[*] gave birth to a vast system of *industrial art*. Half a century ago it was barely possible for friends to visit each other at a distance. Now, by means of railroads, inter-communicating with every city, county and precinct, we have become a nation of travelers. Formerly moving of freight was accomplished by the slow horse cart or ox team, and here we

---

[*]We say so-called inventions, for though popularly accepted as being correctly spoken, we deny its correctness, for an invention would be a creation, when it is nothing more than a discovery, the principle of which existed, only man had not discovered it, and hence all so-called inventions are, properly speaking, discoveries.

can readily see that there was no demand for capital in
founding large manufacturing institutions for the purpose
of building railroad machinery, for the very best reason that
the idea of a railroad had not yet taken material form; the
genius of the *inventor* was yet asleep.

The tallow dip has been grandly superseded by the discovery of principles and machinery in utilizing electricity,
which almost has turned night into day. Millions of capital came into demand to manufacture electric supplies. A
new avenue for skilled artisans to exercise their constructive faculty and thus acquire a new source of subsistence.

**Labor Lightened.** Discovery has lightened labor in a
thousand and more ways. Husbandry
is no longer a synonym for the drudgery and *toilsome labor*
of the farm. The sickle is now preserved along with the
spinning wheel of our grandmothers as a relic of antiquity,
when the world was yet in darkness. A man would reap
from one-half to an acre of wheat in a day; now a good
reaper (machine) will accomplish the work of twenty men.
In those days it took all of a woman's time to run one
spindle—that is, when she spun she could do no more than
attend one spindle or spinning-wheel. Now, in our cotton
factories, one woman can attend to several hundred, turning
out more work than one hundred women could do before the
"invention" of the spinning-jenny, and so it is in every
branch of industry from one end of the land to the other.

The expeditious manner in which everything is done at
this age of activity and enterprise now enables nearly everybody to take a short vacation and visit some summer or
winter resort by the sea, or other places of interest, in different climates, without interrupting their business very much,
and at comparatively small expense, and thus widening
local, financial and social interests, until the great American institutions, States and communities have become as
one neighborhood, and as one family—the people. Now a
man or woman thinks it no very great undertaking to attend
a convention or some conclave five hundred or five thousand

miles away, while not many years ago an errand on business or a visit to friends thirty or fifty miles away caused the family much worriment until a safe return was made.

**Uneasy People.** This wonderfully uneasy and enterprising disposition of our people, urged on by discovery, has given rise, and is still at work, to many manufactories of almost every description, for which there was no demand half a century ago. Extensive mining operations have been inaugurated in iron, lead, copper, coal, silver, gold, etc., giving employment to thousands of people, as well as to the employment of capital, for which there was no demand before *necessity* called it into use. All these various conditions of the rapidly-growing social and industrial systems was created as the legitimate outcome of constant improvements and openings made by discoveries ; new channels for the exercise of man's capabilities in widening industrial resources.

The agricultural worker, whose place was taken by machinery on the farm, has been called into work-shops and vocations of mechanical industry, by which transformation and radical change of the entire social system within the last half century, as a natural sequence has produced a world of wage-earners, and rationally viewing the subject a different system of government, to a great degree, to meet the exigencies of the times, is called for, and must wisely follow, or rather should lead, the star of enterprise and progress.

**Like Thousands of Others.** To exemplify let us think of telegraphy. Before the discovery of utilizing electricity as a means of communicating one part of the world with another, telegraph operators were not in demand. Now this has become a profession. The business of telegraphy is an art of a high order and should be classed with the learned professions. He is, however, a wage-earner, and so are thousands of others who are *high up* in their special line of mechanical art and science. Each in his specialty, for which nature and training have been fitting him from the common workman, or helper, requiring no particular skill or training, up to the expert, who requires years' of hard study to enable him to take a position as a metallurgist, as an electrician, or a thousand other places commanding now in the industrial art, so-called *expert labor*, and however high up in ability or accomplishment in the arts and science of the various occupations, if wages or salary is paid then they are wage-earners, and this applies to all conditions of life, men and women, who do not conduct business for themselves. This latter class may all be working people, but they are not to be classed with those who are employed and receive a stipulated salary or wages.

Having now, though briefly, stated enough to interest our reader, we trust to begin to study, or think further, on the great factor which has filled our country with an element not existing at all fifty years, or even twenty-five, years ago. Comparatively considered a small amount of capital was then invested in manufactories. There was no demand for it. Nearly two-thirds of the population of the United States may be denominated wage-earners, and hence we can readily see, when the subject is fully analyzed, how difficult it is to grapple with the great problem of the philosophic and sociological bearings of capital and labor and reach a correct solution.

**Man's Social Nature.** Besides the inducement of good earnings in occupations there are two other factors that go far in bringing people to locate in cities and enter professions and vocations as artisans. The first we would mention is man's *social nature*, which is more easily satisfied in channels of industry that associates them with their fellow-man more closely in cities, and shops or factories, than is possible in rural life. Then those people who are largely endowed with the social nature seek society, and hence are readily attracted by the glittering promises of a city life.

This is especially true of the young and the rising generation, whose nervous system easily partakes of the excitement and push of the present age, which may be properly looked upon as the *age of electricity*. However, when they get through and reach the years of sober thought, and when they have made the experiment in their search for happiness in the gayer circles of society, they long for a home in the country, and regret that they ever left the business and art of "tilling the ground," where nature is always kind to man, especially to those who make her close acquaintance.

**Relief of Obligations.** It is easier to work for wages than to carry on business; you do not have to think much, only perhaps to study your special work; you do not have to look after the wherewith, and thus the obligations of life are much lightened, and that which will interest them most is to get big wages and put in the time. This is a *growing evil* among the people, namely, a disposition to shift obligations on to some one else, to shirk responsibilities; this is an important consideration with the wage-workers, and is right within a proper limit. This is a study for the wage-earner in order that his hours of hard labor may not rob him of his health, for health is his wealth and comes within the perview of self-protection, for if he does not look after his own welfare who will?* But as we have said that it is a growing evil to shift responsibility too much, for by assuming willingly the obligations of life the mind is strengthened and is one of nature's means of mental evolution. The object of short hours, no obligations and big pay alone is not the proper aim of life, for doubtless this spirit on the part of the wage-earners has brought about a condition that has widened the natural relation of capital to labor so that the result is already being felt.

In the next place we would mention that the social nature being satisfied with city life, and hope of big earnings, it is further argued that there are greater advantages in getting an education and acquiring personal accomplishments, impossible to be obtained in the country. Now this all may be

---

*The subject of long hours is fully treated under the head of " Physiological Limitations."

true, especially since the farmer yields these points and un-
derrates his social standing and place in society. The time
will, however, come in this country when it will be just the
reverse. One thing is certain : that nature has reserved
the American continent as a field for development of the
agricultural science, or the art of husbandry. We never
can become a manufacturing nation more than what we need
ourselves. To aspire to export manufactured goods and
become a nation of factories is an ambition in the wrong
direction.

**The Soil and Climate**. Political campaigns are greatly
enthused with the idea of Ameri-
can industry, looking towards going into the markets of the
world and competing with other nations. Our agricultural
product is that which will lead all other nations of the
world. We have the soil, the climates and every natural
resource to not only grow all kinds of fruit and cereals that
we need, but can furnish more than half the world with
wheat and corn and other products that we can export, and
hence we predict that, as by the many new discoveries and
the openings made for the artisans to exercise their various
inventive and constructive faculties, and for other reasons
we have mentioned, a large army of wage-earners have been
created and cities filled up with them—the time is not long
in the future when there will be an exodus back to rural
life again, and when the farm will furnish sufficient interest to exercise all the artistic faculties of man's nature.
The social institution as well as the technics will all look to
the agricultural art as the leading and highest branch of
all the commercial and industrial traffic.

**Misunderstanding**. Strikes and lockouts are evils resulting from a misunderstanding,
more than any other cause, of the true relation capital and
labor sustain to each other. The idea of co-operative work
is beautifully exemplified by the work done in the human
body, which we presented in what we called a "little story"
in previous pages. Let us now draw another lesson from

EDWARD EVANS.

Plate II–For sketch see page 218.

nature, and we know no better source for correct similitudes than the great book of nature, and the nearer we keep to her, not alone in our every-day life, but in framing our laws and organizing all social institutions, the better it will be for us and the more happy and successful will we be in our undertakings. This time we will draw our analogy from natural science, which will at least arouse a more careful study of the subject, if it is not entirely convincing.

**Lever Power.** Capital and labor, as society is thereby effected, or in the social and commercial sense, may be likened to leverage in mechanics. Lever power is a compound of two inseparable principles. That is, the *lever and fulcrum*. But the moment you separate them you have neither. The lever is no more: the fulcrum is also gone. The moment, however, the two are joined in proper relation you have power, or force, and this also at once becomes operative and can be made to do work. The longer the lever and the nearer the fulcrum to the point of leverage the greater will be the power. The farther they are separated, that is the fulcrum from the leverage, the less will be the force or power. It was Archimedes who said if he could find a proper fulcrum he could construct a leverage to raise the earth. One thing is certain, that these principles in physical science are the most powerful which enter into the mechanism of all machinery known to man.

Now let us call capital the lever and labor the fulcrum, or *vice versa*, if you please; and as in the leverage power they are inseparable principles if they are to be operated in doing work. Separate them and we have neither. Capital is only such when it is in active relation with labor, otherwise there is no capital. The same is true of labor, or work—it is only such when it does something, and when co-operating in conjunction with capital. This is the leverage that moves the world and is the end and beginning of commerce. Now, then, the further you remove these two factors in commercial science from each other the less operative they are and the less force we have.

Unity of principles, in their reciprocal relation, if properly understood become a great help in whatever is to be accomplished. The greatest facility is afforded us by a combined effort of the people in bringing about social reform, or enacting laws which are intended to protect the citizen in all that is essential to the perfect enjoyment of natural rights. As we look about us the idea of reciprocal activity and existence meets us everywhere, and it may be profitable for us to extend our thoughts and notice another striking exemplification of the fact that in unity there is strength.

**Like a Network.** The general law of *correlation*, which is, perhaps, the most universal of all ultimate principles by which everything is governed in its relation to everything else, will apply to governments, peoples, social institutions, the family or the individual.

Every existing thing derives its power, its means of existence and keeping *whole* all of its attributes of individuality from its environment. So in turn it supports some other existence, and so on throughout all the various realms of matter, and the same rule holds good among the gases, the imponderable forces, as also the life-giving elements. Oxygen, in its union with hydro-carbon, gives rise to motion, and wherever motion exists heat is a product, and this becomes at the same time an exponent of force, and nature's workshop is in full operation. Organization, life, electricity, disorganization, metamorphosing, correlation, and conservation, are conditions and principles of rulings and of power that bind *all* together into one grand whole, though made up of many parts. Perfect reciprocal operation governs the whole. Harmony, then, in all relations of existence of our environment, from which we may learn what laws or rulings human beings may best enact to succeed in all social and commercial relations, which, when the whole subject is canvassed, we will find that no one can live alone —that is, no one all by himself. We need each other. The tiller of the ground, the machinist, the scholar, the statesman—all, whatever position may be occupied in the various social institutions of the great *body politic*, are interwoven into one common interest, under the law of correlation, which not only binds together the earth, but puts its arms around man and thus makes him a part of the whole.*

Capital cannot get away from labor, neither can labor get away from capital. The moment either seeks to become

**The Law of Correlation**.

separated a hitch will occur, and if not checked in its first stages serious trouble may result. Whatever the vocation may be naturally each take their respective place in the make-up of the general public. The whole people are in sympathy with all the various divisions and grades of the wage-workers, business men and capitalists. *All* together form a network and interblends, one supporting the other, and one is as important as the other in the make-up of our national commerce, as well as the business of local communities.

Having now succeeded, as we believe we have, in finding and elucidating clearly the proper relation of capital to labor, and also in reaching a correct understanding of ultimate elements, or principles, which together bring before our mind the *normal conditions* of man's relations, all of which, if carried out practically and lived up to, would do away with all quibbles and quarrels which now arise between capital and labor, it now becomes our lot to make further inquiry into at least some of the causes which lead to

ABNORMAL CONDITIONS,

And which have brought about violations of cardinal prin-

* We quote the following from the writings of the greatest law-giver and moralist ancient Rome ever had, if not the world. *Marcus Aurelius Antonius*, a Roman emperor who recognized these principles as early as the second century of the Christian era : "In the series of things those which follow are always aptly fitted to those which have gone before ; for this series is not like a mere enumeration of disjointed things, which have only a necessary sequence, but it is a rational connection ; and as all existing things are arranged together harmoniously so the things which come into existence exhibit no mere succession, but a certain wonderful relationship."

ciples of *good statesmanship* and the normal relation of capital to labor, the result of which has so unbalanced the distribution of *profits* that in so short a time as the last decade alone it is apparent that "the rich have become richer and the poor poorer." If this is so, and statistics seem to show that it is, then we all can easily see in advance where we will land if these *conditions* are allowed to continue.

To avert serious results and "call a stop," so to speak, to the rapidly accumulating power for evil, the *Press*, of Philadelphia, Pa., in an editorial on the labor question, said : " *There is need of a large, broad work of honest education in first principles.*" This is good doctrine and if universally carried out the *nation will be saved.* The people once being fully awakened to a full realization of *danger ahead* some attention may be given to a more active promulgation of "first principles." But may this not bring us too near to the *golden rule*, which we fear would be rather hard to enforce? However, we must not speak ironically when we are dealing with so serious a subject as the one in hand. Moreover we would impress on the minds of all that laws which cannot be enforced had better not be enacted until proper education will bring about a condition of society that a majority can be assured to support the law so that it can be enforced.

**Not Complimentary.** The causes of disturbance among the people may be traced to those *remote* and those more *immediate* in character, and in either case we find that it is not very complimentary to a civilized and intelligent people, for it is true that for nearly a century these causes have been at work and to some extent have been recognized and not corrected. It is admitted that efforts have been made to reform society, repeal those laws which were not in harmony and enact such that are in accordance with "first principles," but the various political parties have in their *demagogic haranguings* so hampered true reform, in this direction, that, comparatively considered, the work of the people in popular education in the true principles of good government has proven almost an entire failure.

We have now reached a point in our investigation which makes it imperative that we *delve deeper*, in order to be better prepared to stake out a *high road*, which will clear the snags and breakers of social discord. Furthermore, it is incumbent on us that we search most diligently for the various causes which have brought about conditions not conducive to the highest standard of social prosperity.

**The Highest Idea.** In the previous pages we have endeavored to find and present to our readers, in the most comprehensive manner, some of the laws of exchange in traffic, and the normal conditions of the sociological structure of *work*, profits and the philosophy of subsisting.

We have, as far as possible, outlined consistent premises from which to conduct a philosophic inquiry, with a hope of reaching a logical solution of the great question of the limited rights of the citizen in regard to just dealings one with another, and the most rational code of legal and moral regulations of the industrial art, in all its bearings, that perfect harmony, the great desideratum of all peoples, may be realized, and thus make this world what ideal poets have sung about it for ages, and our *forefathers* aimed to transmit to succeeding generations, in their efforts to construct a government based on principles of *personal freedom.*

**Cause and Effect.** In our examination of the various causes and effects of the labor trouble we have, and will endeavor to continue, to pursue the course as laid down by good philosophic reasoning, appertaining to this subject, in dealing with *cause and effect* of phenomena elsewhere in nature. We may then either begin our study with the effects and trace out the cause, or, as far as is possible, begin our inquiry with the *effects arising* from causes with which we are already familiar.

What would be considered consistent in all research and investigation of any question of importance is first of all to find a correct basis, or premises, from which to direct our argument. The framers of our Constitution gave us the foundation of institutions *free from imperialism* as far as was possible for them at so early a period in the experiment of a republican form of government, and as far as they had light and understanding on the *normal conditions of man.* It now remains for us not only to *keep green* the old landmarks established by them, but to emphasize those principles and widen the boundary lines by adding new truths, as we may discover them, and as necessity may demand it—to be more vigilant, which we of necessity must be as the nation grows to greatness.

We have, then, already before us quite a broad platform on which to found a course of rational investigation, preparatory and educational. We have examined effects to some extent, and have also been enabled to recognize causes, but now we take a step further and examine causes and effects, with a view of reconciling *primary principles* with *correspondent effects*, and thus we hope to find additional causes, or factors, which have been instrumental in bringing about undesirable conditions in our social relations to finance or business essential to our subsistence.

**Actuating Causes.** In our examination of the subject, we find the actuating causes divided into those having remote origin and those more immediate. Those immediate are far more numerous than the remote.

We will treat of them under their proper headings as they may present themselves while we press onward, guided by the handmaid of sociological philosophy, which we hope will lead us to a *logical* conclusion on which we can rest the case for a just verdict from the general public.

**A Great Desideratum.** It is plain that many subdivisions may be made of the subject under consideration, but like all great issues, or, forsooth, any question or problem for the people to decide, the more *concise* and the more *simple* a basis to which the subject can be brought, the less complicated, the more easy it will be to reach a comprehensive conclusion, especially so in the present instance.

There are underlying principles which, when fully understood and comprehended, enable us at once to master the situation, when successful inquiry will be comparatively easy. One thing more it will be well to remember, and that is that we proceed somewhat guardedly in our arguments in order that our logic may agree with the premises, that our *rulings* come within the provisions of the boundaries of right. The great *desideratum*, then, most of all, is to understand the real cause of the *difficulties*, or social troubles, which we are called upon to reconcile or correct.

**Positive and Negative Elements.** In accordance with our observation and research of the *remote causes* of the social discord, manifested in the form of riots, strikes and the *bugle call* of the soldiery at times when we are at peace with all nations of the world (it is sad to contemplate such a condition), they are traceable to two primary factors, namely: the positive and negative (aspect). These forces are too far apart to keep the circuit complete. Capital and labor are the positive and negative forces in commerce.

Allied to electricity, although recognized as separate and distinct forces, the positive and negative polarities are so strangely alike that scientists have been unable to find any difference in the quality of electricity between the positive and negative, only this, that kindred relations must exist for the manifest current to be possible, hence these conditions cannot be disturbed—that is, the proper polarities are separated and still maintain a continued electric current.

A certain limited distance of the positive and negative electric polarity is tolerated, but when this limit has been reached, beyond which the normal relations of the elements necessary to produce electric current becoming too far separated, straightway the result is disappointing.

Here we have another striking exemplification of the *laws of force* in nature and, hence, when we consider the striking analogy that exists between those elements as actuating principles giving force and activity to the operations of our entire social system we have before us the beginning

**Many Interruptions.** and end of what we are in search of, a positive and negative polarity, a bearing, so to speak (*to compare*); the operations of capital and labor. When the circuit is complete the working power goes on uninterrupted. We are safe to present this comparison; it applies fittingly. When the circuit is broken we have an illustration of the remote cause of the inharmony existing in the industrial ranks of our social system, for in exact ratio as these two forces, capital and labor (positive and negative), become separated their power weakens—that is to say, becomes less and less operative.*

A certain distance (a limit) will be tolerated, though many interruptions and shocks of greater or lesser severity to the *body politic* may be experienced, but when this separating distance is carried too far, that is, beyond a certain boundary line, the circuit once broken becomes impractical. Capital alone, labor alone, can do but little, if anything—become a total failure as a factor in perpetuating commercial integrity.

**Does Not Work Well.** The cause of our difficulty is already discovered. The distance between capital and labor is too great to *work well*, to *blend* in one integral power, in conducting the industrial

---

*Like the qualities of positive and negative, electricity, which scientists have been unable to define as absolute, separate, entities and forces, so statesmen and financial philosophers have been unsuccessful in defining the exact difference, in an elementary sense, in the quality, or personality, of the two great factors of *capital* and *labor*, in the organization of the wonderfully intricate social system which has its primary root in many starting points, and yet in reality but the one, which we denominate *necessity;* and this arises out of the fact of *living* —that is, means of subsisting, clothing, habitation and the faculty of acquisitiveness that leads to ownership; and these altogether enter into the organization of one grand social system, in all of which capital and labor lead the van and regulates them all.

A. WILFORD, HALL, Ph.D., LL. D.

Plate III–For sketch see page 219.

interests of the nation, especially in a country where *personal liberty*, *peace* and *happiness* are the ultimate objects of its government.

**Principles of Human Happiness.** The fundamental principle of *human happiness*, briefly stated, is a condition wherein we are satisfied with *self*, that is, a perfect agreement of one's own personal powers or faculties, all of which implies perfect harmony with ourselves and our environment. Such a state of existence may properly be put down as a *normal life*, and the greatest study of mankind is to learn how to attain to and appreciate what unquestionably will bring happiness to all who can reach that point of harmony with *self* and *surroundings*.

**When in Perfect Order.** It will be evident, then, that if any of the elements which enter into component parts, to maintain a normal state or condition of life, are withheld, the sequence will be disturbance of the harmony, if not destruction. The moment the principles of accordant relations are ignored trouble is at hand. Like electricity, when the elements that produce it are *in perfect order*, it may be operative, but the very opposite will be the result should even a single one of the elements be removed.*

According to our observation, capital in this country is not in harmony with itself, as we shall be able to demonstrate in more instances than one, neither is it in harmony with its compeer, *labor*. Then, if capital is not in harmony with itself, certainly it cannot be in its relations—in its workings as a factor in social matters. We will also observe here that labor is not in proximity sufficiently to blend with the interests of capital, and thereby further its

---

* We treat of the improper distribution of the profits of capital in another part of this work, and show its bad effects on the community, and thus carry out the comparison of the congested condition or unnatural accumulation of wealth, in the hands of a few, as a source of trouble.

*own* interests. The distance is too great between the points of perfect reciprocal unity of the positive and negative impulses of capital and labor, most needful in forwarding those elements that will give to a nation assured success— that is, a healthy commerce.

**The Line of Difference.** Whatever, then, may be the *remote* or the immediate causes of separating these forces, or even widening the distance between them, must be removed in order to avert still greater disruption and restore concordance among those powers whose function is to make happy homes and a happy nation.

We may mention a leading factor, in the remote sense, of disturbance in our social ranks, which has been at work, perhaps, for centuries, but encroaching more during the last half century than any other *time*, which we will denominate *distinction*. For some reason a *person of leisure* has always been a favorite in society, especially those who do not perform *manual labor* to acquire a subsistence. The so-called *capitalists*, or the rich, somehow take the lead in drawing a line of social distinction between those who employ and the employed. This line, it seems, is being more sharply drawn each year, and separates that interest that all of us should have in the welfare of our neighbors.

**Evolution.** It was truly said by a distinguished thinker of New York, in a lecture on evolution a few years ago, that "Society is organized much like a house— having a *bottom*, or a foundation, and a *top*." The general law of evolution applies to the *bottom* as well as to the *top*. Supposing, now, the top of society, which is almost always understood as that class which has wealth, and who can thereby be helped on materially much better than those who represent the bottom of society, the poorer class, and by these helps grow much faster (evolute) in intellect and refinement. Suppose we say by and by the top will leave the bottom so far behind and the distance will be so great between them, the bottom will fall out of society and the entire social structure tumble into ruin. This brings to our mind the fear that those who have been favored by fortune, by circumstances which have enabled them to conserve the profits of their labor so that in every way they can take advantage of environment to lift themselves upward rapidly and thus help on nature's effort in accord with the law of evolution, still, with all this, forget that there are others in the world, human kindred, who are on the same road and must obey the same law of evolution, but are not as happily circumstanced, and must move slow and should be helped on, and were it not good philosophy for those on *top* to remember that the closer *all of us* keep together the more easy will we conquer and overcome obstacles in the way of progress?

**The Top and Bottom.** Should the bottom fall out of society where will the top be? Is it not plain, then, that the failures and the many social wrecks *founder* on the rock of *social distinction?* The line of distinction has been too sharply drawn. The principle of differentiation exists everywhere in nature and constitutes what may be termed education.

Now if the American people desire, and we believe they do, to steadily grow and keep up with the star of enterprise and the work of greatness, growing better, morally and civilly, gaining in power and influence, then we must *keep together* and not allow the top of society to get too far away from the bottom, and thus obviate social disruptions.

**The Intermediate.** Those people who by the law of natural selection occupy the intermediate station of society (the same natural law having placed those in their respective places who are at the top or bottom, so to speak), are going onward—occupying the intermediate. The two points at either end are the factors of trouble or discordance, and require the greatest consideration on our part. Society may be compared to the departments or compartments of our fine ocean steamers. The passengers occupy the upper, middle and lower decks, or first, second and third class. Or again the cabin or saloon—the intermediate and the steerage. Whatever division of society we may make, no matter what station in life *any of us may* occupy, perfect freedom in the pursuit of happiness, within the limitations prescribed by nature, should be accorded to *all men*. Perhaps the greatest happiness that can come to mankind *is* the pursuit thereof.

One seeks happiness in trying to become rich—to amass great wealth. Another finds happiness in trying by every means to deprive the wealthy of that which he has gained. Another chooses the route to vagrancy. Another, wiser than all, finds greatest happiness in seeking to curb inordinate desires, and is satisfied with what may come to him through legitimate channels in business, and thus gets on well in the world.

**Driftwood.** After all the points have been looked over, and after all the *ins* and *outs* of this great social problem of *labor and capital* have been studied, *that* element which *drifts* away from the rest is *that* which brings trouble. But little use can be made of the *driftwood* of a swollen stream. Overcrowded condition of the departments in the industrial system furnish recruits which make up the ranks of the *drifting element*, a sort of prodigal people, who must in some way be induced to return to the fold and home from which they have wandered. Undivided efforts will be required to provide occupation ; institute moral and political reform ; *civic education*, and just legal regulation of disputes, so that a perfect reconciliation may be brought about, and that all of us may understand what is implied in what we define to be the normal relation of the citizen, with the law of integrity, to the *body politic*.

# CORPORATIONS AND WAGE-WORKERS.

*Ownership; Well-Established Datas; Organizations; Companies; Trusts; Pools; Monopolies; Competitive Labor; Poverty, the Destruction of the Poor; Labor Bureaus; Scale of Prices; Organized Labor; How the Evil of Strikes May be Averted, etc.*

"Go tame the wild torrent, or stem with a straw,
The proud surges that sweep o'er the sands that confined them,
But presume not again *to give* freemen a law,
Or think with the chains they have broken, to bind them."

**Ownership.** Much has been said and written on the subject of *ownership* by able statesmen, but whether it has been the logical conclusion of scientific and honest research or not, the dominant idea, as we find it among the people, is still that a man has a right to "get all he can." To tone it down a little, the same idea is expressed in other words, namely : that "all peoples have a right to accumulate all the legitimate wealth that lie in their power."

This is a common saying, and it seems to be the popular idea. In our present undertaking we will not contend for anything more than this : that men may have an *equal chance*, under the law, to make all the money they can, and bring *capital*, in respect to profit-making, on equal footing with *labor*.

As we enter upon the investigation of ownership, several points present themselves for more than a mere superficial consideration. In the first place let us examine the actuating principles which give rise to a desire for possession. There seems to exist in all men a ruling principle which *urges* them on to acquire and own property. In the next place we will endeavor to outline the normal scope for the exercise of these powers or inclinations ; that is to say, find the point where legal interference, or legal regulation, should begin. For it will be self evident, for many reasons, that it is proper and necessary, for man's happiness, to regulate by law those conditions, whose tendencies are to impose on the rights of others.

**Acquisition.** The disposition of acquiring something you can call your own ; to own property, whether you earn it or not, is traceable to the faculty which gives to man the *love of gain*. This, doubtless, begins with a primary law of self-preservation—a physiological necessity. The philosophy of subsisting is the first and most important study of the entire sociological system, for the reason that the first and, perhaps, the last, act of life, is to support the vital forces of existing.

The most important point of all with most men is, in some way, so to conserve their own resources that a subsistence is assured to them, and, withal, to obtain it in the most easy manner possible. These powers are *innate*, and are comprehended under the caption of the faculty of *acquisition*, or *acquisitiveness*, the function or mission of which is to direct man's capabilities in the pursuit of acquiring a maintenance, and also to find ways and means of accumulating property—even to possess great wealth. The love of attaining property, or possessions, seems as natural almost as life itself ; for men fight nearly as hard for their possessions as for their lives.

**Penuriousness.** The direction which this faculty will take depends largely upon the other faculties in their combination, developed in each individual. In the tropics, where food grows almost entirely spontaneously, this faculty is not very strongly developed ; still it is sufficiently so, even among the Fiji Islanders, the lowest in this scale, to cause wars between the different tribes. In this country it forms largely the actuating principle of our great commercial system ; and when not under proper control, individuals become very *grasping*, and in many instances amass not only great fortunes, but do so in a dishonest way.

In and of itself this faculty is blind ; that is, it is void of reason and moral responsibility. Its only object in life *is gain*. Unless it is restrained by the moral and reasoning powers, it knows no limit. For there are persons whose moral faculties are weak, and in such instances legal enactments may have to be invoked to assist them to keep within proper bounds.

But when the faculty is brought under proper restraint, however active and strong it may be, and is governed by the higher judgment attained by the moral faculties, it makes men frugal and economical with a will to make *"little go far"* and give, withal, a feeling of *satisfaction*, which, after all, is the essential point to be attained to insure human happiness. However, as before remarked, unless this faculty is brought under proper restraint, it creates a desire for more and more of this world's goods without a regard to consequences.

### Trespassing on the Rights of Others.

All of the various faculties of the human mind may be the servants of the one faculty of *acquisitiveness*, and thus concentrate all of man's capabilities for the sole purpose of making money—accumulate property—as in the case of the miser. Then, under such circumstances, those who are not on their guard are liable to overdo this work of *money-getting*, and, before they are aware, find themselves trespassing on the rights of others, and thereby become subjects of legal regulation.

### Business Trusts, Etc.

We have now before us, though briefly stated, *datas* which furnish a correct starting point for further inquiry into the evil effects of *penuriousness*. The desire to possess or own property we have successfully traced to an inherent faculty with which all men are endowed, that is, the common nature of man to *own*, to be *powerful, to rule*. We have shown the primary function of this faculty and its sociological influence upon society.

The millions are all bent in the same direction, and everyone exerts his best talent in the race for supremacy. Under existing circumstances *is it not surprising* that not more difficulties arise, where there are so many scrambling for gain, and comparatively so few opportunities? Those performing ordinary bodily labor start out single-handed. Those who have learned a special occupation seek the best positions possible. In traffic every device is resorted to to acquire a subsistence, and besides to gain a competency, and, if possible, riches. The procession, moving in solid phalanx, under the command of acquisitiveness, from the husbandman to the capitalist, is simply great. Many with a few hundred dollars start in business for themselves, and, with good management, succeed fairly well, as far as their small capital enables them to go.

Certain commodity requires expensive machinery to manufacture it. A number of men have each a small capital. Singly neither has enough to start such an institution, so they join forces and unite what capital they have and form what is denominated a company. Any kind of business may be conducted on a more extensive plan by combining capital, and thus increase its power both in controling the market as well as wages.*

We question, however, the moral right to do so, though the legal right is admitted. It can readily be seen that combinations possess advantages not possibly attained by men with small or limited means. Competition is controlled, more or less, by well-organized companies, and, while this is a fact, there must come to our minds another fact, that business men with moderate means, who are not so fortunate as to get into the ring with the combines, can, not compete with them in the markets, are crowded out,

---

* This subject is treated of more extensively under the head of " *Combination*," to which the reader is respectfully referred for a full elucidation.

and they must go to the wall. No one can fail to see injustice here. Yet a fellow man is as much a member of the human family as those who form into great corporations. The weak, in this respect, fail only on account of unequal chance, not that they are not shrewd managers, but on account of the unfair competition with which they have to contend, which makes failure almost inevitable.

Combination of capital cannot benefit the general public, for, unless a fair competition, governed by supply and demand, is allowed to regulate the markets, the benefit must be one sided; the corporations will make all the profit.

## In the End Where is It?

Millions may be made by these combinations. The money is in the country. The nation has materially increased in wealth. But might it not be far better for a hundred or a thousand men, men with families, to make a million of dollars, than for a few to make it, and, by arbitrary means, shut out their fellow citizen from an unequal chance in the markets, and make mere wage-earners of many who with an innate pride and ambition might be their own masters, break down altogether and become mendicants?

We do not hesitate, then, after a careful survey of the question we have raised regarding combinations, to take the ground that a legal charter should be granted only to create combinations in the case, as stated before, where a very large capital is necessary to secure machinery and other heavy investments before the business can be started at all —as in our rolling mills and other similar institutions which might be mentioned. But we have sufficient exemplification to enable *all of us* to think intelligently of the difference we make between an ordinary company in a business (which anyone with even limited means can enter upon) and a combine requiring a large capital, by reason of the vastness of the enterprise and the character of the commodity manufactured; as in the case of a rolling mill or immense smelting works, glass works, cotton factories, etc.

But we ask pardon for this digression, as this subject will be taken up again further on in the course of our deliberation.

**A Stock Company.** We have now in our mind what constitutes a business conducted by individuals taking their chances in the markets of the world unprotected by any organized power that may aid them. We have also an idea, from what has been stated, what constitutes a company; so let us pass on and consider other forms of business firms with which we will have more to do in solving the question of labor and capital than any other.

Where a company is organized by a division of shares, and these shares are held by anyone who may be able to invest to the extent of one or more shares, the capital of a concern thus raised is known as a *stock company*, either limited or unlimited, as the case may be ; and the holders of these shares are said to be stock-holders, for whose benefit a dividend is declared either semi-annually or annually.

**What Constitutes a Trust Company.** Now, in order to make great profits, a number of these companies (though they may be located in different towns or cities) *combine* for the purpose of controling the markets, to raise the price on whatever their commodity may be which they manufacture, and thus keep prices up, as well as to regulate the price of labor. This is called a *trust* company.

The wage-earners who are employed in these institutions are as much at their mercy in regard to the price of wages as on the other hand the public is at their mercy regarding the price of the commodity they manufacture. Then these companies, some of them, at times form what is known in business circles as *pools*. For example, two or more business concerns work to each other's interest in getting *trade away* from others who are in the same business, but are not in the ring, as it is termed. Where it is practical by thus creating an advantage over others, much money is made, and serious failures have resulted to those against whom pools have been organized. The profits are divided *pro rata* among those in the pools who are reaping a benefit from such an arrangement.

**Monopoly.** Where a person has the sole power of vending any species of goods, or manufactures a commodity no one else can, or has the right to handle, such a one, it is said, has a monopoly. Competition destroys monopoly. The more competition is weakened the nearer will you be to a monopoly. To accomplish this, companies, trusts, combines of every degree of power, are organized to monopolize the trade, and thus make a greater profit than where prices are regulated by competition. Thus we may have at once, in these various combinations, not alone a *company*, but *trusts, monopolies*, pools, and when well organized and in good working condition can almost entirely control the markets and the price of labor as well.

After what has been said on this particular subject of combinations, it needs no further argument to show that the consumer pays the cost and labor loses a just profit.

**A Well-Concerted Plot.** The only redress the people have is in the power of suffrage, electing men who will make laws to regulate or abolish these evils. The *evil* is somewhat modified when these institutions fail to agree on a well-concerted plot or plan. A so-called *protection tariff*, improperly levied, will foster and give aid to the very kind of institutions we have portrayed.* Moreover it will fill up the country with corporations, which may flourish for a while, only, however, to react ; and those who conducted them will gravitate to their proper places in the social system, leaving sad remembrances behind them for a disappointed public to profit by in future.

The ingeniously-wrought schemes on the part of the capitalists enable them to accomplish, first, to cripple

---

* The reader is here referred to another part of this work for a philosophic view of the " tariff question."

and avoid competition ; and, second, to reduce wages ; for they well understand that this is a sure way to make money, and make it easy. Capital, naturally the compeer of labor, is still really the most powerful in commerce, but for that very reason it should be willing to take its chances on equal footing with labor in all schemes of business.

Capital, capable and strong in itself, as it is, should seek to organize and combine its forces for the purpose of bringing *to its shrine*, not a foe, but a quondam friend, without whom at last it will be compelled to surrender the battle for gain.

Think of the effects it must have on the ultimate prosperity of the country.

## Ultimate Prosperity.

When, in addition to being already well organized, as we have previously shown, capital, aided by special legislation, either directly or indirectly, can it be otherwise than that by all these advantages it must make rapid and great gain?

Thus capital, operated under advantages not given to the wage-earners, who unavoidably must join to make either available in the industrial art, will far exceed labor in profits, and if permitted to go on and accumulate wealth, and, of course, *power*, any country, under such circumstances, will *fill up* with two classes,[*] either of which is an injustice to the people and a hindrance to the progress of the best and fittest element of civilization.

These two classes we denominate *paupers* and millionaires. The former are mendicants on the charity of the people, the majority of who are economical, subsisting on a narrow margin, while they still have an open hand for a fellow being in need ; and the latter is a *Shylock*, draining the pockets of the honest, industrious classes, and thus both

---

[*] On page 36 we treat of a *drifting element*, and here we speak of two classes, which are at either end of society, who must not be permitted to drift too far away from " first principles " or the government will go to pieces.

mendicants and millionaires are a drain on society, because they never give back an equivalent for what they receive. *

**Neither Work.** Neither of these two classes work, and hence must subsist on the people, for one who does not produce an equivalent to the *cost* of living is consuming the same from a certain reserve fund, which must sooner or later be exhausted unless replenished by profits of some sort. If it takes a certain number of persons to perform a given amount of work, restricted to the proper capacity, making limitations from the standards of health, justice, profits, etc., these being considered, then suppose A or B fall out of line, the work must, however, go on with the task imposed on each individually, and if A and B fail to perform their allotted part of the work, that portion must be assumed by the remainder of the co-workmen, and thus the burden of labor and responsibility would be increased for the rest.

This will be the natural result if A and B do not work, and *work*, as we have elsewhere shown, means labor that produces something, not to draw upon a reserve, for this must eventually end in bankruptcy. Life itself to be normal must maintain a reserve. As soon as by the active operation of living the reserve of the *life forces* are drawn upon, straightway longevity becomes shortened. So it is in regard to capital in carrying on business. So long as a profit is made the solvency is assured. This is the first point a good business man will look after. As a rule capitalists are unwilling to invest their money unless there is a prospect of a profit. Then why should not labor figure from the same premises? The wage-worker has as good a

---

* We would here refer our readers to pages 10, 11, 12, where we define " Capital, its proper place and use;" also the rich and the " Capitalist," for we wish to be properly understood. The millionaires, made in the natural course of business conducted on equitable principles, differ widely from those who make their millions by the help of favoritism, organized corporations, pools, trusts, monopolies, etc. The former builds up *with* the people, the latter *on* the people.

right to demand a profit as the capitalist.   That is, we mean
a profit over and above what it costs to live.   However it
may be, both the capitalist and the laborer are entitled to
a profit if work is performed.   Moreover, they are interested
in each other's prosperity, so that in neither case the reserve
may be drawn on, or rather should be added to than
weakened.

The absolutely poor are not by any means the most dangerous class.   They have comparatively little power or influence ; they simply consume.   But the other class, the
*Shylock*, by nefarious management, furnish recruits for the
pauper ranks, and otherwise cause many unpleasant conditions and contentions among those who naturally understand
and feel the injustice of their operations.

MONEY-MAKING A MONO-MANIA WITH SOME PEOPLE; EDU-
    CATING THE FACULTIES; DISSATISFIED CAPITALISTS;
    WHERE LEGAL RULINGS SHOULD BEGIN; LEGAL AND
    MORAL LIMITATIONS; IRREFUTABLE POINTS ON THE
    LABOR PROBLEM, ETC.

**Educating the Faculties.** Education in the unquali-
fied sense means to cultivate
and strengthen human capabilities.   Proper education
means to cultivate the weak faculties and restrain those
which are too active.   To be well educated is a rare accomplishment.   Such an attainment is only valuable when all the
faculties are equally developed.   It is far better for a person
to possess only mediocrity and be evenly developed than to
force a few of the faculties to the extreme limit while other
faculties remain abnormally weak.   This causes an unbalanced condition of the mind, makes a person eccentric, often
assuming the nature of a *mono-mania* and in many instances ends in crime.   We have such a condition in the
mendicant, who lacks in self-pride and who has but little
desire for worldly possessions ; while, on the other hand, the
disposition manifests itself in an uncontrolable desire to
hoard money.   In the former case this faculty is weak from

neglect of use ; in the latter instance it is too active from the *momentum* it has received by undue exercise or over-work in money-getting.

**A Good Civil Government.** The normal exercise of all the faculties are condu-cive to happiness, and especially so long as they work in harmony with each other the product will be satisfying, but the moment the line of limitation of *moral action*, estab-lished by nature, is passed, the point in a man's life is reached where he is liable to become a subject of legislation, for at the very point or act where the unwritten law of *right* is violated the written law must assume the reign, or else "law and order" are not the dominant principles of good civil government.

So long as there is a cordial relation between capital and labor, or the employer and employed, it will matter but little how much profit capital makes or how much labor may obtain, if there is only an equal chance and an equitable dis-tribution of profits. No colossal or unnatural fortunes can be made under such a *regime;* no great or one-sided institu-tions will form and control the commerce of the land, whose uncurbed power may be exercised for evil.

**And No Return of Profit.** Cordial relations between the employer and the em-ployed *at once* forms a *solid basis* on which to rear a success-ful business fabric. When capital employs labor, where there is a product of profit, the function of capital is widely different from that where it simply is *spent* and no return in profits is expected. In all departments of industry where capital unites with labor, intended to increase the wealth of the capitalist, the function of capital should be governed by the fact that it is under obligations to those that unite with it, in order to make it operative. When we say "obligation of capital" we apply its significance to individuals or cor-porations who own or control capital.

The capitalist may argue that all obligations end with the payment of stipulated wages. We would remind them that there is a jealous principle back of this simple payment of enforced wages. If capital becomes inoperative as soon as the wage-earner steps out then it seems to us there must be an obligation beyond the mere payment of wages. *

**It Cannot Spin, Neither Can It Weave.** Capital, however powerful a factor of social distinction it may be, cannot spin, weave, design, manufacture shoes, cloth, machinery, nor any other commodity belonging to the industrial arts without the assistance of labor, from the common helper to the skilled workman.

**Profit-Sharing.** Profit-sharing then comes forward and presents the claim of labor against capital for *a pro rata* share of its earnings—which is but fair—for the workman's time and labor must associate itself with capital before the wheels of a factory can be put into operation. The argument applies to all concerned, where *capital operates* and *labor works.* But if A employs B to repair his fences for a certain amount in daily wages, the work performed yielding no profit to A, money thus spent is at once entirely absorbed and no division of profit is expected. But if A hires B to *sink a shaft* to mine iron-ore, this ore is sold to C for the purpose of manufacturing it into plows and C sells these plows to D, and each time this ore has changed hands and form, a profit has accrued therefrom, *then* the capital so used performs an entirely different function and changes the relations between the capitalist and wage-earner. In this instance capital works and adds; in the

---

* The obligation we here speak of is that which arises from the common brotherhood of man. If the employer manifests no further interest in his people than merely an apparent selfishness, stimulated simply by business relation, and ignores that social tie of common brotherhood that takes an interest in the welfare of our neighbors, which is allied to family ties, then the employed is made to feel that after all there is but a step between himself and slavery; that amicable relation between labor and capital is not of that strong friendly relation that might exist were the *social austerism* not so strictly enforced between employer and employed.

HON. JOHN WANAMAKER.
Fig. 1.

FRANCES E. WILLARD.
Fig. 2.

HON. DANIEL HAND.
Fig. 3.

RICHARD M. HUNT.
Fig. 4.

Plate IV—For sketches see pages 219 and 220.

former case money was spent, but was not a money-making investment. In the first case the labor performed was simply an exchange of services for an equivalent in cash and did not come under that class of labor in which wages or labor are affected by market prices, while in the other, in case of the price of iron-ore changing, it may affect the wage price of the miner.

**The Farmer and His Plow.** Now in each and every case where capital is invested and labor employed, with a view to increase the wealth of him, or those, who own the capital, in all conditions where both labor and capital do work from which a profit is made—in these cases all competition on the side of labor should be abrogated. For it is now a well established fact that poverty is the bane of the poor. This is fully demonstrated by labor strikes and lock-outs. These, it is erroneously believed, are the means by which capital can be brought to terms. But there are always those ready to take the places of strikers, and as long as this is possible the poor are the ruination of their own class. We say most emphatically that as long as competitive labor exists, by or through which the price of labor may be affected or dictated,

**Competitive Labor.** which in nine cases out of ten is done by hungry stomachs, thus forcing the workmen between two grinding forces—competitive labor on one side and capital in all its arrogance and power on the other, reducing wages on the slightest provocation—just so long the wage-workers of this country must needs feel like giving up the struggle to obtain the rights that should be vouchsafed them under the Constitution of the United States.

It is a wonder that not more violence has been committed by those who must keenly feel what ought to be their portion, see the right socially and morally, of which they are unjustly deprived, but see no civil remedy (alas! who can?) and do not oftener have recourse to their brawny arms and physical powers to be put down by military force!

Let us once more refer back to our miner digging iron-ore, which we have already watched from its crude state to the plow. All along the line the market men, in the different changes of the ore, have had the wage prices regulated by competitive labor.

**The Manufacturer.** The manufacturer, the capitalist, has to meet the markets, where the price of his product is regulated by competition, according to supply and demand. Now if this were *all* much of our investigation would end here. But the major part of the story still remains untold.*

For the present we will only state certain effects of the rise and fall of the prices of wage-labor products and how this might be better regulated. If the price of iron is up and plows are in demand, and the price as a consequence also high, so that each time the iron changes form and hands, from the miner to the farmer who now converts this iron to the use of other productions, the price is increased —then, we ask, if the prices of this iron are high in all its mechanical changes—should not the wage-worker receive a compensation corresponding with such existing prices?

And should the prices go higher will the wage-workers receive higher wages? We know if the prices go *down* his wages follow suit.

**What is Protection?** Should now at this junction a protective tariff be levied on plows by the government and the price of plows, as a consequence, be raised in the same *ratio*, say one dollar on each plow, then the farmer has to pay one dollar more for his plow. This would be denominated a "protective tariff." Now comes the question, how does this protect the wage-worker who has been employed at the different stations along the line from the time the ore left the ground and the wood the forest? Does he receive a corresponding increase of pay

---

* We here refer the reader to the subject matter given under the caption of "Organized Labor"—market prices of the products of factories and the labor that produces it.

for his labor? Who is it that looks after the interests of the wage-workers? Surely not the capitalist. *He* is looking for some one to do his work *still cheaper*, for it is certain the cheaper you can get work done the more money you will make, and it will also be admitted that employers are seldom known voluntarily to raise wages, hence proper legal regulation on this subject may be the right thing to do.

Now, if the demand for raw material is good and prices high, then the man who mines the ore ought to receive higher wages in the same proportion as the capital invested makes a greater profit. The wage-worker, through whose labor the ore is made available, should receive increased pay, or a *pro rata* dividend, as a just portion for his labor, which is *his* capital.

In order that justice may be done both to capital and labor, we would suggest the organization of a Labor Bureau, whose function shall be to regulate the price of labor according to the profits made by capital.

**This Would be Protection.** This would be protection in the interest of the laborer. The capitalist owes proper respect to the workman, whose bone and sinew as an investment is joined to his capital and through which profit is accrued. Of course the workingman must be prepared to meet the reverses caused by the decline of prices, the same as the capitalist, as both are under the control of the same market, governed by the laws of supply and demand. If, however, the price of the products advances, the laborer, who is in working relation with the concern thus favored, should have his wages advanced by the Bureau in an equal proportion. And, we ask, is there any just reason why capitalists should not yield this point and benefit the workingmen, through whose energy they are enabled to increase their wealth? In all law and equity this should be the solution of the labor problem—*an equitable distribution of the profits arising from any work among all who aid in producing them.* Since the whole social system is regulated by supply and demand, then let this rule govern both capitalist and wage-earner; reduction of wages then being a natural sequence to the fall of prices of the products of labor, and being so announced by the Labor Bureau, is not likely that they

### Not Likely that They Will Rush Headlong Into a Strike.

will rush headlong into a strike, nor will the concerns they work for be obliged to shut down, or lock out its workmen, knowing, however, that there are others ready to fill their places at reduced prices. Neither can capital reduce wages at its own pleasure, for no other reason than because there are other persons ready to fill the gap. Thus, if there should be even an over demand for work, the price is fixed by the bureau and the wages will be the same whoever does the work, regulated by the profits made by the concern.

The general public is interested in the successful operation of every manufacturing enterprise, when capital and labor are in harmonious co-operation with the wage-earner, when both are making a profit, great or small, the community where they operate will be in sympathy with them, for every one will benefit by it.

### In a Community Where Capital is Invested.

But in a community where capital is largely invested in manufacturing concerns and capital rules with an iron hand, hoarding money, amassing wealth, while labor, notwithstanding its indispensable fulcrum for leverage to capital, is ground down, wages continually reduced, *there* offended nature will manifest itself in discontent, and smarting under repeated wrongs and injustice, painful to them as the touch of the scalpel when applied to the naked nerve, they will rise up in riot!

This is the course many capitalists and managers of concerns have taken with their employees, and often, too, under the false pretense that there was no market for their products, and wages for this reason must go down. This subterfuge may operate successfully as long as workingmen

have hungry stomachs and sore hearts—for *they must eat!*
But this will not accord with justice and equity, for the
workingman has rights the employer is bound to respect,
say nothing of the treatment that is due him from a humane
standpoint.

**How to Escape Moral Censure.** Now, in order to escape moral censure for
any course pursued by it, not strictly equitable, capital
combines its forces in the form of a "Company" and appoints
a *manager,* who is governed, and governs others, by a code
of rules and regulations formulated by capital itself and thus
tries to shift all moral responsibility from their own shoul-
ders on to *his;* then where is your redress? They operate
within the *perview* of the law, keep on heaping indignities
upon their workmen, until forgetting all else excepting that
they are men, and freemen, too, these workmen, perhaps im-
prudently, rise up to assert their rights, when the local police
or the government troops are called in to *protect* the *capitalist,* but *no* protection for the workmen from either.

**By a Wise Counsel.** Now if all these grievances can be
settled, yea, even *avoided,* by a wise
council or bureau, whose functions shall be to regulate
wage prices, then why not hail the advent of the time and
means when by law, equity and justice in all business
transactions between capital and labor peace can be safely
guaranteed? *Equity* and *justice* we repeat.

If you go forth with an olive branch to meet your fellow-
man on vantage ground you will meet with a peaceful reception, but if you sally out with helmet and sword you invite a fray. The first course we intimated pays well, the
latter results in loss. Hence under all circumstances it is
always more humane to take the peaceful course in settling difficulties than to resort to harsh or destructive measures.

Under such a bureau those who have capital to invest
can know in advance just how to calculate the expense of

running their concern. The price of labor in each special department is fixed.

**Jurisdiction.** The bureau having regulated the prices the capitalist will have no opportunity to reduce wages at any time he may chose to do so, neither will there exist any labor competitive element to work for lower wages. It may be asserted that such a measure would be unjust. How? "Well," says one, "the capitalist should have the right to hire men at wages as low as possible." So he has a right and as long as he has a reasonable profit he should not complain.

The laborer must have a profit as well as the capitalist, and should supply and demand so regulate prices that no profits will accrue to him for a time, the price of labor also being reduced, there is no reason for a shut down by the capitalist on the plea that it *don't pay.*

The workingman cannot reason from that standpoint. Subsistence is an arbitrary power and the laborer cannot say that because it *don't pay* he will *shut down* on eating and drinking and lodging. He *must work or starve!* *

The judicious business man makes a careful inventory of his resources, expenses, profits, assets and liabilities. The wise general when advancing on the enemy provides for proper means of retreat. With a scale of prices before you you cannot err.

**Dissatisfied Capitalists.** If one thing is more apparent than another it is that our wage-workers are, as a rule, employed or controlled by employers, in many of our shops, on very much the same principle as is used in hiring a horse. The first consideration is the *amount of money that can be made out of his services.*

We admit that the hope of gain is the actuating principle of commerce, the natural function of the faculty of

---

* Workingmen should learn to *save* all it is possible so that they be prepared for any emergency. See article under the head of " Cost of Living " for further hints on this subject.

acquisitiveness, and both the capitalist and the workman are different in their relations to their environment. The former is simply actuated by the motive of *gain*, the latter by the force of circumstances is compelled to invest his labor, which is his capital, that he may in some way also acquire the means of subsistence.

The exercise of the faculty of acquisitiveness is the same in both cases, but sustain a *different attitude to* each other,

**A Different Attitude.** the capitalist and the laborer. The common law of humanity, socially and morally, enters into the component parts of either in the exercise of this faculty of acquisitiveness. But by losing sight of the limitations prescribed by the *Golden Rule* men drift blindly into forbidden channels where, as in the barbarous state of man, "might makes right," and when the capitalist says, "I *will* do this," and "I *can* do that," therefore it is *right.* Thus capitalists, little by little, are transformed into a simple *money-making machine* and from the standpoint of the common law of right, which by nature is intended to apply to one as well as the other, assume a condition which may safely be termed a *mania.* In plainer

**Fugitive from Capital.** terms it might be said that this faculty of acquisitiveness has been stricken with *insanity.*

Therefore, we say, that where the true relations between capital and labor exist and are duly appreciated, no discord can result from their application in conducting any business for profit. But since the fact warrants the statement that *humanity* is a fugitive from capital and the wage-worker reduced to the level of the mule, *humanity* and *justice* demand the enactment of laws to regulate conditions intolerable to men who innately possess the spirit of freedom.

**Innate Spirit of Freedom.** The tendency of this unequal struggle for the "almighty dollar," rightfully belonging to him who honestly acquires it, is plain to every honest thinking mind, and to avert a catastrophe *labor organizations* have been created all over the land, originally for protection, but latterly assuming a spirit of aggression. But not, as we are sometimes told, for the purpose of antagonizing capital, but more with a view to cultivate amicable relations, while affirming, by *united* voice, and to enforce by *moral suasion*, if possible, the rights to which they believe the wage-earners are already entitled.

*Strikes* were inaugurated we know, and that this means of settling existing grievances injured their cause we honestly believe. Strikes are not the proper thing for *two* special reasons. In the first place, there are always those who are ready and *eager* to take the place of the strikers. The capitalist, against whom the strike is inaugurated, knows this, and in many instances the workmen are so illy treated that, in consequence of the rules governing the order to which they belong, a strike becomes inevitable, and by precipitating a strike they give the capitalist a ready excuse to fill their places at reduced wages.

Here the hungry men outside cause the destruction of their own interests and their fellow workmen if they are poor. Then in the second place, the **Lawless Element.** moment a strike is "called on," a lawless element, in many instances not members of any labor order, find a ready opportunity to revenge themselves for some real or fancied injury, and in a cowardly manner destroy property and sometimes stain their souls with murder. Public sentiment, of course, will at once condemn the labor organization and acquit the capitalist.

Only the most ignorant and vicious would perpetrate such lawless acts. But here we present two factors, against which our labor organizations must *contend*, and there are yet other reasons why they have not been more successful.

We stated that, to a large extent, **To a Large Extent.** the *avarice* of many of our capitalists is the cause of these troubles. We wish, however, to be understood that we do not by any means class all our business men and capitalists under one caption. Hence we say the avarice of *many* of them carries them to a point in their

C. G. CONN.

Plate V  For sketch see page 220.

operations when they are never satisfied, never get enough, draw the line of social distinction too close, reach out beyond their proper limits, organize "trusts," pools, monopolies, controlling the markets, &c., and these, we say, are simply their own eggs which hatch out all the sad consequences they so bitterly condemn, the natural fruition of their insane desire for wealth and power.

**For Whom Law is Made.** For this class of people we must have laws to regulate and protect *capital* as well as *labor* in their natural rights. This element if permitted to exist and dominate is as much an injustice to the capital, which is willing to make a legitimate profit, in an honorable way, as to labor. It prevents the taking of equal chances in the market, which is, or should be, regulated by the natural laws of *supply and demand.* Under such restrictions or rules the general public, as well as the individual wage-earner and capitalist, will obtain justice.

Before proceeding to the discussion of *legal boards* of arbitration, as the *regulating media* of matters arising out of business misunderstandings or injustice, we will briefly review past strikes and lockouts, their cost and other results.

STRIKES; LOCKOUTS; RESULTS; LOSSES; NUMBER OF STRIKES; IMMEDIATE CAUSES; HOW TO AVOID TROUBLE OF THIS KIND, ETC.

**The Difference.** There is a vast and important difference between a "strike"and a "lockout." A stoppage by the employees, caused by a demand not allowed or acceded to by the employer, constitutes what is designated a "strike." On the other hand, a discontinuance of operations by the employers, caused by a demand or action opposed by the employees, would be termed a "lockout." There are, however, some instances in which the real cause, whether owing to the fault of the employer or the employed, is not clearly defined. This matters but little so long as the fact remains uncontradicted: that whether it be a *strike* or a *lockout*, if inaugurated for the purpose of forcing a settlement of labor differences, the result, almost invariably, will be idleness.

Strikes and lockouts are almost unknown in agricultural sections, while they, only too frequently, occur in manufacturing and mining districts. In 1880 three hundred and four out of seven hundred and sixty-two strikes in this country occurred in Pennsylvania, a manufacturing and mining State. As a rule but few of these strikes have been successful, some were partially so, some compromised, but most of them ended in failure. We speak now from the labor point of view, in which, as a rule, they were a non-success. The census report of 1880 gives for the decade then ended an average per cent. of the successful strikes in New England at 12 per cent. In 1880, as stated already, 762 strikes and lockouts took place in this country, and the number of persons engaged in the different industries affected thereby was 128,676. Of this number 414 returned to their old positions, while 128,262 were left idle for the time being, and unprovided for while in search of other employment. The total loss resulting from these strikes, in wages, if the time were centered on one man, would be 1,989,872 days. The average wages then paid before the different strikes and in the various industries affected, $1.86 per diem, the actual loss, fully calculated on all sides, was $3,711,097. A much greater loss than this was, no doubt, sustained by all concerned and parties involved. In these strikes eight millions have been calculated to be the loss resulting in various ways, directly and indirectly, or through the stolid obstinacy and selfishness of those interested, who might have found a remedy, as we shall show, by which this great loss might have been avoided. This, we contend, might have been done by a legal board of arbitration or a properly constituted *labor bureau*, whose powers and legal function would be to make and regulate a scale of prices and adjust and settle amicably all differences between employer and employee. Besides the direct losses enumerated, sustained by both employee and employer, there are thousands of other persons, not directly involved in these troubles, who are nevertheless seriously affected thereby in many different ways. By lessening trade thousands are injured.

Those striking or locked-out workmen are in debt and cannot pay. Homes partially paid are sacrificed. Merchants fail to collect outstanding accounts and cannot meet their liabilities. Others holding positions in tributary channels lost their employment, even banks lost in falling off depositors, and if all the various losses resulting from these troubles were carefully computed they would amount, for 1880 alone, to *over one and a half billion dollars.*

In 1886 499,489 men were involved in strikes—three times as many as in 1880. The loss was, of course, proportionally great. During the five years, ending in 1890, the number of men directly engaged in strikes and lockouts amounted to the almost startling number of 1,677,162. Counting their families and others affected in various ways, they would number almost as many as the standing armies of the world. If a tax of five cents was levied on each wage-worker, as reported in these strikes, or involved therein, it would aggregate over $5,000 annually—almost enough to defray the expenses of a *board of arbitration,* through whose instrumentality not only money might have been saved, but many aggravating disputes might have been amicably adjusted which terminated not only in loss of money, position, revolts destruction of property, but ended in many instances in bloodshed.

**Labor Bureau.** What the people mostly desire to attain regarding the labor problem, pre-eminent of all points looking toward a successful solution, is to *centre* on some method or way by which, in a conciliatory manner, we can adjust disputes or difficulties arising between employer and employed, so that in no case it may be necessary to resort to lockouts, strikes or violent means in any form. Conciliation, it must be admitted, is by far the *best policy*.

Private *bureaus* have succeeded, in a degree, in France, England and in this country. However, if voluntary arbitration could be made to meet all the exigencies of trouble that cannot be settled amicably by those immediately interested, then nothing safer or better could be desired. Better still would it be for the American people, if a course or system of conducting business could be devised in a legal manner, the effect of which would act as a preventive, that even boards of arbitration, as well as strikes, may become obsolete altogether, a condition of the social system not impossible, for what is attainable by an individual may also be accomplished by the masses.

Since, however, moral suasion and voluntary arbitration have been successful only to a very limited degree, it seems . nothing is left, as a final means of settling these troubles, than *compulsory arbitration*, which may, nevertheless, be conciliatory. We would suggest, to create for this purpose, a legal board or bureau, whose functions shall be to regulate and settle all *labor trouble* in an equitable way, so that justice may be meted out to all parties concerned. It seems to be the only way open to *us* out of a grievous difficulty, which must be brought under control in some way that the peace of the nation may be assured in the future. Laws are enacted for the purpose of regulating human actions, when it becomes a necessity, and, unless there is really a need for new enactments, it is evident that the fewer laws we have the *better it is for the people*. What the nation needs *is* laws that will meet the wants of all people under all circumstances and conditions.

**Experience.** Profiting by experience and the lessons thereby inculcated, we are led to the indisputable fact that the time has come when a broader view of the situation is demanded, and prompt action will be rewarded by a surer way and a "shorter cut" out of the dilemma. As before stated, since there are capitalists who are never satisfied with even enough of this world's possessions and a good profit constantly accruing to them, and who are not willing to abide by the limitation of the *laws of right*, or even willing to submit to impartial and voluntary arbitration to engender a spirit of conciliation, should it not then, under circumstances like these, become plain that the only *and best* remedy remains to us is in a proper and judicious system of *compulsory arbitration?* For another and a good reason this will be the only and best course and the proper thing to do—namely, it is a fact that, as a rule, capitalists object to arbitration, which fact may be used as evidence that they do not want to do the *fair thing.* Or, perhaps, the main reason may be that it seems to them too humiliating to recognize a mere wage-earner (though a fellow-being) by arbitration, which would make them social equals, for too many arrogate to themselves the idea that possession gives to them a rightful social distinction.

**Compulsory Arbitration.** We would then propose, as a means of self-preservation and settling of grievous disagreements, *legal arbitration*, which should, however, be governed by the same rules of equity as in voluntary arbitration, the only difference being that it shall be *compulsory* and final. A *State board of arbitration*, or, as we propose, a board which shall be known in law as a "*Labor Bureau*," composed of six persons,* strictly non-partisan, to be appointed by every State, and shall be authorized to make laws and decide questions at issue.

The members of this bureau, we would suggest, should be elected by the people at regular State elections. (A friend at our elbow suggests that the members of this bureau be appointed by the State Legislature when in regular session, selections to be made from the different national political parties).

---

* We use here the term "persons" for obvious reason. Sex is not expressed, for there is no good reason why a *woman* shall not be eligible to a seat in this bureau, providing she possesses the qualifications required, as we suggest, for its members.

Whatever the best course in this regard may be thought by the powers that be, we are quite willing to allow our statesmen to determine, still we are inclined to the electing of the members of the bureau by the people, the nomination to be made at the regular State conventions of the different political parties; the nomination to be non-partisan, that is, no matter what a man's political proclivities may be, if he is otherwise qualified and worthy, as we shall outline, he shall have his say; the term of office to be for *two years;* three members to be elected each year, and while three or more may be nominated, the three candidates receiving a majority of votes over all the rest shall be considered elected.

**Strictly Non-partisan.** The officers of this bureau may be known as *labor commissioners,* whose salary shall be sufficient to enable them to give all their time to this work, allowing three months' vacation. This bureau is to be strictly non-partisan, if such a thing is possible. The members of the Labor Bureau must not have either direct or indirect personal money-interest in any business coming within their jurisdiction in any of the industrial arts of the character we have defined, viz.: where labor joins capital for the purpose of *gain*, and those institutions over which the Labor Bureau shall have legislation. Moreover, these officers, as they may be denominated, shall not be under *forty* or over *sixty* years of age, and shall have a reputation for honor and knowledge of statesmanship, over which a majority of the voters shall count the same in eligibility as in the election of other State officers.

**The Power Invested.** The function of this bureau shall be to regulate and establish a scale of wages for every degree of skill and condition of wage-earnings, in all business where capital competes with labor for the purpose of making a profit. In deciding on a correct and just scale of prices, both business men and the *wage-earners* can be of great help to the *labor commissioners* by giving them proper *datas* of the markets and wages extant, from time to time, by which the commissioners will soon be enabled to justly regulate the wages by the changes brought about by the markets.

All business, such as we have designated, however limited or unlimited in the amount invested, must register with the *labor bureau* and receive a permit to carry on business, and accept a scale of wage-prices which must be paid to employees. This scale will be subject to changes according as the markets may go up or down, giving to the manufacturer always *his* legitimate profits and to the wage-earner what is justly *his due*. The price of wages, as well as the price of commodities, will be regulated by *location* and *conditions*, much the same as that which is in vogue at the present time, only the great *desideratum* to be attained will be to steer clear of unpleasant disputes and unjust dealings one with another.

This will prohibit the employer from discharging his people and replacing them with cheaper labor. It will also do away with competitive labor. That is, no one can underbid wage-prices, for the employer is not permitted to pay less than the established or current wages. This is the only way the wage-earners of this country can be protected from cheaper labor; since there are always persons who for various reasons would do the work for less than by right should be paid. * This, of course, will, in a certain sense, make the wage-earner a partner in the business where he is employed, as in reality he is, since the fact remains undisputed that without labor capital is inoperative.

The employer will still retain all the rights he now has to employ whomsoever he may, or discharge his people, increase or curtail the number of employees, or lessen hours, run full or half time, or discharge anyone for incompetency, neglect of duty, or any other offense that may in his judgment warrant such a course; but for simply being a member of a labor union the employer can have no say, and con-

---

* This subject is more fully discussed under the head of ''Foreign Competition,'' to which the reader is referred.

cerning any changes of wage-prices he will be wholly controlled by the labor bureau.

*This will put a stop to all strikes or lockouts.* We wish in this to do as we would be done by, and go to the extreme limit of what is *right.* The capitalist says it is *"my money that is invested and I want to feel that I have full control."* And so you shall have, and hence we will go even so far as to suggest to this board that any private personal contract you can make with any of your people shall not come under the supervision of the labor bureau, so long as your actions or contracts do not come under the head of competitive labor, as we have drawn the line, and this must be recognized by the people of this country or there will be no remedy for our troubles.

### The Main Power of the Labor Bureau.

The main power this labor bureau shall be endowed with is to act as a *legal board* to arbitrate, in a conciliatory manner, and impartially judge and decide disputes, misunderstandings, grievances of whatever nature or character arising between the employer or employed. The acts of this board shall be final, for if six just men cannot render a just verdict when all the evidence, *pro* and *con*, is properly presented by plaintiff and defendant, then no higher tribunal among men can be had, unless it may be possibly found in the voice of a majority of the people.

All labor performed outside of institutions, where money is spent in making improvements, of whatever nature, where there is no capital invested for the purpose of *gain,* will not come under the jurisdiction of the labor bureau and will be left wholly to *competitive labor* for the regulation of wages. For example : A has a job for someone to do and B is willing to perform the work for $2.00, and it is really worth $2.00, but C steps forward and underbids B and proposes to A to do the work for $1.50. C will get the job, unless out of purely philanthropic motive A would pay B

BEN TILLETT.
Fig. 1.

ISAIAH V. WILLIAMSON.
Fig. 2.

J. H. STEAD.
Fig. 3.

FLORENCE NIGHTINGALE.
Fig. 4.

Plate VI–For sketches see page 220.

really what in honor the work is worth. This we denominate competitive labor. But this does not affect the industrial arts in general, nor not at all as to institutions, which are, or come, under the supervision of the labor bureau.

By this time our reader will understand the line we draw between the labor that comes legitimately under the regulating function of the labor bureau and that which is left to itself. The institutions registered in the labor bureau, and all labor therein performed, is no longer *competitive labor*. The only competition that can effect it is that which regulates the commodity; the product of its own labor, where it has to compete with the governing or regulating principles of *supply and demand* in the markets of the world, the same competition which regulates the profits of the capital invested. But, as it is now, all such labor, as in the former instances, incurs regulation of wage-prices from two sources, competition met with in the markets and competitive labor coming from its *own ranks*. *Here is an injustice, as all can see at once.* Unfair proposition! Double odds, which the laboring classes at the present time are bound to face, while capital has really to meet but one source of competition, and this is largely modified by uniting its strength in forming trusts, pools and corporations, the power of which is beyond the control of our wage-earners, however well they may be organized. Even the general public comes under the *ban* of the present *regime*, and the only recourse lies in the enactment of laws that will correct the pending difficulties. Certainly no one will think us *hypocritical* when we contend for measures by law to remove *just one obstacle* in the way of our wage-earners to an equal chance with capital to acquire that dollar due to the one who justly wins it.

So long as the wage-earner is unprotected against the competition coming from his own ranks, the capitalist can discharge his people and replace them with cheaper labor. This is the primary cause of strikes and lockouts, and so long as this field is open the present trouble between capital and labor will exist and grow worse instead of better. Labor unions have been organized for the purpose of meeting the trouble face to face, and aim at precisely what we claim; and, although these labor unions have been failures in extant, still it must be admitted, from the facts existing, that these unions have created a public sentiment which, prospectively, it may be said, have been to a certain degree successful. *

**Salary.** The salary of this board should be enough to make it desirable or allowable for a good business man to serve. We would suggest $1,500 or $1,800 a year, making monthly payments, giving them a vacation of three months—the time to be agreed to among themselves. All rulings must be determined when all the members are present, or a *quorum, which shall consist* of all the members, and all actions or decisions must be unanimous, as in the case of a jury.

Then there should be a clerk, and a stenographic type-writer at a reasonable salary. The salary we mention merely so as to proximate the cost of this labor bureau, which should not be much over $11,000 or $12,000 annually. This can readily be made up to the State by a small registration *fee* of the business concerns coming within the jurisdiction of the labor bureau. We would suggest an annual fee of $2.00 for every *thousand dollars* invested by the concern so registering.

The cost of this bureau is very small as compared with the cost of a single strike, besides it will keep the people together more, socially, and create a kinder relation between capital and labor, at the same time materially assisting in furthering the work in hand, for where employer and employed are mutually interested a more cordial and enduring

---

* We would here suggest that our reader turn to pages 58 and 59 where we give the number of strikes, and the number engaged in them, and the cost in money and time, both to the employer and employed, and then think how much better a system of *cumpolsory arbitration will be* when all this trouble can be obviated.

feeling is engendered, and work as a consequence is prosecated with greater rapidity, the results therefrom being larger profits and the retention of a reputation for prompt and efficient execution of orders, which in many instances will bring increased business to the employer and frequently be a great and highly-appreciated accommodation to the party for whom the work is done.

---

*By Way of Desultory Recapitulation we Close This Section With a Few Notes on Compulsory Arbitration.*

**1.**—The law of universal fraternity demands that the people, through their representatives, in a legally constituted state labor bureau, shall *force* settlement by arbitration of all disputes arising between *capital and labor.* We admit *this to be* the alternative, but at the present time and for many years to come it is the best thing to do. If this bureau was a court this could not be legally done, but since it is conciliatory and peaceful there is no obstacle in the way that the mind can conceive of for the state to enforce *compulsory arbitration*—humanity demands it.

It is hoped that wise and honorable men forming an impartial tribunal will render a just and true verdict by which both disputants will be benefited and thus maintain a friendly relation. Then he who asks more than justice, or is not satisfied with an equitable and honorable decision, *is not a good citizen.* It would be far better for society if such a man were forced to take a position in the front rank in battle where he will be the first to fall.

**2.**—Man exists under physical laws which are well defined by physiology. In every sense man is so organized that his environments are not only adapted to his needs, but furnish means of existence, all that is required is to exercise his capabilities to acquire what is by nature his due. By tilling the ground, in return for his labor, the earth brings forth food for his body. Without labor, either mental or manual, he would not long survive. Everyone has a right to use means to *serve* the *end* of existence. In mankind there is planted a consciousness of the faculty of consistency and hence the rational comes uppermost in the mind, so that what are one man's needs, rights and prerogatives are also the ethical and physical attributes of his *brother-man.* Primarily, humanity begins here, and he who wants more steps over the landmark of *consistency.* There are those who are never satisfied though they may possess the earth and are not willing to concede to others what they are ever ready to arrogate to themselves. These are the fractious members of society, and the public sense of what is right may of necessity be compelled to call a meeting of friends to advise, conciliate and thus in the most humane and friendly manner try to adjust and settle difficulties. But should this course prove a failure, to harmonize incongruous elements, then comes the crisis, when the sociological laws of equity may have to be enforced, and we claim that at this point, after all ethical means have failed should be in the form of *compulsory arbitration* in order to put an end to strife and contention.

**3.**—Arrogance and oppression arouse in those who come under their lash the same feeling that is produced in man by a painful application of the whip to the body. The first impression is a feeling of resistance. In the physical sense nature has endowed man with pain which is a warning to him that an attack is made perhaps to destroy existence, against which he immediately musters his forces, debates, examines all points by which he may make a successful defense and thus save himself. Man's ethical nature, if insulted, recoils and does the same thing as in the instance of physical invasion of his rights. The true man never gives offense to his fellow-brother. Those who are so far lost to humanity as to trespass on the rights of others are liable to a trial by a tribunal, established by the people for the specific purpose of maintaining *law and order*. To harmonize incongruous elements in society, who are a source of social disturbance, no one will question the right to legislate enactments by which to preserve social integrity and thus also perpetuate the sovereignty of the state.

**4.**—In the natural order of things, in the evolution of civilization, human history dates back to a time when the strongest and the most skilled in the struggle for existence survived the longest. Quarrels were then settled by herculean "*peace-makers.*" All the world from time immemorial honored the peace-maker and there never was a time when *arbitration* was not in demand.

Prior to the time when gunpowder made its advent as a peace-maker, "might made right." This discovery brought men on a common level in a physical sense. The era of *firearms* transferred the power that tribes or nations possessed in primeval times from *muscle-rule* to the plane of strategem and the use of explosives as a means of warfare. By the continued improvement in implements of war, such an expeditious and easy way of taking life has been brought about in modern warfares that we are rapidly approaching a n **o** e desirable epoch of *mind-rule.*

All former means of settling disputes among men, which we denominate the *era of brute-rule*, will, in the new era, be taken from the domain of *shot and shell* to the realm of the *intellect* where social difficulties may be adjusted by *conciliatory means*, and if nothing better can accomplish the desired end, which is peace, then *compulsory arbitration*, we say, must be enforced. It is better this than civil war. Hence at this juncture of human progress there can be nothing more laudable than for the state to enact needed laws to assist its citizens to arbitrate and settle disputes in the most *manly manner* and thus entirely obviate the use of the soldiery. State troops in the new era will be only an ornament. The exercise in the *manual of arms* is healthful and is a wonderful school for developing the body—*æsthetic culture*. Thus military organizations will be retained in sociology as an art of physical training of the body and not for the purpose of warfare, as hitherto in vogue. *

**5.**—For anyone or any number of persons to step forward and prevent a serious personal quarrel, or to separate men engaged in mortal combat, or to stand between persons so enraged that they may do no serious bodily injury, has always been held to be a humane thing to do. The laws of every land give license for a peace-loving citizen to assume the *role* of "peace-maker" when occasion demands it. Then how can the public consistently stand by quietly and see lock-outs and strikes running on for months, a quarrel which brings sorrow not only to those directly engaged, but to the general public, family and innocent children? Why not in this enforce settlement? Is there any reason why the state should not become "peace-maker"? For what use is the commonwealth? Let the state put an immediate quietus on such pig-headed and unwise actions of these infractious elements in our social system. What shall we do? Call out the state troops? Shoot down one or the other? Settle by violence, or do nothing? Stand by and let the quarrel go on until one or the other is frozen out or voluntarily comes to some kind of settlement? Certainly all who are of good mind will join us in a more humane method. Why have we a government, state or municipal, or why have laws of any kind if we are not to make them available in time of need? We say the very

---

* We would have our reader think of the wonderful discoveries and improvements which have been made in the last few years in heavy artillery. The *segmental wire gun* (J. Hamilton Brown, inventor) is capable of sending a missile six miles and sink an armor-plated ship. Then think of the Krupp gun, the Winchester and Springfield rifles, smokeless powder, etc., and we are again brought *face to face* with a *new era* as we before remarked; humanity demands (since the easy death-dealing means of warfare now at our command) that all these wonderful implements of war *are rendered useless* by taking the wars of nations out of the corporeal battlefields and transfer them into the bloodless realm of the intellectual.

best thing to do is to have a law *enforcing arbitration* before an impartial *labor bureau*, legally constituted, and thus prove to the world that savagery has been grandly superseded by our civil institutions.

**6.**—A lawful settlement of labor differences by arbitration is a peaceful measure. There will be no need for state troops, or a state police, or sheriff's posse to prevent riots or to quiet outbreaks. What matters it by what means the public peace is sustained if at the same time all peoples receive their just dues? Law is the product of necessity. Law is also arbitrary in a sense, but if law is based on first principles it is always just and right. If all peoples lived up to the principles of the "*golden rule*" there would be no need of law. Law is forced conciliation. A man of our acquaintance, not a habitual drunkard, but at an ungarded social good time, with friends, on a new year's day, became inebriated, and though a very fine gentleman by birth and education, became very abusive and combative under the influence of liquor, so that nothing short of handcuffs and a prison cell could be done to control him, where he was allowed to "sober up." When he came to himself and learned what had taken place he said "that he was glad that he was imprisoned for he might, in his inebriated condition, have done some one serious harm."

Compulsory conciliatory measures may seem contradictory, but at least all right thinking people will be thankful, for this will save to them a court case or the loss of much money, valuable time and bitter feelings. The state of Pennsylvania had to foot a bill of over $225,000 to keep the peace at Homestead. The entire Homestead affair was most disgraceful to an intelligent people. If compulsory arbitration had been in vogue millions of money and many lives might have been saved.

**7.**—*Compulsory arbitration* has been tried in north of England and other places and always works well. It is rational, it is right; the aim is equity; it will prevent *arbitrary rule* on the one hand and violence on the other; it is manly and humane; it does not engender revenge; it is not a court where a judge of law presides; its only law is written in every man—equity, justice.

For many other reasons it is right. It is the best for the rich and the poor, Christian or pagan, and should be established in every state in the Union and people educated up to it and put a stop to this everlasting quarrel between capital and labor.

**8.**—Considering the vast number of wage-earners now in the United States and cheap labor imported daily, the frequent *lock-outs* and strikes with their terrible consequences, it behooves the people at once to get to work and fall into line that will bring about a more amicable relation between labor and capital.

Let no man harbor revenge, though he may have been greatly injured. Lord Bacon says: "Certainly, in taking revenge, a man is but even with his enemy, but in passing it over he is his superior, for it is a prince's part to pardon." The same author says further: "That which is past is gone and cannot be recalled, and wise men have enough to do with things present and to come; therefore they but trifle with themselves that labor in past matters." Solomon says: " It is the glory of a man to pass by an offense."

That the business of this country requires for its safe management the highest statesmanship cannot be too deeply impressed on our readers. Everyone for himself should study the subject unbiased by any preconceived notions and take up the subject as it presents itself and be *sure you are right* before you come to a final conclusion. Also remember that what may seem to you to be the right course to pursue may not seem so clear to another; therefore the cultivation of the greatest virtue in the fullest sense is *charity*. Once this faculty gaining control of the hearts of men the fruit it will yield will be reassuring in the hope of a glorious ending in peace and happiness awaiting the American people, but *vigilance* must be the watchword and now is the time to act before it is too late; therefore do not let the opportunity pass by unimproved and think that you individually can do nothing. We need the help of every man and woman. We believe that *compulsory arbitration* will be the *stepping-stone* to a condition of our social system when this method will be displaced by purely voluntary conciliatory measures, which will be the order of settling disputes. The greed of man will then be materially modified and by practical lessons we will learn that it is far better to agree on a *system of government* of political economy that will make none very rich and none very poor.

**9.**—There are those who say that the state cannot force people to arbitrate. We say the state has a right to make any needed law that will secure peace and happiness to its citizens. Every decade brings with it circumstances and conditions which call for special legislation and it is the *duty* of the legislature to fill the indication. At the present time there is great demand for legal regulation of the *labor trouble* to prevent men, who have not humanity as a ruling principle in their hearts, from grinding each other to the quick. The state has always a right to legislate and pass needed laws to assure " the greatest good to the greatest number."

**10.**—It is unfortunate for the laboring classes that they are not better informed regarding personal economy. As a rule few provide for the winter. During the summer when there is demand for labor and plenty of money, is always a golden opportunity to provide for the winter, but too often neglected.

Then it is still more unfortunate, not alone as far as the workmen are concerned, but the general public, that operators engaged in mining and other industrial institutions to shut down in the fall or in the winter and thus throw out of work thousands of people at a time when they are in greatest need and should have employment.

**11.**—Rev. Lyman Abbott, D. D., writes in the '' Arena '' on this subject, and we take great pleasure to quote from this great thinker a few paragraphs in support of our position. He says : ''Compulsory arbitration is simply the application to settlement of industrial controversies of the same essential principle which is, throughout the civilized world, employed for the settlement of other controversies. It devolves upon those who do not believe that this principle can be applied to show why it is inapplicable.'' Of course there are serious objections, and this, he says, '' is generally the case to any plan proposed for securing peace in a community, the individual members of which are covetous, selfish, passionate, ambitious.'' The same writer says that ''Compulsory arbitration is a specific for labor troubles. The question is not : Are there difficulties involved in compulsory arbitration ? but, Would those difficulties be greater than those involved in a system which keep labor and capital always alternating between open battle and an armed truce, and which, in one-half year, has inflicted on the two great States of Pennsylvania and New York the great labor wars of Homestead and Buffalo ? There is no radical cure for labor trouble but character transformed and conduct controlled by Christian principles. Meanwhile compulsory arbitration is a device to protect the innocent from the injuries inflicted upon them by those whose character and conduct are not controlled by Christian principles, nor even by those of Moses or Confucius, but by the devil's maxim—' Every man for himself.' ''

**12.**—We wish our reader to remember that our suggestion on this grievous question, looking toward a final and peaceful ending, is voicing the sentiment of a very large majority of our best thinkers in the United States, and all that is required is a little more agitation and a personal effort of every good citizen, and it will not be a difficult task to ultimately win on the side of right. The profession of the demagogue will, in that day, be no more, for it will be unlawful to ''lobby'' through our Legislatures or Congress laws in the interest of capital or in the interest of any particular class.

# TARIFF, PEOPLES AND WAGE-WORKERS.

*Wrong Government; A Good Government; The Best Policy; Tax or License; Protective Tariff; Free Trade; Revenue; Constitutionality; Effect on Trade and Wages; National Tariff Bureau; Purifying Politics; Etc.*

"*Divide et Impera.*" In English this means "Divide and Govern." "This is the policy of almost all governments. By dividing a nation into parties, poisoning them against each other, the people are deprived of their intrinsic weight, and their rulers incline the scale as suits their caprice or discretion."

**A Philosophic View.** All human institutions to stand must be founded on our intuitive sense of right. The virtue of our nature at once gives support to a *law* agreeing with *some one* of our feelings that harmonize with it, and when these *primary tests* of right are ignored in framing our laws, such laws will not stand, for the reason that the foundation is not good.

Any system of government is wrong under the *regime* of which a single individual can accumulate, by whatsoever business may be pursued, thirty or forty million dollars. Even the possibility of centralizing such great wealth in the hands of a few is dangerous to the liberty and welfare of the people. It is not a good government, we say, where such things are possible. Great wealth is Imperial, Monarchial, and begets Anarchial sentiment among the people.

**Wrong Government.** It is a factor, recognized by the leading minds, that "money is power." If it is in the hands of a philanthropist no wrong need be feared, but in the hands of a Shylock there is no divining the possible evil that may result, not only to local communities, where such wealth is actively operated, but to the general government. The base use of money can so corrupt politics that all the grand principles for which our fathers so manfully fought may be swept away like a Johnstown flood. The bulwarks of a great dam gradually giving way, continually menacing the safety of the people, and when, at last, the crash comes like a thunderbolt, it carries destruction in its way. Then a people who are wide awake to their best interests, and who desire to perpetuate those laws and institutions, based on the natural rights of man, attained by the blood of the founders of our government, must restrain the menacing powers which threaten the life of the nation, and avert the danger in a practical manner by repealing all laws which aid, and possibly foster, destruction, and enact laws that will bring liberty and happiness to the greatest number.

**A Clergyman of Chicago.** In a sermon a celebrated clergyman of Chicago said that "no man can make a million dollars during the natural life allotted to him, and make it honestly, not even, strictly speaking, can it be made legitimately, and surely not morally." This we believe to be the truth ; no man can acquire such great wealth, however extensive his business may be, if he follows the "golden rule."

There are those who amass great fortunes, who, nevertheless, keep within the purview of the law in all their business transactions, and yet are all the while robbing their fellow-men of what is honestly their due.

**Homestead Steelworks.** This is easily done. The Homestead Steelworks are converted, or re-organized, under a legal charter, it is true, into a company (or organized corporation) on a large scale, (combining capital), and, as we have elsewhere stated, works of this sort require an immense capital, even to purchase the machinery indispensable to start the works at all, but this is no reason why moral and individual obligations should not be in full force, as with the rest of humanity who manage a very much smaller portion of the affairs of this world. As a rule these gigantic combines are placed under the control of a so-called management, or agent, whose moral obligations are regulated, or rather relieved, by the combine or company, which in many instances is so in name only, for the purpose of making moral responsibility anonymous, while the head, or those who furnish the capital, may be taking their ease in luxury in foreign lands or at the seaside, or travel for pleasure.

Apparently a very conscientious man, one who gives much to the poor, often receives encomiums of the press for his philanthrophy and public spirit, but how does he obtain his wealth? He has some capital. This is invested in a variety store or some trust company. The undercurrent of these combines is not apparent, at least not to the superficial observer, until by the unnatural accumulation of great wealth their power is beginning to be felt by the money gradually leaving the pockets of the people and pouring into the coffers of these institutions. These corporations have no soul. There is no compunction of conscience, for this faculty has been ruled out by the scheme on which the organization was formed. Legally no member of such organization can be indicted even for the most apparent infraction of the law.

**Not Safe in Such Hands.** Then we would say here that no one who has any interest, either directly or indirectly, in a trust company or a great corporation or combine of any kind, should be considered eligible for membership to State Legislature or Congress. The interests of the people are not safe in such hands.

When we come to look the ground over and view the subject from an equitable standpoint, you will soon learn the moral impossibility for a man to make a million of dollars in the short space of a lifetime, to say nothing of making thirty, fifty or a hundred millions. Then we say again, that there is something not altogether right in a government where men can do this. Of course a man may "strike oil," as the saying goes; or by accident open a rich mine;

or make a great discovery as Edison did ; or make an investment in a few acres of land and a city is built about him,
whereby he may become a millionaire, but the point in hand
is, can a man honestly make millions in carrying on business in a judicious and equitable manner ?  Good business
principles make money, but it also makes it honorably.
The moment you leave these boundaries you pass into the
realm of the gambler, the Shylock, and you depart from
good, honorable and equitable business principles.    In a
true government, then, law must support only those efforts
of its citizens which come within the purview of the elements
or attributes of the capitalist who is willing to take the profits of a business conducted on equal chances with his fellow-beings who are also in business.    All other institutions,
such as we have outlined, which secretly and ultimately
drain the pockets of the people of their equivalent in trade,
and where it is evident that there exists a *focal-point* of attraction for the dollars to accumulate in undue proportion,
should be carefully demarcated in all legal bearings, and if
they cannot be regulated so as to keep within the limitation boundary line of equal rights, equal chance, all things
being equal, then such institutions had better be entirely
prohibited by law.

**Tariff, Cause of Trouble**    One of the most prominent
causes of the stagnation of
business in this country is the almost ceaseless agitation of
the *tariff question*.  Our endeavor to solve the *Labor Problem* would be almost futile should we not dwell upon this
subject in its different phases, and demonstrate the truth in
its political bearings on the question at issue.

We acknowledge that we enter upon the discussion of
this subject with some hesitation and with a full sense of
responsibility, feeling the burden heavily as we approach a
task freighted with the mental ballast of statesmen and
philosopher.  But we cannot for one moment entertain the
idea of passing this milestone on our way, which is one of

the most prominent, pointing the way to the path of safety in the labyrinthian road to national prosperity, and is one of the great breakers over which the "ship of state" finds so much trouble to pass safely, bounded as it is with its labor troubles.

This subject must in some legal way be brought under healthy management in order to meet the demands of a free and prosperous government, such as the constitution of our country offers to all its citizens.

**Every Four Years.** In the course of every four years our country is troubled with the *pros and cons* of a hitherto unapproached or unsettled financial question bearing on the tariff, creating a disturbance and commotion in our financial affairs, which after each presentment leaves the situation of our commercial and industrial interests in a more threatening and hopeless condition than before. If it were not for the many personal or private interests involved in levying a tariff on so many different commodities, it would not be so difficult to determine a correct basis by which other internal legislation might be governed, in order to do justice to all peoples concerned, for it is plain that each presidential campaign seems only to embarrass the business community. The various political parties seem to use the different issues as a simple play of political cricket. Platforms are erected and plastered over with flaming posters full of "Tariff Reform," for or against its characters or "principles," so systematically arranged as political puppets that voters cannot distinguish Jack from Jill, and thus parties gain or lose control in the governmental departments, not by honest means, but by such subterfuge as demagogues resort to for their own personal aggrandizement instead of national or universal benefit. *The people* may by chance be present and hear these bombastic speeches in favor of a *protective tariff, a tariff for revenue only, or out and out free trade.*

Vast sums of money are periodically spent to defray the

expenses of the piratical leaders and for their gladiatorial rehearsals in the political arena to amuse the public.    Nothing more modest can be truthfully said of these campaign

**Figure Heads.** *figure heads*, as far as real education of the people on this subject of tariff is concerned.    From them thus far no intelligent understanding of the subject has been reached.

Surely if the government can once decide on a reliable course to settle the question of an *import tax* that will be permanent, so that it cannot be assailed and altered *ever and anon* for partisan gain or advantage, thereby checking the onward course of commerce and blasting the confidence of business men, then we may expect better times, a more harmonious feeling and a greater activity among the people all over the country.

**A Presidential Campaign.** The tariff question is so profound a subject that the short space of a presidential campaign does not give time enough even to teach the people the A B C of a subject in which the general public should be properly informed and thoroughly educated.    On the "stump" it is treated at best only in a superficial manner and never free from party prejudices.

The proper management of the financial department of a government is one of almost Herculean labor.    The most famous statesmen have been found wanting in this undertaking.    The idea of a *protective tariff* involves so many intricate points, so many financial problems, that even good statesmanship finds entanglements in the network of various business departments, irreconcilable in theory and practice, to puzzle it.    Therefore, taking a philosophical view of the subject, it at once becomes apparent to the thinking mind that a subject so intricate and difficult to handle, involving so much of vital importance to all classes, should not be entrusted to the shallow brains and personal manipulation of office hunters, but should be placed in the hands of

**Office Hunters.** a *board of censors*, whose business it shall be to manage the "import duty" business of the nation, and thus take this question out of popular politics altogether.

The *sole* and *exclusive* business of this *bureau* should be to study the vital points of an *all-beneficial tariff.* Is it not reasonable to come to this conclusion when we know that the general public is too much pre-occupied with its manifold affairs to give ample time to acquire proper knowledge of the subject, in order to cast an intelligent vote for or against in whatever form it may be presented—though the question seemingly may be stated plainly in the different political party platforms?

**Wants His Side to Win.** Those who go forth to present, and argue on, this subject as a campaign issue are, in many instances, governed by personal interests, or the simple desire to have *their* party win, much the same as a man owning a fine horse desires to see his steed win the race, because of the money he will make and the sport and gratification it will give him.

Persons wishing a point of law decided would not be willing to submit it to the issue of a political campaign. They would at once submit the matter to a proper judiciary tribunal, whose legal function and only business is to decide questions of law.

**Extortion and Distortion.** There is both extortion and distortion in politics; extortion in funds, in and out, assessing for the purpose of campaign funds, and distortion of truth, outside especially. Politicians * so cut up, mangle and distort the truth, as a rule, that the general public, whose special business, study or reading does not include *political* economy, is scarcely

---

* The proper definition of the term " politician " is one who is versed in statesmanship, and the term " politics " means the " doctrine " or science of government. A perverter of " politics " is a " demagogue," and hence we often speak of politicians in the popular acceptation of the term when we should use the term " demogogue."

sufficiently informed on the subject to detect even the most apparent discrepancies or falsehoods advanced.    And even should they be bereft of this *campaign weapon* of falsification, *party politics* would still stand in the way of an honest, unprejudiced decision on the vital question at issue.

Comparatively speaking but very few of the people of the United States know much about the *tariff question* and its vital importance, especially regarding a *protective tariff*, and, moreover, will learn but little about it until the effect becomes apparent ofttimes when it is too late to correct the mistake made by wrong legislation if such there be.    Hence it would be far better for the people to leave this question entirely out of *campaign politics* as an *issue* to be decided by voters who know but little about the subject of *tariff*, and especially is this true of newly-made citizens whose education on political economy in some foreign land has been diameterically opposite to our own.

**Purifying Politics.** This will also make our elections more *Republican*, favoring candidates simply for their intrinsic merits, for president or any other prominent position, and framing distinctive party platforms on current national matters, making them as simple and comprehensive as possible.

As it now is parties enter the contest with nothing in view but a place in the White House, regardless of the difference in tariff, high or low, protective or for "revenue only," or free trade altogether, and how all may effect the country so the point is gained.    Whichever party can hoodwink the people most will "carry the day," while in either case business centers will be so greatly disturbed that it will take a year or two to restore its equilibrium, and then before the country fully recovers from the jar another campaign opens and the sad story is repeated.

The proper way out of this national morass is, we firmly believe, to vest our *financial tariff destiny* in a NATIONAL TARIFF BUREAU.

FRANK P. SARGENT.

Plate VII—For sketch see page 220.

**Customs Bureau.** For the purpose of regulating all *import duties* coming within the domain of a protective tariff, so as to take it entirely out of the politics of the country, let there be established, as before suggested, a national bureau, whose duty it shall be to adjust and regulate all matters pertaining to the levying or imposing of a so-called "tariff" or "duty" on commodities imported from foreign countries and intended to enter our markets.

This board, we would further suggest, should be composed of twelve fully qualified members, to be elected by Congress and approved by the president. Or the members of this board may be appointed by the president—as it may seem best in the good judgment of the framers of this bureau; at all events the chairman should be appointed by the president and become a member of the Cabinet as *secretary of customs*.

**A New Cabinet Officer.** In our own opinion we favor the appointment of the members of this "*tariff bureau*" by Congress, save the chairman, who should be appointed by the president and who shall be known as the "*secretary of customs*," and by this act becomes an additional member of the Cabinet. The members of this bureau, we would further suggest, should be selected from the four grand divisions of the Union, namely, from the East, West, North and South, and thus bring together sociological needs and views of the most matured thoughts developed by environment and conditions of a people who are bound together by a common interest appertaining to keeping together the nation as one family, yet in detail there are many local conditions demanding representation in the bureau of social and commercial regulations of the greatest returns possible to the local, as well as the the general public. The term of office to be four years, the

**Secretary of Customs.** sessions of this board to be held the same as that of the *members of the House of Representatives*. All its rulings shall be unanimous and signed by the president.

The duties of the secretary of customs or "tariff bureau" shall be defined by the ordinary parliamentary rules as those of the chairman, and he shall make true and faithful reports of the doings of this board to the judiciary and executive departments. Or the proper legal transaction of this *board* should be submitted to Congress, and we think it would not be unwise for the acts passed by the *custom bureau* * to pass Congress in the regular order, the same as other acts, which by such passage and the final signature of the president shall become law. One *desideratum* above all others in connection with the furtherance of our object in securing honest and just legislation for and in behalf of a *protective tariff* is that this *customs bureau* in all its functions and rulings *shall* be *purely* and *entirely non-partisan.* We regard this as the most vital and essential principle of a good and successful government—cool deliberation and freedom from all party prejudices. The ruling thought in the adoption of means and ways will then not be what "my party desires in the matter," but what is good, right and for the benefit of *all parties.* Experience shows that there is an everpresiding tendency of parties and majorities to exert their power and thence arises the necessity of an ever vigilant watchfulness to restrain those in power or to select only true and good men to make or amend our laws.

**Jurisdiction.** The duty of the *customs bureau* should be to investigate, regulate, amend, relieve or impose such *duty or tariff* on all commodities coming under the head of *importation,* and as it may seem proper in the best judgment of the unanimous opinion of the members constituting said *bureau* and always in the best interests of the whole people of the United States and in accordance with the spirit of the constitution and *never* favoring a class or a political party.

---

* We very much favor the name we here use as being most proper and best understood for it at once expresses its function. Then let it be "*customs bureau,*" and its chairman legally is secretary of customs and a Cabinet officer.

It should be remembered always that this bureau shall have no paramount authority or jurisdiction over internal revenue in any sense. All tariff for revenue only and all *internal revenue* shall remain under the management about as it is now in vogue. We simply desire the tariff question, or all legislation on the subject, to be taken out of the hands of politicians—using the word in the popular sense—and placed in the keeping of non-partisan and honest statesmen.

**Import Duty.** No import duty should ever be imposed in times of peace for the purpose of "revenue only." This levying taxes simply to fill the treasury, then employing it that it may be filled again, breeds extravagance and dishonesty. But whatever legislation may be called for in this department must pass through this customs bureau, or, in simpler parlance, all legislation of a purely *revenue* character does *not* come under the supervision of this bureau. But all matters relating to *tariff* imposed with the specific purpose of protecting our people against the world in all branches of industry *not yet fully developed, and not yet a necessity of the people* shall be under their exclusive jurisdiction. Revenue tax, it should be remembered, is not on that account a protective tariff.

**Strictly Non-Partisan.** The members of this bureau shall have *no personal* interest in any manufacture of commodities coming under their supervision of whatever kind or character, either directly or indirectly. The entire business of this customs bureau must be conducted as far as possible on absolutely non-partisan principles.

This bureau shall set apart a time at stated intervals during its regular sessions for the purpose of giving audience to any respectable person recommended by their own representative in Congress for the presentation of memorials, essays, lectures or addresses on any subject matter bearing directly upon any issue before them or any proposition for special legislation on questions pending with reference to protective tariff.

This method of discussion and inter-change of ideas upon the subject bearing directly on this question will do much towards removing the tariff question from popular politics and enable honest statesmen more fully to familiarize themselves with the actual wants or needs and ideas of the people, and enable them to give decisions and enact laws, influenced entirely by sound judgment, based on scientific knowledge of the best interests of *all* unbiased by *personal* interests or campaign harangues to distract their senses by garbled presentments of political requirements.

**A Glib Tongue.** We take this position on the ground that the tariff question is one too profound and important for the ordinary mind to fully comprehend; especially when subjected to party Don Quixotes glib tongue to discuss it to the disparagement of the truth.

There is no other subject in the whole province of political economy which, by misrepresenting of facts, tends to cripple business as much as the unscientific discussion of the tariff by these *office-hunting* political satraps; bringing it hydra-headed to the front every four years!

A protective tariff would be a beneficent thing, provided it protects *labor* as well as *capital.* To be *just* the enactment and administration of law must affect all alike, the poor and the rich, the weak and the strong. If a given law will make half the individual members of the country five times richer than they are, and the other half poorer by *one-fifth*, the whole would be *six fold* richer, but it would be robbing *the one-half* to *enrich the other one-half.* That is *protective tariff that does not fully protect.*

**To Unbar Our Water Gates.** So long as legislation favors one class only by which they amass a fortune, and no protection is given to the other, whose labor is indispensable to capital, it were better for our government to *unbar its water gates* and let the tide of foreign competition roll in; let the *supply* and *demand* of the *entire world* regulate our markets, yield our sovereignty and collect a tax for revenue only.

This, however, is not our ultimatum. We believe in America ruling America. Let this idea be universally proclaimed and endorsed, that the greatest attainment an American citizen aspires to, is to be, in the full sense of the term, a man. True to himself, generous to his neighbor, but at all times *free to think, free to vote*, and, at all times, ready to do battle for humanity when in the right. Those who wish to come to us from foreign shores are welcome here, as long as they are willing to come under restricted regulations by law, and are willing to join the "rank and file" under the banner that represents true American principles. *

**Is it a Good Policy?** It might be *right* to adopt *free trade*, but, in the judgment of our best statesmen, would it be *good* policy to do so? But until all the world arrives at the same conclusion from which an American argues *his rights* of freedom, it would not be *politic* to establish free trade until all nations become similarly conditioned and adopt systems of government founded on *Republican principles*, where labor is recognized as the *peer* of *capital*, can we afford to open our ports free to the commercial world. As in the case of an individual, *self-protection* is the first law of nature. So a nation has a right, in fact it is a duty, to protect its citizens in all that will assure life, liberty and happiness; though now and then a crisis comes when it is justifiable to take life, but the primary object is to exhaust every means that may maintain peace before such an alternative is resorted to. The primary object of all good civil government is the protection of all individuals and their best interests. Free trade at the present time, and for many years to come, would be in violation of these principles, though ultimately and primarily it would be right, but *not until* conditions and systems of government of other nations with whom we have commercial intercourse are similar to our own.

---

* See the article on "immigration," also on "contract labor" in another part of this work.

**Where are the Dollars?** This question of protective tariff, however, is not altogether the direct cause of the trouble we would here have allayed. The direct cause is *internal*. Tariff is levied on a commodity in order to *protect* the manufacturer to the extent of the amount imposed on it. He does not actually pay it; the importer does not really foot the extra bill. *The consumer pays it.* The wage-worker receives no more pay. There is no more nor less money in the country. But in a few years there is more money in *certain places.* You can readily perceive the rapid increase of wealth in America, but you notice it is in the hands of a comparatively few. The people are no richer.

Then unless there is a correct and vigilant legislation regulating internal affairs, such as prohibiting combinations and the formation of great corporations, who by this means derive the power to control the markets and wages, and certainly they have this for their object or else by combining their strength there would be no advantage. Such a tariff will aid in creating centres towards which by quiet volition the mass of the dollars are drawn as unerringly as the electro-magnet draws the particles of steel and iron that come within its radius of attraction. This is dangerous, it is unfair to the citizen, consumer and the wage-earner. This is the way to make monied-lords and moneyless men.

What little money there is made by those in business who are willing to make a legitimate profit, and who are *not in the ring*, the wage-earners, and we may say the masses, are by these insidious means and management of our financial policy made to *pay tribute* to maintain a monied aristocracy, though not yet so large or strong but that it may be arrested in its course, yet all that is needed now to show the perfection of its evil tendencies is to pass some law creating title of nobility, attainable by so many dollars in American coin the same as they are furnished in Italy, and it will not take many decades to see America a despotism like Russia, or a hotbed of bandits and assassins like Italy.

**A Mere Luxury.** But suppose a protective tariff to be operative as the term implies—we levy a duty on a commodity of industry, a mere luxury if you will, of which all we are in need of in this country can be produced here, the price of which is regulated by the law of supply and demand, and then some one residing out of the United States can and does manufacture said article and wishes to open trade in the United States ; our government imposes a tax or license on this intruder, to be paid into the treasury. The amount to be so levied, and the different commodities to be fixed by our customs bureau and so carefully regulated that the foreigner comes conditioned into our markets on equal chances, if not equal, then nearly so. The home retail price *should not be advanced* by reason of the tariff paid at our port by this foreigner. If our internal legislation is right, *placing all men on a common level*, governed by natural laws of equity, then such a tariff is protection in a proper and true sense.

It should be understood by every citizen that the dollar paid as import duty, if added to the price of goods, is a tax on the consumer and then why call this process a protective tariff when it is a tax on the people who are the consumers ? This is revenue, but we want a protective tariff and revenue according as the country may be in need of means to meet expenses. A tariff as a protective measure should be levied to protect home industries whether we have one hundred million in the treasury or one dollar. If the principle of protection is not good, right and proper, then let us call it by the right name and not deceive the people.

**To Work Well.** For the principle to work well and accomplish what we desire as a people, to be protected against *foreign cheap labor*, and in every way do justice to our own business men and the whole people, and to make the importer pay the tariff and not the consumer, we must by proper enactments of law do away with trusts, pools, corporations and combines, whose sole object is to control our home markets, and who by the help of a tariff are enabled to put prices high up and in this way *fancy fortunes* are made—the consumer pays it all.

No good government will give aid, however indirect it may be, to the harpies that feast on the vitals of our business life. Honest competition is crushed by its very weight, holding business by the throat and forcing it to "deliver or die." The corporations and "trusts" of our land

**An Aristocracy.** may well be compared to the aristocracy of Europe in their relations with the people; both are highly priviledged, though our corporations and "trusts" are more powerful and injurious here than the aristocracy of Europe in their own country are now, for the people are beginning to comprehend the "tricks of the game."

The man at the port is enabled and allowed to add the "tariff" he paid to his goods, and our people eventually pay this tax. Our own syndicates favor this for two reasons, first it will help to put prices up and secondly foreign nations, many at least, are very likely to retaliate and so open another market where the prices go up and consumers there pay the difference and thus our manufacturers are enabled to reap a double profit as the result of this sort of legislation, if they choose to go to foreign markets. With our present price of labor they can, however, only go to markets in countries where a "high tariff" is the law.

**We Are Opposed to It.** We say that we are morally and politically opposed to all *such* legislation, and yet there is no good reason why a "protective tariff" should not be imposed in the true sense on a large number of things, especially on all *infantile industries*, by which to maintain our commercial dignity and prove our faith in the principle of *self-preservation as a nation*.

Foreign nations who sell their products at close marginal profits can still afford to sell in our markets at a small profit and need not, nor will they, cease to employ their capital on this account.

HELEN H. GARDENER.
Fig. 1.

HAMLIN GARLAND.
Fig. 2.

B. O. FLOWER.
Fig. 3.

REV. MINOT J. SAVAGE.
Fig. 4.

Plate VIII—For sketches see pages 220 and 221.

A tariff that will inflate prices is always detrimental to the country. It stimulates manufacturing enterprise and for a time raises wages, but soon over-stocks the markets, and when the reaction comes the country becomes the more prostrated by its abnormal operation. Hence a protective tariff should be levied so as not to affect prices, and it will have no such effect so long as supply and demand governs competition, and then, in a few years, the business of our whole country will become more settled.

A tariff for "revenue only" we apprehend will have a far more deleterious influence on business than the present regime, for many reasons, some of which are self-evident, such as the fluctuation of the markets and the *continued favoritism* asked for by those who want to make *quick fortunes* and do not hesitate to ask the government to assist them.

---

FURTHER ARGUMENTS ON THE TARIFF QUESTION ; DISPUTED POINTS ; THE RIGHT THING TO DO ; A NEW NATION NEAR AT HAND ; NONE EXTREMELY RICH ; NONE VERY POOR ; A PROMISING FUTURE FOR AMERICA, ETC.

**A Different Feature.** A protective tariff differs widely in its nature and operations from that of a tariff for "revenue only." In our political economy they represent entirely different features. All *tariff*, it is admitted, whether intended for protection or not, is a source of revenue. But there is an evident and important distinction between them, and we wish to make this sufficiently plain to the comprehension of all, and thus present another reason why so intricate and important a subject should be taken out of politics and managed exclusively by a board of statesmen, as before suggested and defined.

The money derived from a protective tariff may go far in defraying the current expenses of the government, making the tariff for revenue merely nominal, especially so should our public servants conceive the notion of keeping down expenses. We cannot admit free trade, nor are we able to support an import tariff for revenue only.  *The effort would be clearly deceptive.*

**Material Result.**  All tariff not primarily and exclusively intended as a protection to our industries, covering the business man as well as the laborer, must be considered as internal revenue.  This tax or revenue may be levied as the needs of the government may require, in various ways, in the same manner as a municipal tax in cities or counties is levied and collected.  If a tax or tariff is imposed at a port of entry, be it much or little, it is a source of revenue, but to the exact degree of the amount paid by the importer it is *protective*, hence the material results are similar, notwithstanding the difference in terms applied, namely, "protective tariff," or "tariff for revenue only."

We seriously question the constitutionality of levying a tariff for revenue purposes in time of peace.  But, a tariff with the specific object of protecting home industries, is, peradventure, in accord with the spirit of the constitution and may be imposed by a customs commission.  A protective

**Levying Taxes.**  tariff should, however, at all times be imposed from motives entirely different from those governing the levying of taxes for revenue only; as for example, a tariff for revenue only may be necessary to meet certain contingencies this year and next year this same contingency may not exist, and commodities taxed this year may be entirely exempt next year.  But a tariff levied for the purpose of protecting home industry is beneficial and necessary at all times, as long as any obstacle remains to interfere with the country's prosperity which such tariff is intended to remove.  No import duty should ever be levied in times of peace merely for the purpose of filling a vacuum in our treasury or for personal or partisan consideration, which in political parlance is yclept "class legislation," or simply in point of view of reconciling party differences.  No matter, be there much or little money in the treasury, the motive actuating the levying of a tariff of this kind should be the expediency or necessity arising from a genuine desire to protect our national interests by guarding every vulnerable point in every department of our commerce and industry against unfair competition or invasion

**Foreign Invasion.** of foreign manufacturers in our own markets, which, under their more advantageous conditions and by lower wages paid, the producer puts us to a serious disadvantage and subjects us to a great loss in the sale of our own goods of a similar character. Labor being so much cheaper in foreign countries than here that competition on an equal footing would be detrimental to our own interests and an injustice which it should be the duty of our government to obviate by law in defense of our wage-earners.

**Not to Impede Progress.** If the government needs money our internal revenue may be increased, and it is within the province of Congress to do so, while, at the same time, it is the duty of all officers of the commonwealth not only to provide for every financial emergency, but at the same time to study closely the principles of political economy with a view of keeping the national expenditures down to a proper limit, yet not so as to impede the progress of necessary public improvements however, which a young and ever-growing nation like ours demands. Money spent in the furtherance of institutions meeting the demand of progressive science, art, etc., is always judiciously and profitably invested, but "spending the dollar and saving the penny" is sorry economy.

**Points for Reflection.** We would present, as appropriate matter for reflection as we advance with this subject, several cogent remarks why the tariff question should be in the hands of a *customs commission* or a national tariff bureau, as we have before suggested to be made up of competent statesmen and true representatives of the people.

1st. It corrupts politics. 2d. The question being intricate and of vital importance to the welfare of the nation,

should be entrusted only to able and wise men and not to
political charlatans.   3d. The great majority of the people
are ignorant of its real significance.   4th. Corporations can
"lobby" acts through Congress to favor their own interests.
5th. Many members of Congress are personally interested.
6th. The great difference between a protective tariff and
revenue calls for *different* legislation and by purely non-
partisan considerations.

**Nearly as Cheap as Iron.**   It is contended that a "high
tariff," instead of raising,
really reduced the price of steel rails.   This is not only an
incorrect statement, but is a misapprehension of the facts.
The discovery by Bessemer of a process by which steel can
be manufactured nearly as cheap as iron, and improved pro-
cesses and improved machinery in rolling mills of every description, enables manufacturers to produce steel rails,
armor plates, sheet steel, etc., cheap enough for any market
in the world and still make a good profit.

**An Opportunity.**   Capitalists seeing here an opportunity for a profitable investment,
erected numerous plants in different parts of the country
and over-stocked the market, and here we have another reason why the price of steel rails and other products of steel
is lower.   The formation of "trusts" or "pools," however,
could soon control prices, as was, to a certain extent, done
at Pittsburg.   For armor plates the government pays an
enormous profit per ton, enriching in a few years those who
are fortunate enough to secure a contract to furnish the
same.   This is an imposition on the people.   The government should let all its contracts to responsible and reasonable bidders.   But when there are only a few mills that
have the capacity to build armor plates, and these are under
a syndicate, competition is helpless and the government en-
courages the formation of pools, syndicates and trusts.

**A Famishing Condition.**   As a natural result there is
not much trouble in keeping
the treasury in a famishing condition when anything is

done in the way of coast protection or making improvements. It is not our province at the present undertaking to discuss the particular application of a protective tariff or an internal revenue "single tax," direct or indirect, or any very great change in the method of levying a tax now in vogue ; all we ask is a protective tariff that will protect all peoples alike, in so far as it may be necessary, high or low, and deemed best by a non-partisan commission. We would, however, give our views as to a protective tariff being placed on certain commodities. Those things we actually possess may be subject to taxation, but what we consume (the necessaries of life), should be placed on the *free list.* A customs tax on all articles of luxury and on all undeveloped industries and much of the current expenses of the government may thus be realized, so that an internal tax for revenue purposes will be merely nominal.

**Those From Foreign Lands.** An import duty need not necessarily raise the price on goods so taxed. It will not do so if the law of competition is allowed full sway. Then the markets will be regulated by *supply and demand.* The English or German capitalist, or whosoever he may be, from foreign lands, must enter our markets on equal chances after paying the import duty on his goods. The tariff should be equivalent or more than equivalent to the difference between the wages paid by the operators of the different countries. If, however, capital is allowed to combine at home to control the market then such legislation is a farce, robbing the people of the rise in price to the amount of the tariff.

A license is imposed on one doing an itinerant business in any of our cities or towns. This is to protect merchants who are located and pay taxes. The license is to offset the tax and thus bring even a common hawker on equal footing with those permanently located. It is not for the revenue such license will bring to the city treasury, but it is in justice due to those in business permanently located and who pay taxes to defray the expenses of the municipal government. This license does not advance the prices of the commodities brought into the market by a transient merchant. He pays for the privilege. If he locates he pays a municipal tax.

Then there is no good reason why foreign merchants coming to our markets should not be required to pay for such a privilege.

**Crowding the Market.** Regarding a protective tariff there comes to our mind a very important point that must not be overlooked by "our customs commission;" it is that when the home market is in a plethoric state by reason of over-production. A "high tariff" is now in demand. This will cut off a source of supply. In instances of this kind a "high tariff" will at least decrease importation and give home industry a better chance without advancing prices, as competition under the new *regime*, supply and demand, will have the sway, for foreign competition is diminished to the extent of the tariff imposed.

The tariff bureau will here find an excellent opportunity to exercise its function and to regulate wisely foreign competition, entirely free from the idea of revenue or in the interest of a specific class or a particular political party.

**Laudable Efforts.** A good government is one that will support all laudable efforts of its people to carry on business or pursue a vocation to assure a fair living or secure a competency. As long as they ask no more than that all should be supported by the government on equal chances to acquire the much-coveted dollar, the "bone of contention" between labor and capital, the boon should be granted. Under the constitution the authorities are bound to protect its citizens of the commonwealth (who are the *government* as much as the *governed*), in all rights and privileges bearing upon the happiness or prosperity of the greatest number.

**The Mystery Solved.** National pride, loyalty and true patriotism of the whole people depend largely on the kind of laws we have. The impartial administration of the government binds the people together in true social sympathy with each other. Tariff legislation is doubtless one of the greatest factors in bringing about one common interest in the prosperity of the nation than any other, or the very opposite may be the case according as such legislation approaches nearest to the impartial and non-partisan interest of all the people. Indeed this argument will apply to all laws, and the *secret* of a nation's happiness is *solved* as soon as the day is reached when the legislators are governed in framing laws by a spirit of universal fraternity.

In levying an "import tax" the greatest consideration must be exercised so that it does not create a privileged class. All points must be thoroughly studied. In the first place, the object of such a tariff should be for no other purpose than to protect home industry, and unless all peoples are benefited thereby it is no protection at all. In the second place, if by "customs duty" a limited number are favored by it and enriched at the expense of the rest of the people, then all such legislation should be made unlawful. Moreover, a tariff imposed for the sole object of "revenue only" in time of peace should also be declared unlawful if it is not already considered unconstitutional by the judiciary. The only point covering all forms of "import duty" is to protect home industry.

**That Fence.** The right to erect a fence around your grounds to protect it from the inroads of destructive cattle which might trespass upon your crops is not questioned. It is our right to put up legal barriers against innovations upon our fields of commerce. Self-protection is a law of nature. Impartial justice only is law.

The commonwealth does not represent money. Governments are not instituted the same as a company in business with money making as its objective point. They represent man. Its life and power, its very existence, come from the *people*. Officers of the law are *its* servants. Their *duty* is to legislate for the *good of the people* and administer the laws for their protection—a power delegated *by the people.*

**Curses of Party Politics.** One of the curses of party politics is that the laws enacted by the party in power will, almost to a certainty, be repealed by another party should it come into power. A congressman to receive the good will of his constituency must needs propose some new measure in their interest or repeal some law distasteful to them. A member of some great corporation by shrewd "wire pulling" is nominated and elected to Congress; by means of all sorts of lobby-work and expenditure of money a bill is filibustered through Congress levying a "protective" tariff on certain commodities, in the manufacturing of some of which he is largely interested and friends who assist him. During the time the McKinley bill was pending before Congress over a thousand people, men and women, from different parts of the United States, who were more or less directly interested in the passage of this bill, were in Washington improving every moment in lobby work, spending money (indirectly of course) to pass this bill. All ostensibly for the benefit of the "poor workingman" we are told. Many members of Congress and particular associates become millionaires in a few years, and those who blindly vote for such men have their labor for their pains. Against such villainous *political gymnastics the people must protect themselves.*

**Why so Eager?** Why so eager to have certain "tariff bills" passed? Why spend five or ten thousand dollars to be elected to Congress when the salary is only $8.00 a day? This will not pay banquets, lobby agents, sharp lady-manipulators, often encountered and necessary to succeed in passing a single bill.

All kinds of ventures—imaginary emergencies, harbor defenses, harbor improvements, extravagant appropriations to keep down the surplus, government contractors make immense profits in sub-letting, votes are exchanged in getting a bill through Congress by a common rule of "you

CHRIST EVANS.
Fig. 1.

JOSEPH N. DOLPH.
Fig. 2.

MRS. POTTER PALMER.
Fig 3.

REV. L. ABBOTT, D. D., Ph.D.
Fig. 4.

Plate IX—For sketches see page 221.

vote for my measure and I will vote for yours"—is it all for
the benefit of the workingman? A silver-tongued (?) orator
takes one side of the question, usually the one that pays
him best. Tariff is the issue. High-protection wins. At
another presidential epoch the opposing party wins the contest on a mere *nominal*, or *no* tariff basis. "Divide and
rule," as of yore; but against such mummery the people
should protect themselves.

**Public Entertainment.** This tariff question furnishes
a public entertainment like that
seen in the days of knight-errantry—both parties assuming
characters apparently realistic in the political arena—cutting
and slashing for the amusement of the people. What is the
result? Fire and smoke evince activity of the same smoke-
stacks a little longer, or they cease to breathe. The wage-
earners either gain a short respite or enter the procession of
work-seekers.

**The Tide of Prosperity.** The capitalist can sleep on
his "silent oars; his waters
are calm." He can wait for the return of the "tide of prosperity"—live on collaterals. Capital has no hungry stomach
like labor so often has. It neither weaves nor spins, nor feels
the fierce bite of the wintry blast, when, for proper protection, labor surrenders and submits to the halter of political
charlatanism. Capital tallies another victory, as little by
little these small rivulets of political favoritism swell into
an immense *sea* of social distinction over which none can
navigate unless he has a ticket bearing this stamp : "$—,"
and a good bank account to back it. Is this Protection?

Free-trade you think will remove the cause of these troubles; but it must be remembered that, unless trusts, pools,
monopolies, etc., are absolutely prohibited by law, capital
will immediately form international combines of every sort,
and would then surely assume gigantic proportions. All
combines at home, or those of an international character,
tending to control our market prices, should be prohibited
by Congress. This will bring capital on equal footing in

the markets, and will eventually bring labor on an equal plane with capital by protecting all people alike, especially the workingman, by breaking labor competition.

**High Prices.** A protective tariff that will enhance prices of the commodities on which such tariff is levied is no protection, as we have shown, for the consumer pays it at last. As long as capital is allowed to combine its strength, a tariff will aid in putting prices up. This is liable to cause over-production—an unnatural demand, or rather inducement, for investment of capital. At the beginning high wages are paid—to freeze out rivals—and when the highest point is reached, reduce wages even below what the market warrants. Then comes the "*strike*," and the corporation connives at it. They wish to avoid all the responsibility of a "*lock-out*," so they treat their workmen in such a compulsory manner as to compel a strike, and thus give them an opportunity to hire men at a reduced price, and accuse the workmen of sheer stupidity. Thousands who are unwilling or unable to engage in former pursuits, from which this wild upheaval took them, compete for these vacant positions at reduced wages.

**Signal of Defeat.** Who is to blame? A good government whose financial policy is sound and correct will not permit such disastrous business inundations to overleap the legal barriers. Protection that makes this possible engenders evil. Reaction is the signal of defeat. Corporations are the "decoy ducks" which the government fits out to lure the innocent to destruction. Here responsibility ceases with the general chaos they produced—their unprotected dupes, the unprotected workmen, pay the "piper" for this ghostly dance! The aftermath often reaches to the grave. Corporations should be clothed with individuality, making every member responsible respectively for indebtedness.

The laws of Pennsylvania forbid school directors to have any personal interest in any school supplies. Why should our national laws not prohibit Congressmen from having any interest in any corporation, trusts, combines, demanding legislation in their behalf? We know a Congressman who was honest. His known honesty secured his re-election a number of times; by and by through evil associations at the capitol he caught the popular infection to become rich; he yielded to the temptation, lost his political life. His reputation for honesty, and whatever political glory he had won, was buried with the *debris* of so many other fallen monuments of greatness, overturned by the desolating cyclone of greed and dishonesty.

## NOTE ONE.

**Two-Thirds Vote.** On page 81 of our book we suggested the idea of a unanimous vote in deciding a question presented to the "Customs Commission," in order to legalize it, with reference to any proposed tariff rulings or changes. Upon more mature reflection, however, we desire to modify our views on this particular point. There are emergencies in which our most profound thinkers and wisest statesmen favor a two-thirds vote as the most judicious, for the following reasons:

*First.* They claim that many a good law should be passed, which will be opposed by a few, who may be interested in its defeat, whereas two-thirds of the honest and *disinterested* members may favor it.

*Second.* A two-thirds vote will dispense with the too common and at times ridiculous cavilling and wrangling of unwise but interested parties to put off or defeat a good measure.

*Third.* A two-thirds vote sustaining the measure will make it as binding as a unanimous vote.

## NOTE TWO.

**The Popular Idea.** The popular idea of a tariff is not to favor monopoly, by which the *rich* or the *few* are protected and favored, to the detriment and loss of the *poor* and the *many*, but as a measure by which *all* the rich and the poor, shall be equally benefitted, giving each an equal chance in the market. A tariff should be collected, not on what we *consume*, but what we *possess*. Otherwise the wealthy would be taxed for no more than the poor, if he is satisfied to consume only the same as the poor, and his possessions yield no revenue. The poor man's family may be larger than that of his wealthier neighbor, and consume more, and thus be compelled to pay more tariff money than his rich neighbor.

In this case a tariff for revenue only is as bad as a tariff for protection with incidental revenue. The people must at once see the inequality of such a measure.

## NOTE THREE.

**Campaign Funds.** Some people think to get an office, governmental or municipal, is a big and paying thing. But this is a serious misconception of facts. It does not pay. The salaries paid are really out of proportion with those paid in secular positions, in our social and commercial pursuits. There is big pay and short working hours, it is true, but still it does *not pay*. A friend of ours, who held lucrative offices for twenty years, said the other day, "I would be worth thousands of dollars to-day if I had refused a public office." It is true the government pays large salaries, and in many positions exacts but meagre service, but how many office-holders make or save money—*honestly?* It does not pay in the end.

Almost everyone holding office under the government is assessed by the party for campaign purposes. The spoil system permeates every artery of the body politic. Thus the very money paid into the treasury by the people is paid indirectly out of the treasury to further a political campaign. This is quixotic economy.

Only the rich can secure offices, since it takes money to make the political machinery run smooth and pay your way through the official toll-gate.

> " There's a good time coming yet,
>     A good time coming;
>     The pen shall supersede the sword,
>     And *right*, not *might*, shall be the chord,
>     In the good time coming.
>     Worth, not birth, shall rule mankind,
>     And be acknowledged stronger;
>     The proper impulse has been given,
>     Wait a little longer.
>
> There's a good time coming yet,
>     A good time coming;
>     War in all men's eyes shall be
>     A monster of iniquity
>     In the good time coming;
>     Nations shall not quarrel then
>     To prove which is the stronger,
>     Nor slaughter men for glory's sake—
>     Wait a little longer."

# CORPORATIONS AND UNIONS.

*Man's Natural Endowments; Corporate Organizations and
Labor Unions; Primary Reasons; Driven to It; The
Right to Organize; Good and Evil Effects; The Right
Course; Self-Defense; Political Philosophy; Reason and
Power to Search; Experience and Necessity Elements
of Evolution; How Civil Government was Developed;
State Police; The Difficulty Settled; Harmony and
Happiness the Rule and the End; How Paupers are
Made; Cost of Living, Etc., Etc.*

Search out the high-road to happiness, and when you have found
the way try to remain upon it.—Don't lose your way.

**Mental Endowments.** Man is endowed with the faculty of reason, with which no
other creature is favored.   He alone of all the animal kingdom can think, comprehend and draw conclusions from
scenes around him.   The power of speech and reason is
given to man not only to discriminate for his own benefit
and pleasure, but to impart the result of his researches and
observations to his fellow beings ; and by these powers per-
suade them to become of the same mind, thus uniting their
strength in the same common cause.   These faculties, more
than his physical powers, have made man the king and ruler
of the earth ; he tames the lion of the forest, enters the
tiger's cage, rides upon the tusks of the elephant, or makes
his bed upon a den of dragons.   The fiercer elements are
obedient to his will and allow themselves to be harnessed in
his service like a tame steed.

He has made the lifeless iron a vehicle of speech ; navi-
gates the air as a winged bird ; tunnels the earth, robbing the
high mountain of its staying powers ; bridges the mighty
sea, and links by a simple chain the continents of the world,

wooing them with silent whispers; all through this faculty of reason. He wanders from cause to effect, like a bird flutters from flower to flower, gathering here an idea and there a fact; reaches the solution of a problem by comparison or by experience; encountering doubts, difficulties —at times almost despairing—to hold on to what he has gained, or defending himself against antagonistic forces.

But dauntless and unwearied he pushes on in search of the right—*his* right, his neighbor's right, the rights of humanity—and by his indomitable power and will to seek and to find he brushes the dust from hidden truths, tears away the brambled network covering forgotten principles, opens the barred flood-gates of light, disclosing man's needs and rights, showing men the environment and elements which have long blighted their hopes, and pointing out the road to freedom and happiness.

**Personal Examination.** Men being endowed with reason can and should, by the light transmitted by philosophers and scientists, by statesmen and humanitarians, aim daily to understand better the needs of themselves; examine carefully the elements surrounding them and by all their means strengthen the weak points in their social system. By this means the ego is more sharply outlined and the vital principles of life are better understood.

In the same ratio that individuals progress in understanding the science and principles of good government will nations advance towards the establishment of a government ruled by the people.

**Man is Philosophic.** Man cannot only *find* the truth by searching, but he can shape and govern his life by it. Experience of others is remembered and recorded. Comparison aids men in reasoning intelligently on any line of investigation, and with success.

The lessons learned and taught in the many ages enables the human race to understand at this time what is essential to human happiness. In the face of the wonderful achievements of man in the past in science and art, it should seem but a simple lesson to learn how to adapt measures to improve his social relations. Fire and water have been compelled to take the place of human muscle. The same elements enable him to journey over four hundred miles a day, and take his ease, whereas years ago, before he applied these powers to machinery, he could barely make his weary feet cover a distance of thirty miles a day. Why should he not be able to accomplish similar results in the social system?—He will try, and he will win.

**Self-Defense.** Man fortifies himself against all possible inroads upon or invasion of his domains threatening loss or injury to himself or his.

He erects a house firmly and strongly in which to secure safe shelter for himself and family. He furnishes the doors and windows with complicated and strong locks to bar out unwelcome intruders. Why should he not take equal precautions against the encroachments of men who aim at stealing from him his social rights?

And in doing either he may need assistance. If the enemy trying to rob his house is too formidable to be overcome by his single arm, he calls upon his neighbors for assistance; and if they are good, honest neighbors they will readily respond. The same robbers threaten *their* homes, and they act in self-defense—for if the neighbor is too weak alone to keep the assailant at bay, by uniting their power they overcome him at once.

If a foreign foe invades a domain, not only the inhabitants of the harbor at which they land are expected to drive them back, but the *united forces* of the land are sent against the foe. "In union there is strength."

**Not Only Bread and Butter.** It is not alone a question of bare living or simply a matter of wages that agitates the mind and troubles the heart of the laborer and drives him in self-defense into *labor unions*, or other organizations having self-protection for its object. It is principle!

A true American claims the respect the constitution guarantees to every American citizen when it asserts that "all men are born *free and equal.*"

The moment you attempt to draw a line of distinction you assail his most sacred birth-right and arouse a spirit of just indignation. To be a Roman *citizen*, when Rome was in its glory, was a password of safety and a mark of distinction anywhere, whether that citizen was a senator or an artisan. Why should it not shelter, protect and dignify the humblest American?

There is not another nation on earth that will feel and resent an insult as readily and as forcibly as Americans.

**Their Patriotism.** The American people draw no line of distinction when danger threatens their country. Their patriotism, their pure love of country, their whole-souled loyalty, at once overleaps and levels every barrier of social distinction. No one claims a greater share of the country or asks that only his favorite portion should be defended. All are equal then. Why should it not be so in time of peace? But while the American people are both patriotic and peaceable, they are no less jealous of their rights. While they give the government all the volunteers they need, do it cheerfully, they *will* defend their *individual rights* and firmly uphold their principles.

**Outside Assistance.** Some one may say that it was not only native Americans who fought our battles and achieved our freedom, but we were aided by the aliens whom we now blame for much of the demoralization of our social system. Let us not forget that a century —even half a century ago—the emigrants landing on our shores were quite a different class of people from those now crowding our business centres. A large portion of them were people more or less familiar with American principles and government. They were frugal, industrious, honest and intelligent. Many brought little fortunes with them to invest in their new homes. They *came to stay.* They came to help—and did help us—to build up and improve our country. They helped to frame and support our institutions. They fought and voted for American principles.

**Quite a Difference.** Note the difference between our earlier emigrants and those of to-day. We have already given you the characteristics of the former. Now let us give those of the latter.

The majority of foreigners coming to our country now come not because they love our free institutions, for nine out of ten know nothing about them ; and show, when here, that they *care as little for them.* They come not as patriots to fight for their freedom, as the earlier settlers did. They come when the country is settled, the land populated, liberty achieved, battles fought, the forests leveled, the prairies broken up and productive, furnaces, manufactories and railroads built. They come when the work is done, and the roads are broken, and the feast is ready. They come to enjoy the fruits that others have planted.

Some come from the chattle markets of despotism—from the chain-gangs and prisons, or pauperdom of countries that have no use for them and cast the burden on anyone willing to receive them.

Underlings, ignorant, rude and untutored, brought here by corrupt agents, buyers and sellers of human chattle— which agents the law of the land should banish to Siberia —they come to get *better wages.* They work for any wages they can get, for any amount is far greater than they got at home. They live literally on garbage, spend but a trifle, help to reduce wages, save all they can; then, when they have a few hundred dollars, go back home to spend it.

**The Beginning.** Cheap labor rapidly began to fill up the country when this class of emigrants poured in, more especially during the last decade. A large majority of them settled in our cities as wage-workers. In earlier times it was the reverse. A large majority of the emigrants then sought homes in the rural districts. Many of our western territories were populated by these earlier emigrants. But these later arrivals dreaded the hardships and exposure of territorial life, and, like bees, settled around the visionary honey pots of the cities.

And here our wage-workers met the first charge of the foe which called for united action for self-defense in reduced wages. When it is remembered that this reduced wage element was supported by foreign and American capitalists, forming a union against the honest American laborer, no reasonable man will censure the labor-men, or wage-workers, for forming a union also.

This was simply organizing against an organized force.

Had capital not organized there would have been no cause for organizing labor. But this organization of capital with a view to reduce the price of labor was the potent cause of strikes and labor organizations. It was a great oversight on the part of those who might have prevented it to allow such injustice to be perpetrated against American wage-workers—this importation of contract labor by capitalists, in many instances at least.

**The Trouble Grows.** This was the beginning of the trouble. When these injured workmen—these American wage-workers—saw the coming giant ready to blast their future homes and hopes, without any help from the government they defended, they saw but one remedy—they must defend themselves. Strikes followed. Then the government sent soldiers to stay an insurrection, and *protect capital.*

It soon became evident that "a crust of bread and a bed of straw" was the destiny of the American laborer, as in other downtrodden countries. Something had to be done to avert such a direful catastrophe. It seemed near at hand and action must be taken to stay its progress. Some slight efforts were made by the government. Contract labor was prohibited to a great extent. But by the help of protective tariff, foreign labor, trusts, pools and other capital formations, the evil was not abated and no legal remedy found sufficient to heal the sore, and labor unions were the result.

**Mutual Attraction.** Man is a social animal. He needs companionship, without which he is not contented. Then the keen sense of justice instilled in every man urges him to protection or self-defense. Alone, he may be too weak to protect his interests, and he appeals to his neighbor. People moving in the same social circle, travelling on the same road, governed by the same interests or circumstances, naturally attract each other. They feel the same injustice and they affiliate. From the millionaire to the pauper, in all the divisions of classes, or society, there exists a sympathy which leads to fraternal friendship and closer organization, by which instinct they maintain a special distinction of rank, a tendency towards ownership, a wish for supremacy, &c.

There seems to be a disposition to look up to those who belong to the winning class, or those possessing wealth. This is largely owing to a misconception or perversion of the true idea of what makes life a real success. The greatest evil permeating society is the almost universal desire to amass wealth, or want to become rich. Fine clothes, fine houses, fine carriages are alluring, and frequently questionable means are resorted to in order to acquire them. The wage-worker cannot keep up appearances with the rich; hence his deeper sympathy for his own class, and hence these organizations.

**Their Effects.** Primarily organizations are an evil; temporarily they have their influence for good. These organizations, if properly conducted, are schools in which adults may learn many lessons of benefit to them in their calling and station of life. Societies conducted peaceably, with a view to do good to all are blessings to a community. Organizations of a belligerent character will engender strife. Any organization of capital or corporation that discharges a man simply because he belongs to a labor union invites resistance, for a man has a right to belong to any society he chooses as long as he performs his duty as a citizen and attends to his business.

**Labor Unions.** In the foregoing chapters we took occasion to speak of corporate organizations and merely briefly referred to labor unions in the abstract. Here we desire to discuss labor unions more in detail.

**Circumstances Made Them.** Organizations are the result or outgrowth of some prevailing evil having existence somewhere, not only in our social system, but permeating our financial, commercial and political principles and even our governmental acts. The organization of unions seeking protection of special interests is not what the normal condition of man would require. The normal condition of man pre-supposes *perfect freedom* in all conditions and stations of life. The normal prerogative loses its prestige as soon as an individual, or a class of men, assume an arbitrary position, in society or in business circles.

The normal condition of mankind can be enjoyed and preserved only under equitable rule and equal rights, which, under all ordinary laws of nature, operate *for the good of all*—the heritage due to every man, woman and child.

As soon as law or custom favors any one particular class more than another, so soon the sacred rights of man are invaded and subverted, and the neglected or slighted portion resorts to abnormal means also in the simple spirit of self-defense and protection, then such action is justifiable because it becomes a *necessity*.

All antagonism, however, not exercised in honest competition, seeking its own advancement at the price of another's loss, is abnormal and criminal.

The *real* fundamental principle which must govern any good business policy in order to satisfy the normal condition of man, individually, socially and politically, is to make him the rightful, undisputed owner of the *profits of his own labor*.

If you defraud him of this you take away all the instincts, all the attractions that in his normal condition bound him to, and made him happy in his life and associations.

Under these adverse circumstances all manner of means were resorted to for the purpose of regaining their lost prestige or to ameliorate their changed condition ; and from this desire soon were called into existence Labor Unions, Lodges, Granges, Knights of Labor and similar organizations all over the land.

**An Old Idea.** This was by no means a new departure. The idea of organization and concentration is as old as the solid phalanxes of the Romans. Our country formed a federation to protect its rights and a union of states to perpetuate its power.

Our military, police and civil officers are organized bodies, intended to defend and maintain the rights of *individuals*, which, were the power given *them* to do so, the aid of soldiers and police and labor unions would never be needed.

**Give the Laborer His Own.** We have already said that every man should be the absolute owner of the profits of his own labor and every vocation *should* yield a profit. But labor and capital must make a profit or they must cease to exist. The natural outcome of every judiciously-managed business, or work, is a reasonable gain, or profit. All legitimate investments should be made with the *reasonable assurance* that a profit will accrue therefrom. Wages, in the same manner, should be so regulated that the wage-worker obtains a reasonable profit on *his labor*, which is the *capital invested by him* in the same enterprise.

Immense profits for the speedy acquisition of great wealth cannot be made while labor and capital maintain normal relations to each other.

**How Much is Due the Laborer?** What is really the profit of the laborer, based on his apportionment of the capital invested by each party? It is certainly something more than a bare living— merely the necessaries of life. This much is given to your dumb cattle!

The cost of *individual existence* is not the total of the laboring man's necessity. His necessity includes an honest and comfortable provision for the members of his family; and if all he receives for his labor, judiciously expended, barely suffices to support his family, where are his profits? The capitalist is not satisfied if he simply realizes the amount he invests in an enterprise with the usual rate of interest. He wants a *profit* over and above that. The laborer deserves the same. If he gets no more than a bare living he realizes only what he invested in time, skill and muscle, and where is *his profit* then?

Certainly economy should be practiced in their expenditures. But even this has its limits. We cannot see why the capitalist has license to live better than the laborer. Roast turkey and champagne no doubt would tickle the laboring-man's palate as pleasingly as the capitalist's. But nature has certain laws and requirements which no capital or poverty can control. The laboring man, no more than anyone else, can afford to subsist on less than physiological laws demand.

His family must have *enough* healthy food to eat and comfortable clothes to wear, and do this in accordance with the laws of health. Scanting themselves in food is injurious. A *low diet* is the precursor of disease. A plain diet is healthy, but you must have a *sufficient quantity* of it. Good, nourishing food is just as necessary for the laborer as the professional man. While a plain diet will suffice to recruit his physical powers, more nourishing food will add additional vigor, by which he may apply himself to higher education in the branches

**Branches of Study.** of study pertaining to his particular vocation. It requires additional nourishment when both the physical and mental powers are placed in requisition. Then to work faithfully and study the laws of nature governing his physical being and the science connected with his own business or vocation demands more than the means required for the bare necessaries of life.

The wages of a laboring man then should never be less than is required to maintain his family comfortably *and leave him a profit.*

After acquiring this point a man's earnings may be governed by competition. Skilled labor may exact a premium where it is specially required, always regulated by the demand and based upon the prevailing scale of prices legally adopted. But while this may operate to increase the profits of more skillful men, it would in no wise deprive any wage-worker of an honest share of profits.

This provision would stay the production of paupers and strikes and contract foreign labor. The wage-earner will then feel secure, assured that his daily wages are sufficient to keep himself and his family respectably and procure some such small luxuries as books and magazines for the improvement of the mental faculties, while he would still have a little money to put on deposit at the end of each year for any future emergency that may possibly arise.

**Make a Standard.** Let us make a legal common standard of wages, below which wages cannot go. Make that sufficient to support an ordinary family comfortably and still leave a profit. Calculate it so that a man still has a profit, no matter how small it may be.

Then let honest competition come in. If we then have a job which any common laborer can do, requiring no particular skill, and the work is worth $1.50, and it will require eight hours' diligent labor to do it, we should be required to pay that man the amount named though a dozen men stand ready to do it for less.

We contend for a minimum price for common labor; in fact, a standard price in every branch of industry, below which no capital or competition can bring it—where capital and labor are united to make money.

This will take the laboring man at this point out of the hands of oppressing capitalists as well as the greedy range of unjust competition, by law.

This would be absolute protection to labor and is in simple justice due to the laborer, his family and the nation. This would remove the struggle for mere existence to a more noble ambition for honest possessions.

Spencer and other scientists claim the struggle for existence to be one of the primary causes of evolution. It arouses the energy necessary to urge mankind to action, in order to outdo one another; gives strong impulse to work, an incentive to outrun each the other in the race of life. If this is true in the mere struggle for a meagre existence, how would a hopeful struggle for the higher attainment of personal possessions arouse the dormant energies of the wage-workers of America!

**Reduction of Wages.** A good business man will not only look after his own interests, but he will also consider the welfare of his workmen. Philanthropy enters into almost every business transaction made between men, more especially in determining the proper remuneration of the wage-earner. Whatever adversity employed capital may have to meet in the market, labor cannot justly be reduced below a certain limit. Capital does not suffer privations of the necessary comforts of life if it does not make a large profit or if it cannot be operated for more than cost, so long as its owner makes a living. This, however, will not occur under good management on the part of the capitalist and the right kind of tariff and labor legislation on the part of the government.

Regarding labor, wages cannot be reduced below a certain minimum, which the business man must take into consideration, for the wages must always be considered first in managing capital, for the wage-earners must live; and there should be a law prescribing a standard limit, or at least a precedent established by the *labor bureau* that the price of labor cannot be reduced below a certain point in all concerns where labor *joins capital* and where capital is worked with a view of making money.

GEN. RUSSELL N. ALGER.

Plate **X**-For sketch see page 221.

**Limit of Wage Reduction.** A man who learns a trade so he can take a position as a learned mechanic cannot justly be classed among the common laborers and should be able to get something for skill. It is not just for this man to have to contend against too much competition with cheap labor. Then there is a difference in how people live, as to whether they can bear much reduction or compete with labor less accomplished. A man learned, ambitious, who values personal accomplishments, studies the arts and sciences, wants his family properly educated and cared for, as well as those who are rich.

---

## THE WORK AND COST OF LIVING.

"'Money is a good servant, but a bad master.' It is useful when well employed, but mischievous when men devote themselves wholly to its acquisition."

**To Satisfy Hunger.** It is not a difficult task to ascertain the cost of living with the knowledge we have at the present time of the mysteries of the human system. Physiology, chemistry and the science of *force*—power—give us all the *data* we need in determining the quantity of food necessary to sustain that activity of our body called *life*. The cost of clothing and habitation can also readily be figured out, and hence we can at least approximate, at a minimum limit, the wages a workingman must receive to live half-way comfortably, and below which a reduction of wages is inhuman and cannot be tolerated even though capital should not make a profit. Then, as we have already exemplified the subject under the head of "profit sharing" of the wage-earners, the workingman should and must make more than the bare cost of living, for there may be a time when he can't work; besides every head of a family should have a home.

For a man to do a good day's work he must be well fed on good, nourishing food so the system need not draw on the reserved forces of life and thus shorten life. An underfed man is shortlived; moreover, he is predisposed to disease. Then it will be the duty of our *labor bureau* to carefully study this subject that no injustice is done. In all institutions where *capital unites* with labor for the purpose of gain, this matter can readily be regulated so that labor will receive its just share in the profits. Yet, whatever may happen to capital, there must be a limit established below which wages cannot be reduced.

**The Science of Living.** Life is an activity dependent on physical conditions. These conditions must be in harmonious operation in order for life to proceed in regular order. Living beings are not unlike machines. It takes force to run them; it takes fuel to produce force, and this must be constantly and regularly supplied or the machine will not run evenly or it may stop altogether.

To produce force something must be consumed. For example, steam is the product of burning fuel, which, when mechanically applied, becomes force. Motion is the beginning of force. Motion develops heat and this is convertible into force. Heat itself is a mode of motion and, therefore, it is proper to say that heat is an exponent of force. When force is mechanically employed, the amount used will equal the consumption of fuel in its production. Life is dependent on the same source for the supply of force necessarily expended by the process of living. Without air, wood and water we cannot have steam-power. Unless air, food and water combine in the living body to support combustion, the human machine, like the former, the engine, would soon come to a dead halt.

**Capacity, Power, Work.** To perform a given amount of work to be done in ten hours by an engine of one-horse-power capacity, the combustion of fuel must be sufficient to equal the amount of force expended. Hence, if we employ a horse to do the same work, it will take corn and oats to feed the horse, from which, by the process of digestion, this food, with water and the union of oxygen given to it in the lungs, is converted into force. The ultimate of the combination of *food-fuel* is the same as in the former instance; the only difference may be in quality and cost of the fuel.

Perfect combustion is a saving of fuel or food in producing force. Less heat is given off from your stove or fire-place if the wood or coal is not thoroughly burned. The same is true of digestion and assimilation; if this is imperfect, not as much life force is produced as when in a normal condition. Force, when applied mechanically, will do work equal to the supply and no more. The faster a machine runs and the more work it does the more it wears and the greater amount of force it takes to run it; the greater the amount of work there is to do the greater amount of force will be required to do it.

**Average Amount of Food.** Force is the same, whether it is produced by vital or animated or inanimate machinery. The primary source is also the same. Some change of substance in the form of combustion must take place to produce force or power. Vital force in living bodies is evolved from food, air and water. This runs the body.

The average amount that will keep an ordinary working-man for one day is about three pounds of solid food and two pints of water. If heavy manual labor is performed he will require something more. If he works at a furnace he will require more food and water than if he works in an even temperature of seventy degrees. If he works in a much lower temperature he will require more. If he gets eight hours' sleep and eight hours' rest and works eight hours, all things being equal, the former estimate will be sufficient to keep a man in good condition, providing his digestion is good and the food of good, nutritious quality.

Where men work hard and perspire freely much more water is demanded by the system than under ordinary circumstances; and when the food consists largely of fruits and garden vegetables, about four pounds of food and a

little less than two pints of water will keep a man sufficiently well fed.   The kind of business or work men engage
in, their habits and quality of food will largely modify the
quantity of food necessary to produce vital force enough to
sustain life and the amount of force to do the work required
of them beside the simple process of living.   It should be
remembered that those who live a life of leisure do not
require as much food as when actively employed.   In mental
activity, as in case of the mind workers, more food is
required than in a life of leisure, but not quite as much as
when manual labor is performed.   This is a study, if people
desire to live in accordance with nature's laws.

**Too Much Food.** A large majority of the people eat
too much.   If one eats more than the
system demands to keep the vital machinery in good working order, more than is required to perform the work that
is to be done, then the stomach will have to work too hard to
get rid of it.   As we have said, food produces vital force.
If we eat more than is required the body will either grow
obesic (if digestion is good) or the system will have to throw
off the superabundance of material which has been unwisely
supplied.   Besides, this is a source of disease.   It is unfortunate for a man if he has to work so hard that three
pounds of good, solid food in twenty-four hours will not
keep him.   For the work of the system to convert so much
food into force weakens the nervous system as well as the
stomach, and it is for these reasons liable to shorten his life.

If the surrounding atmosphere is warm and dry the
evaporation from the body is then greater, and from two to
four pints of water is necessary to be healthy and strong.
As a rule people are more apt to eat too much than to drink
too much.   For good health and strength food and water
must be sufficiently and regularly supplied.

**Children and Food.** Children require more food comparatively than adults for the reason
that they have to furnish the system with material for growing the body in addition to running the little vital machine.

During youth the body is more rapidly metamorphosed, and good, substantial food is necessary to grow the body, to reproduce tissue, supply the vital force and keep up repairs. Old people need less food for the reason that the body changes or wastes very slowly.

If the body is not supplied with food, or in cases where food is not properly digested so that the supply equals the expenditure of force, the reserved material of the body will be drawn upon to support *combustion*, the tissues will be consumed, thus to generate force enough to accomplish the work to be done.

Over-work, under-feeding, over-feeding and under-work are conditions that violate the laws of health.

Three pounds of good, solid food, with two to three pints of pure water, properly digested and assimilated, will keep a man in good condition, performing a reasonable amount of manual labor eight hours each day, and with eight hours' rest and eight hours' sweet sleep. This will not shorten his natural longevity, providing his habits otherwise are within physiological limits. He will have at least six hours each day for recreation, outing and social enjoyment, two hours of which, each day, should be devoted to mental improvement —some educational study, some branch of science—sociological science. Mental labor is then to the workingman a source of rest, and in fact is as necessary to good health to the wage-earner as to other people ; and one can always find some time for mental improvement each day, if people will only learn to divide up the time at their disposal and live methodically and systematically.

**Cost of Living.** The *average* cost of living, as we estimate it from the basis of a family of five keeping house—the actual cost of food and the cost of cooking it, where the wife does the cooking, or, in another way of writing it, where the housekeeper is one of the family and does not have to be hired, is about $18.00 per month. Where the family has a kitchen garden—and every well regulated family should have one—this sum can be reduced several dollars during the summer months. **But** the extra cost of fuel during the winter will **make the** *average*, as we have stated, at about $18.00 per month.

This, of course, will not give the family many costly luxuries, but it will furnish good, wholesome food. Still hundreds of families are obliged to subsist somehow on much less.

The next item we will mention is rent. This we place at $8.00 a month. Of course those who own their homes will save the larger part of this item. The item of clothing we will place at an *average* of about $65.00 a year for the family of five. This will aggregate $377.00. The wages paid by our railroad corporations to their employees, whom we will take as a criterion to give us a starting *data* of what is considered generally by the wage-earners as reasonably good wages for unskilled labor, is $40.00 per month. Here we have now the head of this family receiving $40.00 per month, and if nothing happens, no time lost, no sickness, there will be a saving, or profit, if we may call it such, of $103.00 a year.

**Incidentals.** Now, shall we include incidentals in the sums we have stated as the cost of living, or is our figure already large enough to cover little wants that come up every day which we never know of beforehand? Little presents for the children, a brief outing in the summer, or a short vacation, which is only to break the tiresome monotony of life. Then every family should buy a book or two each year, keep one newspaper, a good family paper and one good monthly magazine. For these latter items, and some unavoidable loss in time and possibly unforseen mishaps, we will deduct $47.00, and we have now in the savings-bank $56.00, which, if carefully invested each year, will in ten years make quite a sum toward paying for a vine-clad little home, where the days of ripened years may be spent in comparative ease, enjoyment and independence. Many peoples get more wages than we have calculated and many get much less. Under all circumstances and conditions peoples should not neglect a careful study of *household economy* that they may shape their *mode of living* to suit their income.*

"Agur's prayer," says Colton, "Will ever be the prayer of the wise. Our incomes should be like our shoes; if too small, they will gall and pinch us, but if too large, they will cause us to stumble and to trip. But wealth, after all, is a relative thing; since he that has little, and wants less, is richer than he that has much, but wants more. True contentment depends not upon what we have, but upon what we would have; a tub was large enough for *Diogenes*, but a world was too little for *Alexander*."

Horace.—*We cannot refrain from quoting the words of one of the wisest authors and thinkers the world ever knew— the great* Horace. *He says:*

" Whoever makes choice of the golden mean, safe from all the ills of poverty, is not compelled to dwell amid the wretchedness of some miserable abode; while, on the other hand, moderate in his desires, he needs not the splendid palace, the object of envy."

> "The man, within the golden mean
> Who can his boldest wish restrain,
> Securely views the ruined cell
> Where sordid want and sorrow dwell,
> And, in himself serenely great,
> Declines an envied room of state."

## HOW "TRAMPS" ARE MADE.

**What is a Tramp?** A person who journeys on foot is called a pedestrian. Those who go from place to place, having no particular destination, are wanderers. If obliged to travel on foot for want of funds and no specific object in view, peregrinating from place to place, such are vagrants, popularly called "tramps." This country has altogether too many so-called "tramps." Many start out in search of employment with a view of bettering

*We take up this subject again in the department of *"Random Thoughts,"* in this volume, under the head of " The Chemistry of the Kitchen" and " How to Make Little go Far," to which we refer our readers.

their condition. Others are forced to go forth to find work, and soon their funds give out and they become "tramps."

**The Voluntary Tramp.** We have the voluntary tramp, who prefers to tramp and beg rather than to work. The primary cause of such a condition is perhaps outside of any philosophy by which to solve the mystery other than that there is a constitutional indifference to self-respect and an innate laziness, for which there seems to be no remedy other than perhaps a strict legal prohibition of vagrancy. If every city, town or precinct enacted a law, and enforced it, that all strangers having no visible means of subsistence are apprehended and required to comply with the law, soon this evil might be materially modified, if not entirely driven from the land.

**The Involuntary Tramp.** Then we have the involuntary tramp, who enlists our sympathy. Thousands of this class are distributed throughout the country and are *made*, in many instances, by circumstances over which they have no control—bad luck, as goes the word. An extensive manufacturing establishment burns down, throwing a hundred, perhaps a thousand or more, people out of employment. The works may be rebuilt, but the chances are they are not; at all events these people who have no capital to fall back on must work to live, and it is more than probable that not all can get a job in the town in which they live, and so they start out in search of work. This is not so discouraging as long as their money holds out, as when, by and by, they are broken in spirit and in purse, absolutely become disheartened. No hope, no prospect, no one to speak kind words—all is given up for lost. He enters the ranks of a tramp.

Once in this line, or lane, it is a long run before a turn is likely met with.

**Another Way.** Another way involuntary tramps are made: A town is boomed by some enterprising speculator, hundreds flock in with a hope of bettering their condition, often leaving a good situation, only to find they have been misled and may, before an oasis is reached, become tramps.

Another factor to the entrance-way of the bourn of the tramp, from which few ever return, is: We are acquainted with a rich farmer and real estate speculator, near the city of Dayton, Ohio, who had a very faithful farm-hand, whom he hired in the month of March at $20 a month by the year. The work-hand did all in his power to please his employer and even when, during the harvest time, he might have earned big wages, went right on, however, with his work, hoping and feeling assured that he had steady employment. But to his surprise, about the first of November, when the farm work was pretty well out of the way and when he might have had an easier time during the winter, his employer thought now that there was not much else to do than to feed the stock and care for the horses—and he himself could do that—discharged him, with the remark that if he was out of work in the spring he could get back to his old

**In Search of a Job.** place. Now what was this man to do but to start out in search of a job? At this season of the year it was almost impossible to get work, unless some one else would step out of a place and let him step in. He had saved his money, but sickness overtook him, and before spring we met this same man in Terrehaut, Indiana, broken-hearted, in search of work. He had then tramped it for over a week, and totally out of money. We paid his board for two weeks, when he was fortunate in getting employment.

A man with a large family is employed in a Wisconsin lumbering factory. He gets good wages, but he is on for twelve hours per day's work, and thus he alternates with another. He is induced to buy one of the company's tenement houses on the installment plan. Now it is well known that this kind of work is not very conducive to health. Some last longer than others, but the average is about four years, when he begins to break down; now and then fails to

**By and By.** take his place for a day or two. By and by he is obliged to "knock off" for a week and longer. He loses his place. He is discharged. His little home is not yet all paid. He starts out in search of lighter work, but after awhile any kind of work, if he could only get it. He thinks he might be able to stand anything to save his home. His wife takes in washing, or sewing —several of the children are beginning to earn a few pennies. A mere living is made, but the payments on the home can no longer be met; interest, insurance and taxes are beginning to be compounded in such a manner that under the circumstances it is impossible to ever liquidate the indebtedness. For a while this family is tolerated as trespassers, just long enough to keep down moral censure, but at last the mortgage is foreclosed, the family is evicted, and the property is again sold to another who is willing to take his chances to cope with the situation.

**Stay Where You Are.** A good rule is to stay where you are. If a change is contemplated, every side and point should be well considered, from before and after thought of view, and then act. A judicious business man never rushes headlong into new adventures, and a common laboring man should be equally careful, for his labor and his health are his capital, and, by injudicious management he may be just as unfortunate as the man who has more money than forethought. A celebrated writer on "how to get on in the world," says that there are two ways to get on in the world. One way is to stay where you are and the world will come to you. Another is to go out into the world, to go forth, to move, to venture.

> The busy hands that restlessly unfold
> To labor—though they gather little gold—
> Work for the world a benefit untold;
> Cheerfully aid the weak, uphold the strong,
> And, by their work, help industry along,
> Are worthy of the poet's sweetest song.
> When man and master—if a master be
> To claim a peerage in humanity—

With one accord, in peaceful harmony,
Work each to the same end—each one to gain,
Unchecked by classes, or distinctions vain—
That which was meant each factor to sustain,
That freedom, with its all-pervading grace,
Assigning each its undisputed place,
Will "*Work and Capital*" at once efface.
When each in his own sphere is satisfied,
Their work and means to the same end applied,
There is no line their honors to divide ;
Then labor, to the humblest of the free,
A crown of glory, just as bright will be
As that surmounts the head of royalty ;
Its blessings bring the toiler recompense
More noble than man's worshipped pounds and pence.

**Monstrosities.** There are monstrosities in every department of nature. A monstrosity is a thing out of the common order of nature. The word is applicable not only to beings but moral conduct—monstrous brutality and monstrous education. South says: "We often read of monstrous birds, but we see a greater monstrosity in education, when a father begets a son and trains him up like a beast." We erroneously limit the meaning of the word to things hideous in nature: deformities of body, cruelty of character, ferocity of animals, &c., or to high stature, or enormity of size ; but it is equally applicable to things of a less repulsive nature. Dryden says: "Who with his wife is *monstrously* in love," using the word in the sense of extravagance, excess. Thus a mountain or a man may be of monstrous size, while a person or a dog may be monstrously cruel.

The general idea of monster, however, is a great, hideous, overgrown being, animal or thing. Giants of old were called monsters. The leviathan and the behemoth were monsters in the animal kingdom. But there are moral monsters—persons with monstrous principles. There are monstrous creeds, doctrines, theories and laws, as hideous and cruel in their influence as the monsters in the forest and the great deep.

**Evolution.** The monsters of ancient times, described in mythology, or the pseudo historic works of some of the ancient writers, are now extinct, if they ever existed.

That giants existed is proven beyond successful contradiction. That the leviathan of Egypt or the behemoth (the Arabian ox, or elephant) was not altogether a myth, scientists will admit. But they have passed away with other creatures of the antediluvian age.

Goliath—the children of Anak, as big as trees,—Milton's

"Giants of mighty bone and great emprise."

and the giants who built the great basaltic pillars in Ireland's famous "Causeway," are known no more, save in history. Their day of usefulness is passed; the world needs them no more.

**We Need Them No More.** By a general law of nature all physical and mental existence not needed gradually becomes extinct. Monster animals, huge lizards and birds were mere scavengers of the soil builders—races of men living ages ago, having passed away, as the Indians of our country will soon do. And in the track of the red man follows the solitary relic of the vast herds of buffalo once crowding our prairies. We need them no longer. Extermination, propagation, wise generation, civilization and domestication of man and beast have all a tendency toward the useful and the good. Republics rise upon the ruins of fallen monarchies. Persia, Babylon, Greece, Rome served their day, then departed, while new republics are born almost every year; and we may safely predict that before America celebrates the second anniversary of the declaration of independence nearly all the strong monarchial governments of Europe will be metamorphosed by the principles underlying the civil government of our country. Evolution pursues its course of changing and improving the world silently but surely. Behold its work of a century only! A monarch, in either church or state, dare not place his foot on American soil and exercise the imperial functions of his office. Princes are aliens in this country, and lords, aside from their good qualities of manhood, are only birds of plumage. Ostentation is tolerated and nobility admired

**Admired Only by the Vulgar.** only by the vulgar and the vain ; the nobility only affiliate with the rich to secure their shekels. The march of progress displaces or eradicates all these civil and social monstrosities as well as those existing in physical nature. Why not accompany evolution in its course, allow ourselves to drift along in the safe current it pursues, instead of clinging to monstrosities, moral, social and political, which, while they must eventually die, may still for the present do us great injury?

In some countries where these titled men and women display their pomp and royalty, exists another lawful monstrosity of these titled "lords of creation," which we sincerely trust evolution may soon pass out of existence. This monstrosity is known by the name of "pauper." During the last decade these lords and potentates have been painfully impressed with the idea that these paupers are a great nuisance to them, and instead of waiting for the regular course of evolution to extinguish them, they most earnestly recommend emigration, particularly to America. How successful they were in this movement the influx of tens of thousands

**The Influx of Tens of Thousands.** demonstrates. Counter force should be brought to bear by our government in this case. At least we think the time has come when emigration should be regulated, if not prohibited, and none be allowed to land here unless possessed of certain qualifications. This is one of our social and political *monstrosities.*

It is a gross injustice to the wage-workers of America— especially if they are Americans—to allow the cheap labor of Europe, or any foreign country, to come here and enter into unequal competition with the skill and industry begotten with time and patience on our own soil. With entirely different tastes and education, with different habits, formed through life, it is impossible for our laboring men to meet them on equal ground. An American workman is accustomed to a good, substantial meal, and a comfortable home, a clean bed, and, if a typical son or daughter of America, the enjoyment of an annual vacation, and the reading of a book, or regular perusal of a good magazine —while these foreign competitors are content with a bed of straw, make their meal from a battered pail between their knees, huddle together and live in squalor—thus being enabled to live on half the wages human cleanliness and social decency require.

"But," asks one of my opponents, "if their mode of living is good enough for them, why not for our workmen?" Let me answer that question by asking another: "If some men make a living by stealing, why should not all men be thieves?" That idea is one of the grim "monstrosities" of the age, which must and will be evolutionized. The spirit of the age calls for *elevation*, not *degradation*.

For the avoidance of this pauper-emigration "monstrosity," evolution in the shape of protective tariff is a farce. You must put up barriers and close the gates. But this monstrosity must become extinct, for

> The evil, be it of what sort it will—
> Social or civil—known as *evil* still
> Must die. E'er since creation's birth
> The evil that has cursed our mother earth
> Has been short-lived—while true and good
> Has lived to bless our human brotherhood.

# COMPETITION; EIGHT HOURS.

"Easy is the descent from Avernus to the lower world; but, to retrace one's steps and escape to the upper regions, this is, indeed, a work of difficulty: this is, indeed, a task."

**The Life of Trade.** Man by nature, in his most advanced physical condition, is but an imperfect creature, untamed, unlearned and inexperienced. In all his various exigencies he is still in want of something and knows not how to find it. Had he come into existence perfected he would have remained without wants and, perhaps, without ambition. But the necessities arising daily in his material life, and the desire to supply those necessities, makes him alert and watchful to discover the means to that end. By this his utility is developed. And while each of his neighbors and acquaintances are equally bent on the same achievement, it behooves him to do his utmost to keep pace with or, if he can, outdo all of them. This, of course, awakens activity, causes "hustling," and, as in primeval times, the fittest gets the most.

Competition creates activity and activity creates business and trade. Then don't be afraid of competition, though this may cause friction, for, from the very fact that such is **It Stimulates.** the case, it will stimulate improvement and make industry and trade more active in almost all departments. In fact competition enters into and is largely the actuating principle of almost all commercial enterprise. As soon as the rudimental principles underlying the possible construction of a sewing-machine were discovered, competition was aroused and scores of dormant minds were awakened and engaged in the further development of this desirable industry. Before long various and still much-needed improvements were made, the demand was increased, manufactories sprang up all over the country to supply the demand and business was stimulated in various departments of iron and wood products. The introduction of sheet steel, sheet copper, galvanized iron, by late discoveries in metalurgy, the further practical developments of the usefulness of electricity, has stimulated business by calling into action additional capital and capitalists, requiring men and skill in the production of articles long in competition in the markets of other lands.

**Men Will Do Their Best.** As long as man has needs that must be supplied, self-preservation will impel him to find means to supply them if possible. A man will under all circumstances give all in defense of his life, and as long as there are means available to preserve it he will make use of them. While in all ulterior matters he may be indifferent or careless, when ambition, with clipped wings, hides itself after failing to attain to fame or power, the absolute necessaries of life still goad him on to renewed efforts to help himself and those depending on his endeavors. He may exhaust all his resources and yet be unsuccessful against all adverse circumstances or overwhelming opposition, still battling manfully and honestly with the available forces at his command, he has done his best and must be exonerated from blame if he fails in the attempt.

**The Government Can Do No More.** Men often blame the government for not doing more than it does to stimulate trade, and, while it must be admitted that it might do more than it does, with all its machinery employed in the interest of political advancement for its favorite party and political *proteges*, still, if the government could for a little while forget its political

G. M. PULLMAN.
Fig. 1.

P. M. ARTHUR.
Fig. 2.

MRS. MARGARET GIBSON.
Fig. 3.

JOHN P. HAINES.
Fig. 4.

Plate XI—For sketches see pages 221 and 222.

foundlings and magnanimously look to the interests of its laboring classes, they could do no more than to encourage honest competition. This is all the people can expect the government to do, unless it is to give them an open field.

**An Open Field.** The government should, and *must*, guarantee to its people a fair and open field for the exercise of their political and business functions. As soon as it creates barriers or obstructions, so soon it commits commercial suicide. When it opens its gates to unlicensed and indiscriminate traffic, it kills honest competition. When it favors the *wealthy few* and ignores the industrious many, it abuses its power. When it protects all alike in honest competition, its prerogative is honestly exercised. Destroy competition and anarchy stands ready to speed the arrow of destruction.

**It is an Educator.** No matter how high or how low the standard of a man or a nation may be, practically there is always room for improvement and advancement. Education, in commerce, mechanism and science of living, is just as essential as in the most abstruse problems of astronomy or physiology.

"'*Tis education forms the common mind*" from the mastering of the *Alpha* to the *Omega* in the lessons of human life. It is unsafe for the solon or the booby to jump at conclusions. The greatest achievements of this, or any age, were accomplished by study. And in all the various epochs of history competition accomplished the greatest results. Demosthenes, while declaiming to the sea, climbing mountains with pebbles under his tongue to improve his speech, pursuing his studies in a hermit's cave, was actuated by a spirit of competition. His country boasted of its orators; he competed with them in greatness. Education and training made him the ruling power of a mighty empire and *competition* spurred him on. Then let the workingmen of America educate themselves for the work before them. Utilize their time, their opportunities to understand the advantages competition offers them and let its various oper-

ations—as it certainly will do if properly studied and understood—educate them in the science of economy; and the
lessons they will learn from this spirit of competition will
make them stronger and nobler in the battle for their
"inalienable rights."

### Friction Will Bring Out the Best.

You may place two solid sticks of
sound wood side by side and they will lie in close proximity
until they decay without showing any activity. But should
you take those two lifeless sticks and rub them vigorously
against each other for a time you would then see the life in
them. First they create warmth, then the sparks begin to
fly, and ere long they will kindle a fire larger than that
which burned down a great city. That is friction, which
serves the universe in so many ways through its mysterious mechanism. And that is what competition arouses.
If all the means and advantages in the business or commercial world were left in the hands of a few passive or inactive
men, our industry would lose its name in idleness—but
once let the vigorous hands of competition begin to pumice
them, then life will permeate the dead bones, open the
closed arteries and start new life in business avenues. By
all means give us more *friction* by giving us more honest
competition. Competition is not only a lever to a man's
activity, but it is the ambition of a boy.

### The Ambition of a Boy.

From the earliest childhood
contests for the largest piece
of tart or the largest share of jam down to the battle with
the last champion of life, man has been in competition with
man.

The boy in his school days is ambitious either to be
at the head of his class, or to beat his comrade in marbles,
or to "lick any boy of his size in school." If of a studious
nature, his ambition is to outdo his classmates in all their
studies; and, if it is only for the love of study, the good it
will do himself and—by proper application—to others, his
ambition is laudable. If, on the contrary, his object is

selfish, only to gratify his own vanity, the spirit of competition he manifests awakens a corresponding degree of
activity on the part of his classmates and urges them on to
greater efforts, thus doing good to both parties. So even in
boyish ambition competition has its salutary effects. The
dreams of boyhood ambition have often been realized in
manhood days. But it was done by the hard rubbing
against opposing obstacles, the polish of friction and the
firm but honest competition with which he urged his way
onward and upward. No great man ever attempted or
gained his greatness without being influenced by a spirit
of *competition.*

---

## THE EIGHT-HOUR SYSTEM.

"Wise work is *useful.* No man minds, or ought to mind, its being
hard, if only it comes to something. Of all wastes, the greatest waste
you can commit is the waste of labor."—*John Ruskin.*

There has been much said and written on the eight-hour
system, *pro* and *con*, and while both sides advance arguments worthy of more than a passing consideration, we
think the system is one that, if adopted and properly managed would result in great good.

**Fundamental Reasons.** The many discoveries, both
in science and general mechan-
ism, were, as we believe, intended to lighten the burden of
manual labor. Every thing exists for a specific purpose
and is intended for the good of mankind. "So far shalt
thou go and no further" applies not only to the dashing
billows of ocean, but to every object or purpose in which
mankind has an interest. The tide may harmlessly rush
over its usual boundaries for a time, but in the end it may
do much mischief by robbing us of much otherwise available territory. Ten hours' work may not perceptibly immediately manifest its debilitating influence upon the hardy
sons of toil, but, like the slow washing of the sea, it will
make its mark upon the generations to come.

The discoveries of late years were intended to lighten labor. For what other purpose could they be intended? By them more work can be accomplished in eight hours than could be performed without them in ten. And as these labor-saving machines are intended to lighten labor the time should be shortened. The primary object of labor is to make a livelihood and the exercise it gives is intended to promote health, not to injure it by undue exercise of physical power. Labor has a right to benefit by these discoveries. Capital should not absorb *all* of it, for the purpose of amassing wealth more easily and rapidly. Its advantage lies in the saving of expense, life and energy; and the laborer as well as the capitalist has a right to share in these advantages.

**Physiological Reason.** In the prime of life and the vigor of manhood a laboring-man can do more, accomplish and endure more, than when years have told on him. The power of endurance becomes exhausted, if overtaxed, much sooner than if his physical powers are carefully husbanded. Life carefully preserved in youth will give vigor and strength to old age. Extravagance in anything depletes. Anything overdone can never be renewed. As the water which has once passed the mill can no more be used to run its wheel, so physical energy once spent can never be recalled. A worn-out, tired man cannot study, his mind cannot retain a lesson. He may attend a lecture replete with well chosen and eloquently expressed thoughts and ideas, embodying exactly what concerns his individual welfare, but in his tired condition it falls upon listless ears and unimpressive mind.

**Moral Reason.** Knowledge is free to all men. We go further in this statement; since knowledge is free to all, and so easy of access, and comparatively inexpensive, we deem it almost criminal for any one in the nineteenth century to be entirely ignorant. Not all laboring-men can attain to great heights of education for want of proper time or means. Even here monopoly comes in and education is monopolized by the wealthy. The poor man, it is true, has his free schools. But the wealthy are not satisfied with these. The fact is in these schools the young children are simply prepared for learning. The real fields of learning, the colleges and universities, are fenced in for the wealthy. Still, much can be learned by the laboring classes if you give them two hours per day more time to do it in.

These men should study natural philosophy, a broad and fruitful field, from which they may cull many a flower and pluck much fruit to make life more pleasant and themselves more useful. There is much they could learn if their task-masters gave them two hours less in the labor tramway.

**A Personal Reason.** There is no nearer kin to a man than *himself.* A man can voluntarily injure himself for the sake of gain. A man has no right to turn himself into a cart horse, whether he be a capitalist or a laborer. If it is possible for a man to make a living in eight hours, why should he work ten? He simply attempts to move ponderous bodies at the expense of his intellect. It is the duty of man to work, not only to supply himself with the necessaries of life, but to develop his physical powers and retain his health. But when he does this to the neglect of his intellectual life, that higher and nobler part of man, he does it to the detriment of his highest welfare. Man has no right to work until his physical or mental machinery breaks down. It is just as sacred a moral obligation on man to rest in season as to work.

The merchant sees this, for

**Stores Close Early.** The merchant of the present day has learned that it is not only possible, but really desirable, to close his store at 5 or 6 o'clock instead of keeping it open until 9 or 10 at night, thus giving his employees from three to four hours more time for study or recreation.

At first this movement was met with the bitterest opposition; some met it with ridicule, as a great absurdity; some with uplifted hands, as a dire calamity. The merchant prophesied great reduction of sales and inevitable loss in business. The buyers said it would be impossible to make their purchases during the day—"they had no time;" "it was too hot," and a dozen equally ridiculous objections were made against this early closing movement.

**The Public will Soon Learn.** With a painfully cautious movement, the more progressive and intelligent business men went into the experiment with a feeling something like a person experiences when he first dips his feet in a cold stream preparatory to taking a bath, but they soon grew bolder and more confident; they saw their clerks more pleasant and cheerfully active in waiting on customers and ready to do more work in view of the shorter hours; their gas and coal bills were much lower; they relished the additional hours of rest themselves, and their sales were just as large. The public found they could make better selections by daylight; they could find plenty of time to make all needful purchases during the hours the stores were open, and instead of spending their evenings shopping,

**The Wage-worker will Have a Chance;** the mechanic and laboring man will be able to spend his evenings at home with his wife and children, or take them to hear a good lecture, or accompany them to some place of innocent amusement, or, if he cannot or does not care to indulge in these things, he can devote his leisure hours to something better still:

**To Acquire Knowledge.** He can spend these leisure hours in useful study. No matter how intelligent he may be, he can always learn more about his own work or profession; about the history and laws of his own and other countries; about his own body and its needs, its wonderful mechanism, and how to keep it in order.

The wage-worker has a perfect right to the inexhaustible resources of literature.

**The Wage-worker Must Have a Mental Profit.** The laborer is not only entitled to a profit in the labor products of his work and skill, but he may also justly claim a share in the mental profits of the day. By right of the laws of nature every man has a claim to a share of the knowledge so lavishly scattered all around us. The wealthy can get the lion's share of it in the form of costly libraries and leisure time to read the volumes therein; but how shall the laboring man get his share if he has no books to read or no time to study?

**It Takes Time for Mental Culture.** "Rome was not built in a day" is a somewhat hackneyed quotation, but it is convenient for application to almost any subject involving the crowding of much into little time. A man cannot store his mind with much useful knowledge in a few hours. One little stream does not make a river, but our great rivers are made of *many little streams.* If one hour cannot give you much mental culture *many hours* can, if you use them properly. Give us the eight-hour system and you give the wage-worker (deducting Sundays and holidays) six hundred hours a year for study, of which the ten-hour system deprives him now. If he uses that time now he robs his employer or his family of just that much. We mean eight hours for a day's work.

**The Law Must Favor It.** It is a problem. This eternal law, law, law! It stares us in the face no matter where we turn. Right or wrong (and how often it is wrong!) it must be obeyed. The law certainly should favor the eight-hour system, and we think if the wage-workers learn right, vote right and act right, it soon will.

---

## EDUCATION, INTELLECTUAL MONOPOLY, TRUSTS, MENTAL PAUPERISM, Etc.

**Why Should a Man be Cast Down?** "Man, amidst the fluctuations of his own feelings and of passing events, ought to resemble the ship, which currents may carry and winds may impel from her course, but which, amidst every deviation, still presses onward to her port with unremitted perseverance. In the coolness of reflection he ought to survey his affairs with a dispassionate and comprehensive eye, and, having fixed on a plan, take the necessary steps to accomplish it, regardless of the temporary mutations of his mind, the monotony of the same track, the apathy of exhausted attention, or the blandishments of new projects."

**The Greatest Danger.** This blessed land of ours is menaced by many dangers, internal if not external. Some think emigration is dangerous; others are afraid such or such a tariff law or theory is threatening disaster; while the more bigoted, or superstitious, prophesy our downfall because of the fearful immorality of our people. The danger we refer to as the greatest is the cause of all these other evils named. We mean *ignorance*. It is this evil which makes so many blunders in the formulation and passage of our laws; it is this that makes emigration dangerous, and it is this that breeds and sustains immorality.

**More Than One Kind of Ignorance.** This evil is not that which makes men cruel and uncivil as often found among the reeking haunts of vice, the social lepers, banished from all intelligent society. Nor does it apply only to the innocent ones, reared in the wild woods, deprived of all the benefits of more advanced civilization.

But there is an ignorance more dangerous than that implied by want of education. A man may be educated in certain branches and yet be ignorant of those things of the most vital importance to himself and his country. The common interpretation of learning or education is a something intended for the ignorant only. This is a mistake. There is such a thing as educating the educated. The men

**Harmful Education.** and women who are truly, positively ignorant, being even unable to read and write, are not the most dangerous element of society. There *are* those in society who have learned just enough to become expert pick-pockets, swindlers and tricksters. It is

GEN. JAMES B. WEAVER.

Plate XII-For sketch see page 222.

among those who are in some sense bright and intelligent that you find the most dangerous and successful criminals. It takes an intelligent burglar to pick a complicated safe lock.

"A little learning is a dangerous thing," our juvenile school book taught us, and these smart scamps have only learned those things pertaining to their vicious calling. Not only is this simply learning the things especially suited to an unlawful calling, but it is dangerous.

### Learned Men Make Mistakes.

Men may be learned in some branches quite well and yet in other departments closely allied to those branches in their application be very deficient. For example: Our best educated men, in drafting or framing our constitution, made a mistake by the simple scratch of the pen which caused a bloody war. They may have lacked a statesman's foresight, or they may have been ignorant of that particular branch of education only, but it illustrates the great importance of being well versed in those matters especially in which a whole nation is concerned.

### Political Campaigns.

The deplorable results of a "little learning" is too often seen in political campaigns, especially among political leaders and speakers. The effect of their teachings upon the ignorant portion of their hearers and followers is often disastrous. Men who are perhaps learned in various branches of science or literature, but woefully ignorant of the true principles of political economy, or the issues before the people; or knowing better, but presuming on the ignorance of the people, willfully misrepresent the true features in the case, and thereby mislead them, simply to enable their own party to come into power.

### Demagogism.

There are demagogues in every political party, and their great aim is to rule; by fair means if they can, but win they must. Of course, they have their followers and adherents. Some follow them and obey their behests for the loaves and fishes. The more ignorant are driven to the polls by more arbitrary measures—threats of political excommunication, loss of work, &c.—while a large number of the illiterate, and some with a fair learning, deposit their votes in good faith, against their own personal interest, because they believe their leaders, lacking intelligence sufficient to decide clearly for themselves.

These men should be met by the wage-workers with at least equal, if not superior, intelligence or education.

### Whose Fault is it if you are Deceived?

It may be dishonest on the part of these demagogues to thus mislead the masses; but that will not exonerate the duped themselves from blame. When a man is brought before a court of justice, charged with the violation of a law, his plea that he did not know of the existence of such a law, or did not understand its purport, will give him no release. The court will tell him that every citizen is expected and supposed to know the law. Hence ignorance of the law is almost, if not quite, as culpable as the violation of the law. The same thing may be said concerning the violation of the natural, physical and social laws. You are expected to *know them.* When you bear in mind that the men who frame our laws and control our finances are not ignorant men, you should at once realize the absurdity of ignorant men questioning their methods and actions. You must meet the enemy on vantage-ground and with his own weapons. In other words, you must be intelligent yourself.

### Educate Yourself.

As soon as the laboring man learns what constitutes right, what is good for himself and his class; in short, as soon as he knows as much about *labor, tariff, finance* and other vital questions of the day as the would be political demagogues, then there will be some chance of him getting his rights. "When Greek meets Greek, then comes the tug of war!" There has thus far been really no war between the two factions. It was simply a charge on the part of intelligent leaders and an ignominious retreat on the part of the ignorant. Again, let us say to the wage-workers of America : *educate yourselves!*

**Public Sentiment.** The masses of the working classes are governed by public sentiment. This is not always safe, for public sentiment is often divided equally and yet diametrically opposed. There were two public sentiments at the outbreak of our Rebellion, yet only one proved to be the right. Careful study of the mooted question, intelligent statesmanship and stern honesty of principle, in defiance of all public sentiment, made the war a blessing, instead of a curse, to our country. Public sentiment is often created by public desire, political charlatanism, or " mushroom growth ;" the result of special excitement, the impulsive throbbings of an unhealthy heart. Public sentiment made the ancient philosopher recant his doctrine of the earth moving on its axes. But it moved in spite of public sentiment. Intelligence was in the right. Of course public sentiment condemns or approves. But its judgments and decrees are not always right.

There is an instinctive sense in every human being which seeks to discern the right or the wrong in all things, but only when properly educated and directed will it be a safe guide to the truth.

**College Education.** Most of our American workingmen have had a common school education; thanks to that grand provision of free schools in our country. Few of them, however, have had the advantages of a college education. A college course is very desirable, but it is not really essential to good citizenship, office qualification or business success. Don't misunderstand us. We by no means contend that the different branches of learning taught in a college course are not essential to qualify a man for the higher duties of life, but we do say it is *not absolutely necessary* to go through college to acquire such learning, since you can obtain it outside of college walls. And after all it is *the man* who is studious while *in* college as well as *out* who becomes proficient; the same text-books imparting knowledge in the college furnish the same information at your home.

A college education is a good thing to have. It is like getting married. If you marry for love—as you ought— and you get riches with love, it is doubly gratifying. But if you wait for riches, you may never get married. If you want to marry you had better marry for love and try for riches afterward. If you depend exclusively on a college course, many of you will never amount to much or accomplish any good. If you have true ambition you can educate yourself. Almost every opportunity is at your hand; avail yourself of it.

**How to Educate Yourself.** Taking for granted that the eight-hour system is adopted—and here let us make a short digression to say that this very education we so urgently impress on you is intended to enable you to accomplish all these desirable objects as soon as you are able to present them intelligently to the world. Supposing then the 600 additional hours this system would give you, each year, were devoted to study, what an immense amount of useful knowledge you might acquire in a few years—and even with the leisure time you have now much might be accomplished.

You need not aim to become a great savant, a famous scientist or a grand philosopher, but you can become an intelligent man. If you have a special hobby, or a particular talent or love for any particular branch, make that your more especial study. But above all things select only the best and most useful subjects for reading and study. We would recommend some of the subjects we consider the most beneficial in what may be called "university extension."

**Natural Philosophy.** In our catalogue of subjects for study we commence with the practical, because, for the laborer or mechanic, we consider them the most profitable. We give natural philosophy as a general heading, under which are grouped many separate divisions. This science covers all the laws of phenomena and matter, including man. One of the most important and interesting departments in this is physiology.

**Physiology.** It is truthfully said that "the greatest study of man is man," and there is no study in all the range of intellectual possibility that is as important and as obligatory on man to understand as *himself*. Physiology shows us how man is constructed, gives a comprehensive idea of all his functional organs, how he breathes, smells, tastes, hears, sees and feels. It shows him how he digests his food, what is the best food to eat, what gives him nourishment, and what gives him pain, and enables him to outline a safe road on which to travel in order to *live happily* and *live long*. Whether he works eight hours or ten, it will tell him when to continue and when to stop. It gives you the operation of the brain and function of your nerves.

After studying and understanding the immediate wants of yourself physically, your next great desire should be the good of mankind, socially and generally.

**Political Economy.** This subject in times past was considered only an adjunct to or a disintegrated part of other branches of general governmental philosophy, but now it has become a distinct science. It teaches us the principles of good government, the proper levying of revenue, the careful management of our national resources, our productive property, our labor interests and in short the careful and honest management of all our national affairs *for the good of all our people.* This is a subject that should interest and be fully understood by all wage-workers, for on the proper administration of these affairs depends all they hope to achieve in the future.

**Mechanism.** But there are other studies of practical value to the workingman. The mechanic, positively, and the laborer, incidentally, will find in the study of mechanism much, not only to aid him in his present department of business, but enable him to improve and enlarge his opportunities and business. To learn the principles

of proper construction and adjustment of parts, to apply and
increase power or motion to machinery, to overcome friction,
to make lifeless iron subservient to his will, and so infuse it
with his own intelligence that it becomes an active, living,
almost human power; to accomplish this is worth hard study.

Every workingman should study the different branches of
mathematics. They teach you how to measure distances,
lines, surfaces, solids, &c. The carpenter, the mason, the
architect, the bridge builder and every mechanic should learn
this. Even the wages of a common laborer would be valued at a higher figure.

**Chemistry.** Chemistry is perhaps the most instructive
and certainly the most important of all scientific studies. By this you can discover the nature and prop-
erties of bodies, of material substances, in solid or liquid
form, by analysis. This is useful in any department of
business. By chemistry you can create forces unknown
and produce results nature has hidden for ages. It has a
thousand charms for the student, the inventor and the practical business man.

The study of the general formation and structure of the
earth, its chemical affinities, by which the minerals are
formed and crystalized; the story of the silent, mysterious
work of ages—all these present an interesting and instructive study in geology and mineralogy.

The lover of the beautiful in nature will find a grand
field for study in botany : the various structures, color and
classification of plants and flowers; the homes in which
they grow, the endless variety ; the propagation of new orders and the many uses to which they may be applied. Not
only the farmer who makes it his special business to till and
cultivate his farm, and specially interest himself in the quality, quantity and price of his products, will find much to interest and benefit him in the study of agriculture ; but it is
of some interest to the laboringman to know which is the
best way to prepare the soil in his little lot, or garden
patch, what to plant in it to yield the greater profit.

All these branches of study to which we have briefly referred are more or less of a practical nature, but interesting and instructive.

**Collateral Branches of Study.** To look at the glittering heavens on a clear night and 'see the myriads of twinkling stars without *knowing what they are*, deprives a man of a great amount of pleasure. Astronomy furnishes us with the name, place and motion of the most conspicuous stars. It tells us their size, their distance from us and the invariable course they travel. If you take Jupiter, for example, and learn that that little shining light is a body 85,700 miles in diameter (eleven times as large as the earth), that it is 483,000,000 miles away from the sun, and that each revolution it makes around that centre of light occupies twelve years, you can form but a very faint idea of the sublime lessons taught by astronomy. These studies inspire the mind with admiration and a full appreciation of the beautiful and the good. It brightens up the intellect and by a little economy of time the workingman can hold his own with others who by having money can avail themselves of an education.

**Literature.** Here we strike a dangerous current. There is perhaps nothing more elevating, more efficacious in educating men and women to a higher standard, socially and morally, than *good, sound* literature; and, contrariwise, there is nothing more pernicious, more productive of vice and misery, than some of the light, frivolous, senseless, insipid, so-called literature, based upon nothing that is truthful, void of science or history, without instruction or amusement, neither "pointing a moral or adorning a tale." This more than worthless so-called literature is a social abomination. Cultivate, therefore, a taste for the *solid* literature of the age; read no other.*

---

* We would here call attention to the article under the head of *"Random Thoughts,"* in this book, entitled "The Workingman's Library."

We have many very good newspapers, family papers, weeklies and magazines. But learn how to discern between good, useful literature and the abominable, trashy stuff that is liable to poison the mind. There is as much care necessary in guarding the mind as the body. Good, solid literature that gives to the reader and student knowledge, strengthens the mind the same as good, nutritious food, will build muscle and brain.

**Be in Earnest.** It is a mistaken *idea* that many working people have regarding education. Many think that there is no use in studying different branches of education outside their particular line of business or vocation; that it cannot benefit them and hence is a mere waste of time; that it will not enable them to rise in the social scale, since it seems that possession is the main qualification for social recognition. But it should be remembered that the very process of acquiring knowledge is a source of happiness. The mind is employed. This builds character. Knowledge getting strengthens memory and brightens up the face. Knowledge is the wealth of the mind. The greatest inventions of modern time were originated by intelligent workmen. Wage-earners have risen in the *wealth of this earth*, and wage-earners have risen in the wealth of the mind, of soul and greatness of individuality, and we take the position that all peoples can accumulate knowledge, little by little, that they may keep apace with the intellectual march in line of evolution. You may not be able to do much now, but the question is not what you can do, but what you can *learn* to do. This is progress.

Before passing on to our next division, "Immigration and Suffrage," we would add one word more that will help every one amazingly in getting on well in the world. Education, qualification and perseverance; it should all the while be kept fresh before the mind that *integrity* is perhaps the most essential of all personal attainments. Cultivate a habit to make *your word good* and establish a reputation for truthfulness and you will never lack for a position. Work and trade will come to you. Be honest and truthful

HON. WALTER Q. GRESHAM.

Plate XIII  For sketch see page 222.

in dealing with others and with yourselves. *Simms* says: "Nothing will more rapidly loosen a man's hold upon prosperity than such behavior on his part as leads to his being accounted unreliable in his dealings." Let, therefore, the foundation of your life-structure be a fearless love of truth, honesty and justice, with an implicable hatred of deceit, chicanery and meanness.

" For without interest (profit) the accumulation of capital is impossible ; without capital there can be *no co-operation* of anterior and present *labor;* without this co operation (of capital and labor) there can be no society ; and without society man cannot exist."

## IMMIGRATION AND SUFFRAGE.

Nations, like individuals, are gauged by what they are, and they are what they make themselves. "*Learn,*" therefore, "*the right of all things.*"

> Blest, too, is he who can divine
> Where real right doth lie,
> And dares to take the side that seems
> Wrong to man's blindfold eye.—*Faber.*

**Why Foreigners Come to this Country.** The "immigration problem" has become of late years a study of much political interest; in fact it has grown into undue proportions, and yet only quite recently the question has been formulated as to whether immigration shall be suspended or otherwise regulated by law or not. Foreign immigrants figure largely as a factor in our labor troubles, and the time has come when our government can no longer *pass by* unnoticed the hitherto indiscriminate influx from other nations of the earth to the United States.

It is in justice due to our wage-earners of America to regulate immigration in a proper manner so as to obviate conditions which may either directly or indirectly lead to disturbance among our people.

It seems this country is a kind of an *oasis* for the foreign emigrant, unrestrained almost entirely, until in recent years we were driven to prescribe conditions, and will be forced to more strict regulating measures for obvious reasons. A great majority of those who come to this country from foreign shores do so for three special reasons : first, to better their financial and social condition ; second, to enjoy the blessings of liberty and freedom ; and third, because they have no opportunities in their native land to rise and do anything for themselves.

**The Galling Yoke.** The motive prompting the first class is natural and laudable, for each individual seeks in some way to better his financial condition, since that, in our day, is looked upon as the *open sesame* to all of this world's greatness and happiness.

The reason governing the second class is still more praiseworthy. Whatever their untutored idea of liberty may be, one thing is apparent—the most intelligent class is the one attracted by that object. They feel the more keenly the galling yoke of monarchial rule because of their intelligence. To come away from its lashes and burdens and find respite in a free country is safer and cheaper than to foment a revolution, sacrifice their possessions, if not their lives, and then, perhaps, fail to accomplish their desire to gain freedom. The inborn desire to *be free* prompts many a noble man, with his family, to sacrifice all to gain it ; like the eagle, preferring the rough, rocky heights, away from the comforts of the flowery valley, in order to breathe in the mountain air of freedom.

**Prohibited Class.** The third class, wandering like birds of prey, to pick up whatever they can find, is an element troublesome and dangerous to any land. It is true that the law of our country, as it now is, prohibits the reception of paupers, or such as threaten to become public charges ; idiots or insane persons ; persons suffering from infectious diseases ; those convicted of crime and all forms of what is known as contract labor. A searching examination of emigrants, before embarking for this country, must be passed to ascertain if they do not belong to this excluded class. This prohibitory law, imperfect as it may be has none the less accomplished some good, and we sincerely hope it may grow in compass and keep on doing good work.*

But while legislation has closed the national gates against some objectionable classes, there are still further precautions to be taken to make the work complete. It is well known that since the Act of March, 1891, the character of the emigrants arriving in this country is greatly superior to that of many previous years. As we have stated, what our government should strive to do is to raise the character of our immigrants rather than to reduce their number.

There is a certain class coming to our country who are neither criminal nor physically disqualified, but who, nevertheless, are very objectionable and in a degree dangerous.

**Ignorance.** We refer to that class who are abjectly poor and lamentably ignorant and who, in their social degradation, care very little whether they improve their condition or not. Those belonging to this class do not, as a rule, make good citizens. Against this class some legislation should be directed in order to protect not only our own wage-workers, but all our national interests and reputation.

Let certain qualifications be peremptorily required for citizenship or domestication in our country. Let it be requisite, in the first place, that each foreigner wishing to make his home in this country, as the head of a family, possess at least two or three hundred dollars to commence his new life with so as not at once to become a subject of public regulation. And then they should at least be required to know something about the history, the government and the laws of the country they wish to adopt as their own.

---

* It has been estimated that since the Act of March, 1891, over 55,000 applicants for emigrant passage to this country were rejected, and nearly 4,000 of what is known as the prohibited classes were returned. The Commissioner of Immigration reports that this law has had a wholesome effect, for the character of the emigrant coming to our shores is vastly superior to those of many years previous.

**Let Them Come.** We should rather feel disposed to elevate the character of the emigrants than to reduce their number.

It is almost an established *truism* that our foreign people are honest and industrious as a rule, and soon infused with the spirit of enterprise and above all filled with true patriotism and willingness to defend the principles of their adopted country. So, while there is much to be deprecated, there is also much to be admired, in those especially who have families.

Many with lofty ambition, oppressed by monarchial insolence and wrong, finding nothing to approve, much less to emulate, without any incentive to greater action, or encouragement to loftier endeavors, find their hearts expand with new life as they breathe the exhilerating air of freedom, and become our best citizens. Among this better class are the young men and women, many of them bringing aged parents with them or waiting until by industry and economy they obtain sufficient money to send for them.* Many foreign people have sacrificed not only hard-earned money, but even the ordinary comforts of life to enjoy the liberty of this country.

* *United States Senator* HENRY C. HANSBROUGH, *in North American Review.* This excellent writer and thinker expresses our views on this subject. The true statesman point of view, with humanity largely interlined, is the only tenable ground that we can assume in regulating immigration to this country. We do not want Europe's criminals, her insane, paupers or the *indigent* in any sense, and in justice to our *American wage-earners* the government must suspend the importation of cheap or contract labor of whatever kind.

We quote from the Senator rather at length his own words. He says:

" The patient, delving European has been the fulcrum and American brains and enterprise the lever of our great progress. If we hope to continue our marvellous development we must not turn the emigrant away. He is a necessary part of the human machinery that causes the commercial and financial world to revolve in its daily orbit. The place that he is content to occupy in trenches cannot be filled by the native American, who has moved up to a higher plane and to more congenial employment. The versatile, wide-awake Irishman, the

**Shall Immigration Be Suspended?** Yet with all this filial devotion, all this love of country, all this industry and economy, there lurks that one grim ogre of foreign labor, competition. For, in order to keep their aged parents or to get money to bring them here, and many times for other reasons, they will work for almost any price, thereby, perhaps, innocently doing injustice to our own wage-workers. This is a matter for further legislation and could be regulated by the *Labor Bureau*, referred to under a special head in this volume. But there is great need of legislation on this subject of immigration, and a vigilant Congress could soon discover where it could be better regulated and readily supply the legislative want. All we can do as a people is to direct their attention to the matter and by virtue of our American citizenship demand the needful laws and regulations the welfare of the country requires.

**There Is Room for All.** We American people are not at all selfish. You will not find a more generous, kind-hearted and hospitable people in the world. But we are sensitive. We don't like foreigners

---

sturdy, stalwart Scandinavian ; the frugal, persevering Germans, who are among the best of our emigrants, furnish the basis of a higher order of citizenship ; they are the substratum of society. The immigrant built our railroads and opened our mines, and now his children, advancing with the general progress, are teachers in the public schools and practicing the skilled professions in the cities and villages, while his grandchildren are foremost among scientists and rank high as authors and statesmen.

The general belief that immigrants are not immediate contributors to the wealth of the country, but bring with them only the rags upon their backs, is erroneous. As an example : For the last half of the fiscal year ending June 30, 1892, the 152,360 immigrants over twenty years of age who arrived in the port of New York brought with them $3,060,908 05, or $20.09 each. The adult French immigrants brought an average of $55.67 ; the Swiss are next highest in the list, the Welsh third and the Germans fourth. Hungary, Italy and Poland are lowest, showing an average of $11.75 each adult.

to come to our homes, have a free run over our house and grounds and then sit down and deliberately rob us of our most precious fruit.

No one will question the right of our government to designate what class of people shall come to live among us or even to *prohibit immigration altogether*.  But this, we think, would not only be bad policy, but it would be inhuman, morally, and disgraceful, politically.  It would demolish all our boasted doctrine of friendship and neighborly love and dim the lustre of our national escutcheon, so proud of the "home of the free."  And really there is as yet no cause for alarm.

**No Trouble Yet.** The country, thus far, has no special cause to complain as to the *number* of immigrants.  In fact the tide of immigration thus far has not damaged our shores as much as some timid or over enthusiastic politicians would have us believe.

The total immigration from Europe and all other countries during a period of seventy-three calendar years, from 1820 to 1893, aggregates only a little over fifteen millions.

**Numbers Arrived.** Immigration has been gradually increasing, year by year, from 1820 to 1882.  Since then it has averaged the same or, rather, de-

---

But the strong, honest, healthy immigrant brings more than the paltry dollars in his pocket.  He brings value difficult to estimate. In a book published in 1870 by Frederick Knapp, then Commissioner of Immigration of the State of New York the average economic value of each immigrant is given at $1,125.*  Norwegians who come here have very little money, but they are the least illiterate of any of our immigrants, and experience shows that for industry and frugality they are unexcelled.

Our best immigrants are those who bring their families with them, and, when they have earned sufficient money, send for their relatives. It is interesting to study the official figures † in this respect, for we discover in them the motive of the immigrant, and when we find his motive we may judge of his worth to the community.  Of the 51,383 Irish who came during the past fiscal year, 25,684 were females. There were 119,168 Germans, of whom 52,271 were females.  Italy

creased to some extent. In 1820 there were only 8,385 immigrants, while in 1882 there were 788,992. The total number of immigrants to this country during sixty calendar years was 11,597,181. Of this total Ireland and Germany furnished the greatest number, aggregating almost all from the other nations. Ireland furnished 3,063,761; Germany, 3,002,027; England, 894,444. Taking all the European countries together they aggregated, during the time designated, over 9,500,000, while the remainder of the grand total came from Asia, Africa, British America and other American provinces.

This immigration from other countries is, after all, not as disastrous in its effects as some political prophets represent it to be, when we learn that we have available territory enough to settle down readily and comfortably provide for *five hundred million people*, without crowding them as closely as our foreign neighbors do. We can give them, *per capita*, over two acres of tillable land more than England or Germany now can give to their people *per capita*.

**Our Resources.** Supposing that in the spirit of progression, for which America is now noted and feared by the nations of the world, we should still continue

---

sent 61,631 in all, only 14,232 of whom were females. These figures by contrast conclusively show the necessity for extraordinary care on the part of the government in making selections of those who are to people this country. The immigrant who brings his wife comes to stay. He assimilates rapidly and his offspring make good Americans.

That Congress has the right to pass laws for the suspension of immigration, and that such laws would not be in contravention of treaty obligations, will scarcely admit of dispute, but that the enactment of a measure of this character would be in the interest of sound public policy may be very seriously questioned."

* What is the economic value, says Mr. Knapp, of each immigrant to the country of his adoption? We are perfectly familiar with the estimates which, during the existence of slavery, were made of the value of negroes. A good field hand was considered to be worth $1,200 and over; a good cook was valued higher; and a seamstress or housekeeper was, in some cases, held at even $1,500 or $2,000. In order to obtain a proper idea of the importance of immigration to the

to increase in the same proportion, year by year, as steadily as we have during the last decade, it will still require 1,000 years to fill up this great country, allowing each inhabitant three acres of land to settle and live on.    Have our readers even a faint idea of the magnitude of our territorial extent? This United States, with its fertile and scarcely fully explored territories, represents a mammoth farm, covering *three million, twenty-five thousand, six hundred* (3,025,600) *square miles.*  Cut this up into acres and see the result.    It will give us *one billion, nine hundred and forty-two million, seven hundred and thirty-five thousand, two hundred* (1,942,-735,200) acres of land.    Three hundred million sections of 642 acres each !   But what additions may be made during the centuries to come !   "Westward still the car of empire rolls !" the poet exclaimed long ago.   But the spirit of a republic like ours will seek and find kinship in the four quarters of the globe.   There is no danger of crowding us yet !

In the face of the foregoing statistics we feel disposed rather to favor immigration than to legislate against it.   Still, some better regulations might be adopted to make immigration not only safe, but more respectable, as well as profitable.

United States, we must endeavor to capitalize, so to speak, the addition to the natural and intellectual resources of the country represented by each immigrant.

Dr. Engel computes the cost of raising a manual laborer in Germany at forty thalers a year for the first five years of his life ; at fifty thalers for the next five years, and at sixty thalers from the eleventh to the fifteenth year, thus arriving at an average of fifty thalers per year, or 750 thalers in all.  From my knowledge of German life I consider this estimate as correct as it can be, and assuming that in this country subsistence costs about twice as much as in Germany, I do not think I shall be far from the truth in doubling Engel's estimates, and in assuming the expense of bringing up an American farmer or unskilled laborer for the first fifteen years of his life to average 100 thalers per year, or a total of 1,500 thalers, equal to about $1,500 currency.  Following Dr. Engel's estimate, an American girl will be found to cost only about half that, or $750, for the reason that she becomes useful to the household from an earlier age.   Allowance must be made, it is true, for the fact that about one fifth of the immigrants are less than fifteen years old ; but this is fully balanced by the great preponderance

Instead of receiving a heterogeneous collection of paupers, criminals and vagrants, with a small number of really intelligent and worthy persons "sandwiched" among them, all packed like herring in vermin-infested and disease-breeding holds of vessels, bringing them here half starved and demoralized—instead of this the government should fit out suitable vessels for this special business, select the best emigrating material only, refuse all objectionable characters, and do it with a clearly decided plan as to their destination, work and personal safety when here. Select the people most useful and desirable here.

Surely a nation having the power and the right to close its doors to every one has the undisputed right to select whom it pleases if their desire is to come.

Let these vessels be commanded by competent U. S. officers, to examine into the moral and social character of these emigrants; with competent physicians to judge of their physical condition, establish sanitary regulations on these vessels and attend to proper fumigation or disinfection of ship and luggage. Make these vessels clean, neat, attractive as a parlor, so that the very passage may impress them

of men and women and by thousands who represent the highest order of skilled labor. Hence, I feel safe in assuming the capital value of each male and female emigrant to be $1,500 and $750 respectively, for every person of either sex, making an average for both of $1,125.

† In the following table will appear the number and per cent. of immigrants of each sex, from the leading countries of Europe, arriving from 1881 to 1889 inclusive.

| Country from which arrived. | Males. | Per cent, males of total. | Females. | Per cent. females of total. | Total. |
|---|---|---|---|---|---|
| Germany | 836,290 | 57.6 | 616,680 | 42.4 | 1,452,970 |
| Ireland | 334,229 | 51.0 | 321,253 | 49.0 | 635,482 |
| England | 395,273 | 64.3 | 249,407 | 38.7 | 644,680 |
| Sweden and Norway | 346,862 | 61.0 | 221,501 | 39.0 | 568,362 |
| Italy | 243,923 | 79.4 | 63,386 | 20.6 | 307,309 |
| Russia, including Poland | 174,481 | 65.8 | 90,607 | 34.2 | 265,088 |
| Austria | 142,221 | 62.9 | 83,817 | 37.1 | 226,038 |
| Hungary | 94,243 | 73.8 | 33,438 | 26.2 | 127,681 |
| Scotland | 91,752 | 61.6 | 57,617 | 38.4 | 149,369 |

with the taste, the dignity, the cleanliness and the intelligence of the country they mean to adopt; and give them an idea of what may in due time be expected of them.

How much better for the immigrant, after landing, if he (the immigrant) could "read his title clear" before sailing.

**Start Right.** Let these vessels not be the old worm-eaten hulks, picked out of the naval bone-yards, but safe, seaworthy-going steamers, able to make the trip in two weeks. Let them carry but little freight outside of the personal effects of the emigrants.

We would suggest three routes : Land those who desire to settle in the northwest at Quebec or Ontario, tapping the Northern Pacific R. R. Those destined for the Eastern and Middle States land at Philadelphia, Boston, New York, and Baltimore; for the Southeastern States, New Orleans and for the southwest. Let there be vessels for each of these routes, making monthly trips, and carrying a special class.

**Settle Them.** This is of course only the first step in the arrangement of immigration. We must dispose of these immigrants when they arrive; in fact some disposition should be made of them when they start.

With large available territory like ours this is an easy problem to solve. *Colonize* them on our western lands,

**Colonization.** help to cultivate the idle acres, build up new towns and cities, as others have done before them. Those with families and a little money capital prefer to settle in these localities—of colonies. Immigrants with means enough to be independent can choose their own place and vocation, but for the masses we advocate *colonization.* It will not require much money to start them. Our capitalists can soon follow them and put up mills ; railroads will soon be needed. A smart German can make a good living on 40 acres of land ; so can a Yankee! Forty acres is all that should be allowed a man by the government in *one tract* or railroad grants. It is better for 16 families to occupy and improve a section of 640 acres than to entrust it all to one man. This will at once form a neighborhood, enabling them to unite their work, assist and encourage one another, have social advantages and friendly intercourse. Americans will soon follow their example and settle among them, and it will not be very long before these colonies are Americanized. It will be advantageous to the immigrant and to the government to aid such a project.

But *let the government put its foot firmly down on land syndicates and "land sharks" of every description!*

**Make a Charge.** By this method of colonization, and by proper care and industry, every head of a family can, in five years, become comparatively independent, have a home of his own and be no longer the slave of any man, as a large majority of our wage-earners in our large cities now are. But we do not mean that the government should give this land and go to all this trouble and expense *for nothing.* The charges should, however, be not in excess of the actual cost of conducting this special work and made payable in such a manner as not to oppress or embarrass these colonists in their early struggles.

**Immigrant Bureau.** This work should be entirely entrusted to and managed by a special *Immigrant Bureau,* under the control of the Department of State, as international questions may arise where their diplomacy may be needed.

This will protect the immigrant against the wiles and swindles of willful, self-appointed agents, who so often rob the poor, unsophisticated stranger when he lands in our midst.

**Qualification.** Our government and its perpetuity are based upon the character and intelligence of its subjects, or citizens. Then, for the welfare of our republic, it is of vital importance for our citizens to learn and understand the fundamental principles thereof, know the meaning of and what constitutes a *free* government. For this reason we should require an *educational qualification.*

As to the proper qualification, we would suggest that we have as much as we now can do to supply the wants of our own poor, and there is no moral or legal reason why we should extend our generosity so far as to take care of other nations' poor also.

We cannot afford to educate other nations without some compensation year after year. We have enough to do with our own. A foreigner, to become a citizen of our country, should be intellectually qualified and should have a clear moral record and correct habits. He should be able to show a *tax receipt* (after being five years in this country he ought to be able to own something on which to pay taxes) as an evidence of his industry, &c. In fact he should have all the characteristics of good citizenship to obtain the right of suffrage. This is only just and equitable; as these are the prerequisites of our own American-born people to the full rights of citizenship. We, as a nation, certainly have a right to prescribe rules and what conditions whereby aliens can only be fully qualified for and clothed with all the prerogatives of native-born citizens.

**Don't be Narrow.** We labor to destroy *distinction based on possessions.* Let us not draw the line too finely in this direction or we shall have intellectual paupers next, and this would be equally unpalatable. But we must have a certain amount of education to be safe and prosperous. For this reason we are opposed to annexation of neighboring islands or countries whose people are ignorant and lack the elements which fit them for affiliation with our own intelligent people.

We do not favor a change in the present law which requires a foreigner to live here five years before he can exercise the right of suffrage. But we would require a more rigid examination of his qualifications by the courts, as we have stated.

A very large majority of the people of this country will concur with us in our views on the immigration and suffrage questions, for no better reason than, as Mrs. A. W. Moore, in a lecture, puts it all in a few words.  She says : "A great many foreigners, having been born and reared where they have had no rights as individuals, are unable to understand this grand idea as the Anglo-Saxon understands it."

We ask nothing unreasonable.  It is our duty and prerogative to guard all vulnerable points and remove all perilous conditions that we may be true to ourselves and to our fathers, who looked forward for the welfare of generations whom they believed would not only look back to them, the founders, with pride, but honor their declining years by perpetuating the government which was sealed in their own blood and hard-earned sacrifices.  Shall it be so?  It shall; then what are we doing?

**What Are We Doing ?**  Are we educating and training the young men of this generation to be party-men or patriots?

Pure, strong, noble patriotism must be instilled in the *boy* if we wish to behold its grand spirit exercised in the *man*.

If we fail in this we present to the United States government, at the age of twenty-one, not a *patriotic* and *useful citizen*, but an *individual* for whom American citizenship is *given too cheap*.

It is too cheap for the immigrant or the native-born whose soul is so dead to the glory and greatness of his country and its institutions that he has never said with glowing eye and joyous heart:

" This is my own, my native land !"

**NOTE 1.**—There is a prevailing idea that the right of suffrage is a natural right and that to rob a man of the privilege to cast a ballot that his natural born rights are invaded.  This is incorrect, for if it were so then every man, woman and child, black or white, would have a right to vote.  But the fact is the right of suffrage is a delegated right, delegated by the state to the citizen, under certain conditions.

Then a foreigner comes among us as an adopted citizen, and as long as his rights as a free man and his interests are well protected he ought to be satisfied, for it is only the simple right to cast a ballot which is reserved until he earns it.  This right he must earn, and all right-thinking foreigners will soon see the necessity of this course, and if it makes a better man of him to vote, let him study and acquire the necessary qualification and then comply with the law.

**NOTE 2.**—When we were 21 years of age, and on the day we cast our first vote, which was for "John C. Fremont and Jessie, too," we remarked to a friend that we hoped to live long enough to see the day when we would be permitted to step up to the polls along by the side of woman and exercise the privilege of voting together as citizens. The little, blue-eyed, rosy cheeked, dimpled chin and wavy, golden hair had to wait outside while we performed the proud prerogative that makes a young man feel very patriotic. She had also just come of age, and there is not the least doubt in our mind but that she was quite as competent to vote as we were. From that day to this we have done nothing that would in the least retard the incoming era, when there will be *no sex* in politics. Women have correct ideas as well as men. We now think that we will live to see that day we hoped for while yet a young man, although the *goal* is almost in sight. Six to ten years more and women will enjoy the right of suffrage in every state in the Union as a fully recognized citizen of the United States. We take great pleasure to quote a thought from a lecture on "Shall Foreigners Have a Right to Vote," by *Miss Louise Earle*. She said :

" If, now, we consider the often repeated assertion that America, the land of freedom, should be an asylum for all who are oppressed, we shall find that this statement is in no sense an argument for the naturalization of foreigners. Both the persons and property of aliens are well protected here ; and they themselves, moreover, share in the benefits of all our public institutions. There is, therefore, not the slightest reason for granting them the citizenship before they are capable of discharging its duties."

**NOTE 3.**—A very remarkable change has taken place in England, during last year, in public opinion, and in the position of Mr. Gladstone himself, regarding the *eight-hour* system. At first Mr. Gladstone did not take kindly to the compulsory eight-hour rule ; but after making the proper research, he is in favor of a sort of local option law to make the eight-hour system compulsory as it may suit localities. Many corporations have for some time adopted the eight-hour rule ; that is, eight hours shall constitute a day's work, forty-eight hours a week's work. A bill before Parliament brings a day's work to an eight-hour basis. The vote was very close, and it is believed that on another occasion this will become a law in England. The question is much agitated in all civilized countries. Over 450,000 miners in Great Britain are now on the eight-hour basis. If this rule is adopted it will give work to a large number who are now idle. "We must not grow discouraged if the tide seems to ebb sometimes ; it will return with renewed power."

> " It is we must answer and hasten
>     And open wide the door
> For the rich man's hurrying terror,
>     And the slow-foot hope of the poor.
>
> Yea, the voiceless wrath of the wretched
>     And their unlearned discontent,
> We must give it voice and wisdom
>     Till the waiting-tide be spent."

# MORAL, SOCIAL, FOOD AND BODY.

*On the Moral and Social Effects of What We Eat and Drink; The Comparative Value of Different Articles of Diet; Chemical Analysis of the Body; Fancy Groceries; How to Economize and Still Be Strong; Home Fabric; Something About Social Life; The Drink Habit, Etc., Etc.*

"That which before us lies in daily life,
Is the prime wisdom; what is more is fume,
Or emptiness, or fond impertinence;
And renders us, in things that most concern,
Unpracticed, unprepared, and still to seek."

**Oh! What Are We?** There is a reason why we exist, or else why should we? There are certain conditions under which we live and there are certain conditions under which we die. Our body is composed of the substances of this earth. Matter or substance has been found to be made up of different elements. Of these elements, it has been found, exist, as far as is known, about sixty-five in nature. About twenty-two of these elements have been found in the human subject. These substances or elements are gradually sublimated and refined, brought *up* from a low and inorganic state to a higher, by a principle or force we call life. Life is everywhere at work in converting earth, air and water into organized beings. Then comes the law of support—one thing supporting another. In the vegetable kingdom the cereals are the highest expression of life. The dove is the highest representative of the bird kingdom; the salmon of the inhabitants of the sea, and men of the mamalians. Man may be considered as an *epitome* of existences.

Life may also be spoken of as a property of matter. The body has been analyzed, and so have other animals and things—birds, fishes, vegetables, the cereals, fruit, etc.    It has been found that the different elements and substances of the earth are variously represented in the almost infinite

**Living Matter.** variety of existences, where life is manifest.   Where matter is associated with the life activity of organized beings it is called living matter.

The expression of life differs in degree of intensity and activity, according as the chemical equivalents of these elements are united with *life* in quantity and quality.

Living matter, then, differs in its property and nature according to chemical equivalents, which explains the cause of the almost infinite variety of forms and appearances of existences, and hence, also, the differential expression of life.

Accordingly, then, as things differ in their appearance so do they differ in their component parts, affinity, differential elements and substance out of which the body is built or grown.

Living beings manifest different degrees of activity, from the slow-going snail to the swift, arrow-like pigeon darting through the air.   The difference is produced by the different equivalents of the *phosphates*, and this is dependent on digestion and power of assimilation.

**So We Differ.** It is plain that things widely differ, one from another, physically, and we find that this differentiation holds good in the realm of the intellectual.   Then as physical conditions are changed so will the mental or intellectual phenomena change correspondingly. Different kinds of food and drink affect the passions, instinct, reason, power of thought, health and strength of the body.

It is now well understood what kind of food will supply material from which bone-builders, so to speak, will be enabled to construct a good, strong *osseous* structure ; the same holds good regarding muscles, brain and every tissue of the body.   The brain is the organ of the mind.   We can then readily perceive that as people differ in their diet so will they differ in power of thought.   Nations exhibit differential characteristics, traits of character, etc.  Meat-eaters

HON. WILLIAM B. ALLISON.

Plate XIV—For sketch see page 222.

are courageous for a time in the battles of life, but they do not have the reserve force of life to draw from which those have who live on a vegetable diet and flesh of animals but sparingly.

**What We Eat and Drink.** That what we eat and drink does effect character can no longer be questioned, since the *datas* we have are overwhelmingly on the side of the affirmative.

Food is that which, when taken into any living animal organism, makes blood, bone, muscle, integument, hair, brain, life, etc. It stands to reason that character and disposition must be largely influenced by the kind of a body that is built up for the mind to occupy and through which the mind must operate. A change of diet will change the constituance of the blood, and a change of the blood produces a change of thought.

Dryden ate raw meat on retiring that he might dream of tragedies; that he might, from his dreams, make his tragic scenes more vivid in his description.

**A Sensible Man.** A quiet, sensible man becomes as a demon as soon as a few glasses of strong drink have passed from the stomach to the blood.

The effect food and drink have upon character is no longer questioned, since physiology has *delved* into the deeper mysteries of human life. All of our scientists who have given the subject much thought teach, since it is a fact, demonstrated before our eyes, that our bodies are built out of the food we eat and absolutely verified by chemical analysis.

**Absolutely Verified.** How, then, can it otherwise be, than to draw a correct inference, since it is a verified fact that a person's conduct is widely different if a radical change is made in food and drink. Some years ago, while practicing medicine in Chicago, we gave this subject some special attention. We visited the prisons and police courts frequently and in the course of two years—special time set apart for this work—during which we devoted much of our time to the study of the different *phases* of crime according to organic condition of each individual.   We extended our visits and observations to the prisons at Milwaukee, St. Paul, Minneapolis, St. Louis, Cincinnati, Columbus (Ohio), Cleveland, Detroit, Jackson (Mich.), Michigan City, and while we did not keep an accurate diary of the number of examinations we made from which to make up a table, and give nationalities, sex, age, trade and circumstances which lead these people to commit crime, the point we were in sea.ch of we attained to our full satisfaction.

From the knowledge we had of physiology, we were strongly inclined to the belief that peoples who are reared on, and after maturity continue on, a vegetable diet were not so liable, or rather disposed, to commit crime, especially those crimes of a murderous nature.

It is surprising to state that out of the many hundreds of criminals into whose habits and mode of life we made particular inquiry, on this one point of diet, *not one* could be found who was strictly a vegetarian.

In many instances a number of the most hardened, guilty of capital crime, were inveterate meat-eaters.   A large majority of these criminals lived on a low diet of animal food, only sparingly intermixed with vegetables and this of the most difficult of digestion.   As a rule they were woefully ignorant of the simplest rules of hygiene, irregular in their habits, especially in their meals.   Particularly was this the case regarding those who lived in the large cities.   The bath was scarcely known to them and nearly all were addicted to the *drink habit* and used tobacco in one form or another.

An eminent author says, "according to the nature of the food eaten will be the idiosyncrasies of the eater."   There is danger of going to extremes.   One has to understand physiology scientifically, avoiding, as much as possible, speculations; form for yourself correct premises and then look to it that you do not get too far away from your premises.   Heredity does not operate in the *per se* sense ; for example, a man living on the flesh of swine, it is not claimed that he will become a hog, but this is argued and held as reliable doctrine of life that a low, imperfect or unhealthy food will build a body corresponding to it, and this will weigh on the mind.

"He is a chip of the old block" is an old saying and answers our present purpose. Caligula was Rome's most blood-thirsty ruler in all her history. His parents were well-disposed and loving people, but while a nursing babe, and until matured years, fresh blood from animals was part of his diet, and Dion tells us that it was believed as far back as ancient Rome that drinking fresh blood had a tendency to make men courageous. Some years since, we can well call to mind, a craze got among the people that drinking fresh, warm, beef's blood would cure consumption. This was practiced by a large number at Cincinnati, O. While we were there attending medical college, over thirty-five years ago, two young ladies, where we boarded, went to the butcher's slaughtering house every morning and drank a glass of hot, fresh blood. There was a regular bar over which this blood was sold, and hundreds tried the remedy. The two young ladies, we remember well, picked up, gained in flesh, but they became irritable in disposition. The young ladies were cousins and dear friends, never quarreled until they began the fresh-blood treatment for a lung difficulty they believed they were ailing from. They quarreled so that they separated, and they also had trouble with their landlady.

**Prior to the Whiskey Era.** Before distilled liquors came in vogue, men, on special occasions, when they wished to strengthen their heartless nature, or to render them courageous that they might become blind to humane treatment of prisoners, women and children, or an enemy against whom they were preparing to move and meet in mortal combat—one thing, on many occasions, that they provided themselves with was to drink fresh blood of animals. The blood of lambs was not considered good—too tame—but if the blood of a wild boar could be obtained then those who were fortunate enough to obtain a drink of this blood they would be sure to win in battle.    However, since distilled liquors have come into use, the blood drinking has been discarded.    Liquor is more sure and it is drank many times by people who are planning to perpetrate some hideous crime.    A drink or two of whiskey will deaden the moral sense and they succeed to commit the crime.    Whiskey acts on the base of the brain and on the spine, thus arousing the animal propensities, and men become brutal, for the higher faculties of the mind lose their control over the lower and the animal brain.

**How He Prolonged His Life.** Dr. Jennings, of Oberlin, Ohio, was a hopeless invalid at forty.    One day, by way of a little exercise, he fed the pigs their usual allowance of corn, and, as he was thus engaged, the thought came to him (and we give it in his own words) and he said to himself : "How foolish I am ; here is this corn, pure, undefiled, free from disease germs, feeding it to these unclean animals and then take it back to my system second-handed."    From that day the good Doctor resolved never to eat animal flesh again, and from that day his health improved.    He became healthy and useful, reaching the grand old age of over eighty, and died of old age and not of disease.

The Greek philosophers were vegetarians.    Our forefathers, the early settlers, ate sparingly of flesh food ; corn bread, mush and milk, oats, beans, potatoes, cabbage, and, for a change, good all-wheat bread ; that is to say, temperate eating, no adulterated luxuries, fancy groceries, no complicated dishes ; was as much a help as the well-directed shot that won the victory that made America free.    Poor, weak France, a devouring, meat-eating nation.    An old horse worked nearly to death and disabled is fattened a little and sold to the butcher.    Compare and think of the Scotch, a people who have been beaten but never conquered ; almost vegetarian in their diet. Really Scotland to-day may be mentioned as the representative of the highest attainment of civilization.

**National Characteristics.** Germany, under tyrannical rule, when the royalty absorbed all the good things of the land; when the object was to keep their subjects down to bed rock; when a workingman was glad to get enough to furnish the family with vegetable soup; bread was scarcely obtainable at all. Germany retrograded, but during the last century a nobler type of people, faithful and true, have been developed on a much improved diet. The German is trustworthy; is a good friend. There is comparatively but little meat eaten in Germany—more in England. Dr. Johnson, who always had a prejudice against the Scotch, on one occasion defined the term "oats." He said: "In Scotland it is for men, in England food for horses." "Very true, Doctor," replied a lady, "but where will you find such men and where will you find such horses?"

Only the lower classes in India eat flesh. Did you ever see a cattle ship? The animal, imprisoned, feverish and in a suffering condition, reaches the stall in the London market. Wheat and corn will not deteriorate by shipping it. Cereals furnish man with nerve and brain power. The spirit is not gone. Distill grain and the spirit is gone. The residue will fatten animals, but the higher principle is gone. Animals use up the higher principle of food, and when we eat their flesh we get a lower grade of food than if we relied more on good vegetable diet. Feed the people of Mexico and Spain on a cooling vegetable diet and in ten years the arena of the bull fight will go out of use for want of patronage.

**Animal Food a Necessity.** It is only those who are not informed, who are not students in physiology, who will argue that animal flesh as a food is necessary for health and strength. We have not the space to argue this question at length as we would like

to do, but there is no argument necessary when a few facts
cited are sufficient to satisfy the mind that, since hundreds
who are strong, healthy people, who, from childhood, lived
a pure vegetarian life and who made life a success. Dr.
Simmse's daughter, a young lady of 19 years, was traveling
with her father, who was delivering lectures on anthro-
pology at Grand Rapids, Mich. She had one of those huge
so-called Saratoga trunks, the terror of baggagemen. Two
expressmen found much fault with her large trunk, that it
was more than two men could handle. The young lady became impatient and said to the two men to take the one end
of the trunk and she would take the other end, which they
did, and she threw her end on the wagon first. It was
about all the two men could do to put up their end of the
trunk. The young lady never in her life ate meat. Those
men, as we knew (for we saw the circumstance we have related), were not very careful in their habits. They smoked
and drank, ate meats, and, of course, they were weak, for no
one is strong whose blood is poisoned.

Some of the greatest minds of the earth were vegetarians—
Alcott, Swing, Newman, Trall, Harvard, Franklin, Wads-
worth, Hawthorne—and, in a word, more than two-thirds of
the educated classes, in which are included many mechanics
and some very hard-working people who are vegetarians.
Then think of the horse; and had we not better, like the
horse, take our food first-hand from nature? Why does the
horse get on so well without flesh food? We think man
henceforth had better be classed amongst herbivorous animals in place of omnivorous. What would be nearer right,
is to place man in the class of *cerco-frunivorous*. Meat flesh
is stimulating, excites the system to an unnatural activity,
while vegetable diet is cooling and nutritious.

**For Whose Benefit ?** We introduce this subject to
help the wage-worker all we possi-
bly can, for a dollar saved is a dollar earned; and then in
regard to the diet of a workingman, much is to be considered: 1st, to know what the best food is ; 2d, how he can

save and still be fed so that he has strength for his work, and 3d, his health must be of first consideration. All meat-eating animals (the carnivorous) are scavengers. Their function is to eat the carcasses and thus prevent stagnating the air by the decaying dead in open air. It would not be a very high compliment to humankind to be classed with the scavenger animals.

Herewith appended is a scale giving the comparative value of the leading articles of diet so you can have something of a guide to a systematic and scientific way of living, economize (save money) and yet live well:

### CHEMICAL ANALYSIS OF FOOD.*

| | Phos. | Nigt. | Carb. | | Phos. | Nigt. | Carb. |
|---|---|---|---|---|---|---|---|
| Beef | 5 | 15 | 20 | Wheat | 2 | 15 | 63 |
| Mutton | 3 | 12 | 40 | Corn | 1 | 12 | 12 |
| Lamb | 3 | 12 | 30 | Buckwheat | 1 | 8 | 15 |
| Pork | 1 | 10 | 50 | Barley | 3 | 17 | 10 |
| Veal | 4 | 16 | 16 | Oats | 3 | 17 | 10 |
| Codfish | 6 | 14 | 5 | Peas | 3 | 22 | 60 |
| Salmon | 5 | 20 | 10 | Rice | . | 6 | 80 |
| Herring | 5 | 10 | 10 | Potatoes | . | 1 | 22 |
| Oysters | 2 | 10 | 10 | Sweets | 3 | 2 | 26 |
| Clams | 2 | 12 | 10 | Turnips | . | 1 | 21 |
| Egg (white) | 5 | 16 | .. | Cabbage | 3 | 20 | 46 |
| Egg (yolk) | 6 | 18 | 20 | Starch | . | 1 | 22 |
| Wild Duck | 6 | 11 | 16 | Corn-Mush and Milk | 2 | 15 | 20 |
| Goose | 1½ | 16 | 24 | Celery | 3 | 12 | 8 |
| Catfish | 1 | 11 | 40 | Apples | 1½ | 8 | 35 |

Food containing the *hydro-carbon* furnishes the warming principle of the system. Food containing *nitrogen* furnishes muscle-building material. Food containing *phosphorus* or the *phosphates* furnish brain, bone and nerve-building material. Animal flesh contains the first two mentioned, namely, *carbon* and *nitrogen*. Vegetables contain these elements and all other elements necessary to good health and strength of the body. Animal flesh as a food does not contain all the elements necessary to life, while a vegetable food does, and hence is not only reliable,

---

* The chart given above is divided so that at a glance you can discern the article of food you may need, making your selections intelligently from the (leading) articles we have here selected. The first column (phosphorus) gives the bone and brain-building value; the second (nitrogen the muscle, and the third column (carbon) the heat-producing principle.

better and healthier, but is very much cheaper.   For breakfast begin with fruit, whatever may be in season, then a dish
of oatmeal, two eggs, home-made bread and a good cup of cof-
fee, or hot water or milk.   This is a good breakfast for any
workingman or anyone else, but the point we wish to give
here is, that if we have a meat diet the meat alone will cost
more than the rest together and you will not get as much
strength from the meat as you would from the purely vegetable meal.   We would not exclude eggs.   Two eggs will
give a man more strength than he can get from a pound of
beefsteak.

### GONE TO THEIR LONG HOME.

**$1,200,000,000 Per Annum.**   Having shown the effect
of *food* on character and the
purse, we will take the liberty briefly to say something on the
"*drink habit.*"   Viewing the subject from the financial, humane and physiological standpoints we will cover all practical argument in favor of a total abnegation of an indulgence
that leaves its millions strewn all along the path of life.
One by one they drop out, one here another there, as the
result of the use of distilled liquors as a beverage.   Every
wage-earner in the land who will make this subject of "*Scientific Living*" a daily study (practically) he for one will
be able to break the *line* of distinction.   No man can do
more than to do right, and none can rise higher in the social
scale than one whose conduct is beyond reproach.   *Marcus
Antonius* says: "Be simple and modest in deportment, and
treat with indifference whatever lies between virtue and
vice."

The lives destroyed each year by the drink habit in this
country amounts to over 120,000, and the amount of liquor
consumed in 1891, taking the revenue report and estimat-
ing it at a low average, and we have the enormous sum of
$1,200,000,000.   This amount of money spent annually
for intoxicating drinks alone, if properly invested, would secure a snug little home, costing a little over $850 each, to
one million families, and counting five persons to each family

(which is the average estimate given by the census reports) and we have a comfortable home given to over 5,000,000 of people ; besides, if this was saved by a thorough reform in the drink habit, another vast sum annually could be added to the above, for no estimate is yet made of the probable cost incurred by every community where liquor is sold in prosecuting and supporting criminals and paupers. Think also of the orphans and widows and countless miseries that follow as the sequence of the unholy traffic.

There were manufactured in the United States, in the year 1891, 91,157,565 gallons of spirituous liquors. If this was sold out, averaging sixty drinks to the gallon and at ten cents per drink, the amount realized would figure up $546,945,390. This is only for one class of drinks. The estimated expenditure for fermented liquors, at five cents a drink, will foot up for the same year $586,487,856. And if we credit revenue statistics the *drink habit* is really on the increase. M. Fillmore Brown, in the *American Journal of Politics*, makes the statement that during the last four years the *liquor traffic* has increased at the rate of almost $100,-000,000 per annum. These figures show a sorry condition of our people. Notwithstanding the laudable work of the temperance element, there is but little abatement in the consumption of stimulating drinks and tobacco. The only point that has been gained is that the line is more sharply drawn between those who indulge in these destructive habits and those who do not.

We stated that over 100,000 lives are sacrificed per annum to this terrible drink habit; but you say lives have no financial value. Then, if that is so, the loss of life can only be considered from a moral point of view. In an article we wrote for the *Vincennes Commercial*, on the "cost of an idea," a few years since, we showed by careful computation that it cost to raise a man or woman from birth to thirty-two years of age (which is the average longevity of people who indulge in spirituous beverages), everything considered, about $3,000. This would aggregate, at a low calculation, another annual sum of $10,000,000, which is an absolute loss, as are also all the other sums we have shown in actual mathematical calculation, for none of these firey and stimulating beverages, whether much or little, nourish the body in the least, but absolutely shorten life.    Premature death is a loss to the community, for a man pays taxes, brings up children, cares for his family, helps on humanity, and hence we are justified in speaking of loss of life.    Here we are menaced by a dangerous foe, which it is incumbent for our government to abolish and thus to protect its citizens. Morally speaking, it behooves every individual *wage-earner* of America to guard against the drink habit and at once identify himself or herself with that organization or movement on foot which looks towards total abstinence and the abolishing of all stimulating beverages in the form of *liquor traffic* from the land.    For it can readily be seen that the subject needs no further argument to convince even the most incredulous that our position is correct, especially since three facts present themselves as a self-evident truth, namely: 1st, the use of liquors as a beverage does not furnish substances necessary for the nourishment of the body; 2d, the drink habit does harm; in place of prolonging life by supplying the needs of the system it predisposes all who indulge in these stimulating drinks to disease, and for this reason no one can take their chances and expect to come out all right; 3d, the extravagance that must follow habits of this kind, in spending money for anything that does not give you value received in any sense, is like throwing money away, and far worse in this instance, for if you indulge in spirituous liquors you do not only lose money, but your health and life is injured thereby, and hence a judicious business man will at once form a correct conclusion. He will take his pencil and figure out how much he can save in the course of years by abstaining from a thing that does no good, but does him great injury, and, besides, robs him of not less than $40 a year—$400 in ten years—and at the same time he is in danger of the habit growing on him, that long before ten years are reached the cost of the drink habit will double on him twice to three times and he will curse the day when he first began the habit of drink.

Another habit, as the one we have just treated of, is the use of tobacco.

*Physiological points and axioms bearing on the subject of a good, strong mind in a good, strong body.*

Gross food will build up a gross body and in so far as the organic structure is of a low order, the product of a low order of diet, the character will be affected to a very great degree. A highly refined fibrous structure (high-toned) of body is, as a rule, found in people who live on a carefully selected diet, consisting mainly of fruit, cereals and vegetables. In this kind of diet, with a view to enjoying the blessings of refinement, health, strength and long life, we almost entirely exclude animal flesh from the menu, especially from children. Animal food is never admissible in the diet of children until the lapse of at least eight to ten years of age. There is not much difficulty in permanently laying the foundation of refinement and an even, happy disposition in children who are properly fed. Whatever the habits may be of the child, the after life will largely be what is implanted during the period of youth. Then there is not so much importance to be attached to the kind of food as to the way food is prepared for the table. Good cooking is as much a science as the proper selection of food. The very best food, brought up to us in purity and perfectness by nature for our use, is destroyed by the cook on its way through the kitchen from nature's laboratory to the table. Complicated dishes, richly mixed, over or underdone, and we wonder not that men sometimes step over the limitation line of right, although the will power is strong and the moral sense acute.

Correct formation of habits, as also character, during the childhood years, and there will not be great necessity for the reformation of persons brought up in the right manner, physiologically, morally and æsthetically.

All peoples should be familiar with the natural laws of life and learn well the *axiom* that *the highroad to health leads also to wealth.* The Greek philosophers valued the enjoyment of health far more than even great wealth. Theophrastus was the author of the following invocation :

**Invocation.** "Health! thou most august of the blessed goodness, with thee may I spend the remainder of my life ; mayest thou benignly dwell with me ; for if there be any pleasure to be derived from riches, or children, or royal power making men equal to the gods, or longing desire, which we hunt after with the secret nets of Venus ; or if there be any other delight bestowed on men by the gods, or respite from pains, with thee, blessed Health, all these flourish and beam effulgent like the spring arising from the graces : without thee, no one is happy."

*"Now comes the winter of my discontent."*

WHERE THERE IS MUCH SMOKE THERE MUST BE SOME
FIRE !

" Evil events from evil causes spring,
    And what you suffer flows from what you've done."

**Something to Think About.** We cannot well pass by a subject of so much importance to our wage-earners, and do justice to all parties concerned in our work—*the tobacco habit.* This subject, you may say, is an innovation, but you will decide otherwise when you think for a moment of the enormous traffic and commercial commodity tobacco has become, and our wage-workers should understand scientifically the effect tobacco has on the health of the one who uses it. We all should labor as in one common cause, which leads to the emancipation of all men from slavery. We can conceive of no greater millenium than that which will make *all men free* and equal, practically as well as theoretically. It has been the great desire of our life to see all men drop the shackels of servitude, the ostracism of *caste* and class distinction, and the time when only the laws of nature shall govern us all alike—when human slavery, subject to ancient royalty, or modern aristocratic chattledom, seen in its original form in our own country, and aped after still, shall cease to exist.

It has always been our aim to oppose slavery in whatever form it appeared, national or personal. "A fellow-feeling makes us wondrous kind," and the reason we advocated full freedom for all was, perhaps, because we enjoy it ourself.

The time *was*, and, alas! to some extent still *is*, when the wage-worker was a slave to capital. In this respect, however, he is becoming yearly more independent.

"The *freer* you make men the *better* you make them," Matthews truly said long ago. False education—dogmatic belief—is slavery, but there is no slavery more abject and humiliating than that by which men and women bind themselves to their own follies and habits.

Emerson says: "We are all slaves to our organism;" that is, we are absolutely servants of our own body, in that we cannot escape obedience to the natural laws which govern life and a happy perpetuity of the various faculties which are the attributes of the individual being. It is about all that we can do or have time to do to meet nature's requirements, but when, in addition, we acquire habits not included in the bill of fare, the unavoidable, then is when we are enslaved, and, worst of all, the victims of our own follies.

A source or cause of pain, suffering, sorrow and premature death is in your own hands, and yet, alas! you *will not*, you think you *cannot*, and yet *you can*, free yourself from its servile power. By so doing you may save your life— spare yourself to your family and the world and save money besides. What money you *save* you need not work for. A dollar *saved* is a dollar *earned*. Spend no money unless you get a commensurate return for it.

In a commercial sense you get an equivalent when you buy cigars or tobacco, but you don't get "value received" for the money investment, in a physiological sense. On the contrary you are *injured* by the transaction, if to be used by yourself.

All the tobacco in the United States would not make a drop of blood for you. One thing it will do. It will make the heart go faster, and the faster you run any machinery the *sooner it wears out*. This is an axiom requiring no proof. Tobacco will cause heart disease. A smoker's lungs will become as fumid as a piece of smoked meat. This excessive inhalation of tobacco fume hardens the lung tissues to such an extent that normal elasticity is gradually destroyed, the lungs are discolored, until they are almost as black as Erebus. The blood becomes poisoned, the nerves shattered and the breath offensive through the use of this favorite "weed." It affects the brain and cripples your mental powers for want of pure brain vitality. Let us take a practical view of this tobacco question and give you a reason for our faith on this subject : *

Three cigars a day, costing five cents each, will, in a year, amount to *fifty-four dollars and seventy-five cents*. If you are more exquisite in your taste, and indulge in "ten centers," your annual cigar bill will be $109.50. Quite a nice little sum to blow in the air! Now by freeing yourself from this social slavery you have just that much *less to earn*, or *more to save*. This sum will clothe your family and yourself nicely and do away with that stale excuse for not going to a public lecture, that your clothes are too poor.

Why, the young man smoker could in a few years save

---

* *Roger S. Tracy, M. D., Sanitary Inspector of the New York City Health Department, and author of Hand-book of Sanitary Information, etc., says :*

"Of tobacco it may be said that, although it is a poisonous weed, and, when first used, produces alarming symptoms of nervous prostration, it is soon tolerated by the system, and becomes a source of great comfort and satisfaction to those who use it habitually. The excessive secretion of saliva, however, in those who chew it produces extreme thirst, and may thus lead to the habitual use of alcoholic stimulants ; while tobacco smoke, constantly irritating the mucus membrane of the throat and nose, produces chronic catarrh of those parts. It is said that no habitual smoker has a healthy throat. It has been abundantly shown that the habitual use of tobacco stunts the growth, and it should therefore be shunned by the young."

enough money to give him a nice little start in life and share it with his little sweetheart by furnishing that romantic "cottage," so often quoted by romancers. At any rate, by giving up tobacco you will have a cleaner mouth, sweeter breath and better appetite and more respect from the ladies.

It is estimated that over one billion dollars is annually blown in the air as tobacco smoke! This would feed and clothe over 120,000 families each year, yet we grumble when we have no ready spending money.

Every person who is a victim to the tobacco habit is in greater danger when illness overtakes them than if they did not use it. But you may say that some people have lived to a ripe old age and had always used tobacco freely. Well, we admit it, but you will also admit, that having lived so long *with* tobacco, they would have lived *longer* and *better* if they had never used it.

" Nothing is so indicative of deepest culture as a tender consideration of the ignorant."

**Homespun.** *Dress becomingly* and in accordance with your business and station. To dress well and at the same time to do so cheaply is quite a study. A study of the decorative art will be a great help in making cheap goods look well. This is economy. A man is estimated to a great degree in society by the clothes he wears, but not so much by the quality as by the fitness of what he wears. The artistic taste of an individual is discerned at once by clothing being properly fitted to his person ; it evinces an *artistic mind*. With the wealthy the item of cost is of little concern, but they, as a rule, give to the subject of dressing becomingly much study from the artisic standpoint.

The wage-earner is obliged to consider the cost, therefore the more he knows of the decorative art the cheaper he can get on and yet appear well in society.

In this respect the indications are that we are getting back again to first principles—homespun will be preferred.

It is an axiom with a large majority of our best people that goods at a medium price are the best for wear and the cheapest in the end. The main point we contend for is this : That, however cheap a fabric may be, the wearer of the same will pass for a cultured person if his clothes are becoming, artistically made up and properly fitted to his form.

Cultivate, therefore, good taste in these matters and learn how to buy, so that what you buy will do you good service. Clothes should wear out and not give out. The wage-earner then should endeavor to master *three points* in dress, namely, *cost, service* and the *artistic*, which will put money in his purse and at the same time he will appear well in society.

**Public Lecture Halls.** It has long been a favorite theory with us that for effective
**Civic Education.** work in disseminating knowledge among the people the easiest way, the cheapest and most efficacious, is by public lectures, given by persons who are qualified. One can learn more in one evening in the lecture room than from books by two weeks' reading and hard study. University extension practically means to extend university education to the people by the graduates of these institutions, imparting their knowledge in a popularized form to the citizen, by giving popular lectures. In other words, university extension is a system by which knowledge getting is made easy and cheap, and people can keep up their studies after they leave school, and after they are married, and during their business career. This may be more properly called *civic education.* It was a grand conception of the mind of those who first introduced the so-called "university extension lecture course," and when once fully developed promises the most satisfactory results than anything yet attempted in the promotion of *civic education.* Here is a movement for the commonwealth to lend a helping hand. There is no good reason why a certain sum should not be set aside from taxes accruing from liquor licenses to

HON. JOHN GRIFFIN CARLISLE.

Plate XV—For sketch see page 222.

pay some of the expenses of these lectures. It is important **By Whom.** always to be well guarded against wrong education. In acquiring knowledge it is very unfortunate for any one to learn, after a few years, that you have to *unlearn* what you were lead to believe was correct knowledge. It takes about as much of our time to unlearn, that is, to disabuse our minds of erroneous ideas, than to learn the truth in the first place. *No* learning is better than *false* learning. The most ignorant and untaught are more easily taught the truth than those who are learned but *falsely taught.* The value and importance to an individual, whose first impression, or *concept,* is correctly and truthfully made in the first place, cannot be estimated or expressed by word or pen.

Hence it will be incumbent on those who manage these *"extension lectures"* to invite to the platform speakers by whom (as we believe) the truth—reliable, verified knowledge—is to be given to the people. These lecturers, men and women, should be experienced and qualified by education. They need not be graduated from a university, but it should be well known that they are capable—specialists high up and strictly in pulse with the ever-growing science.

**The Counterfeit.** Knowledge-getting is like working for money. If the money you get in exchange for your labor is counterfeit, then you will not only lose your labor, but your time is gone where the "woodbine twineth." The labor you can give again, but the lost time can never be recalled. These lectures should assume the *academic order*—purely secular, free from far-fetched theories, personal "axe-grinding," dogmatism or party politics. (Politics is a proper subject, but must be free from the narrow ideas of "party").

**Public Halls.** In every community, town, city and ward there should be a public hall, built by the public's money, and if properly planned will be self-sustaining almost from the beginning. The size (capacity) must be governed by the population, extending your calculation into the future somewhat, for the country is growing rapidly. These public lecture halls should be built over two fine storerooms or in the rear, if the lot will permit. The storerooms will readily rent and this rent will go far towards defraying expenses of the lectures. Every township should have a public lecture hall. The usual municipal officers can take care of and manage this work in spreading knowledge. We would suggest the appointment of an executive committee, consisting of five ladies, whose business it shall be to manage the entertainments, to correspond with and invite lecturers from time to time. A very large number of lecturers and persons to read and give elocutionary entertainments, as well as concerts, would be glad to lend their help free of charge if unavoidable expenses are met by the executive committee.

Home talent should be encouraged as much as possible. Joint debates, for a change, may be of much educational good, if properly conducted, though we do not think debates, as a rule, are conducive of much good. Papers read, essays and lectures may be criticised in five to ten minutes, speeches by the audience following the speaker, giving the speaker ten minutes to defend his position and close. Choir singing at the opening and closing of each of these meetings will make the place attractive and entertaining. We would set apart two evenings in the week for these lectures and other entertainments—Monday and Friday nights. The other nights the hall may be rented and thus add to the income of the enterprise. This property should be free from taxation. In the saying of an ancient philosopher we close our remarks on this subject: "*Nemo solus sapid;*" that is, *none are wise alone.*

# RANDOM THOUGHTS.

*National Park Improvement; Work for the Jobless Man;
Four Months Each Year; Less Than Half a Million;
Landscape Art; All the World will be Attracted
There, Etc., Etc.*

"The wealth of a nation, its peace and well-being depend on the
number of persons it can employ in making good and useful things.
Employment is the half, and the primal half, of education."—*Spencer.*

## LET THE GOVERNMENT HELP.

**Improvement is Wealth.** The government can do
much toward helping the
common working people to get along in the days of their
dire necessity without any real loss to the public *treasury.*
(Improvement is never a loss, and, as Spencer says, it is
"the primal half of education.") If, as it presumes, its
business adherents or its allied manufacturing industries
should lend them a helping hand, why not give it? The
government of any country is supposed to be the *protector*
of its *people.* If then its citizens are to bear its financial
and commercial burdens without its assistance and co-operation, why have it at all? If the *people* are to do everything
necessary for the welfare of the *people* without any claim
on the *government,* then the government is a *nonentity* and
loses its significance and power. The government of a free
people is not intended to be a *driver* or *tyrant* to lash its
people on to slavish obedience, but to govern and control
them in all things for *the good of its citizens,* and to protect,
defend and assist them in all matters by which they can be
prosperous and happy.

**What Will He Do in the Winter?** Now, our government could
furnish a large number of workingmen with employment

on public improvements during the winter season. There are at the present over one hundred thousand people in the employ of the government, mostly people who are appointed to positions, and a large majority receive wages for skill and professional attainments. There are many thousands of clerks, so called, who receive reasonably good pay in the government's employ. It is doubtless truthfully stated that all this great army of officers and government employees are unavoidable; are necessary to run the government. Still let us see if not another class can be provided for under contingent circumstances—the man with his shovel and pickaxe.

It could profitably employ about 5,000 of our laboring men during four months of every winter—just on its public improvements. Put them at work on the *National Park*. It will take them from the street corners, out of the alms-house and police station, where so many seek shelter when other help fails them. A man out of work is dangerous. Idleness is the stepping stone to crime. Something to do for the man with his shovel and pickaxe, the roughness of the craggy rocks and the wild appearance of a landscape, where nature has already done more than half, can be em-bellished so that we can soon boast of the finest park in the world and the finest that the world ever saw. (We refer to the National Park in the Yellowstone).

By thus improving what nature so kindly gave us for our adornment we add beauty and interest to our country, bring tourists from other countries to feast upon the novel won-ders of the New World, as we do upon the antiquities of the old, and create a source of enjoyment and pride to our own people. It would attract settlers to build up and improve that section of the country, enhance the value of land and invite all kinds of industry.

**Landscape Gardening.** Let the government appoint or employ competent and experi-enced landscape artists to lay out the grounds artistically and manage the work. Gather in the jobless workmen with their idle picks and shovels, put them to work leveling and plotting and planting flowers, trees and shrubberies, and by so doing save them from starvation, or vagrancy, or crime. The money saved in the payment to the *National Guards* to cool the ardor of hunger-stricken laboring men will go a great way in defraying the expenses of creating a *National Park*, an improvement that will not only do honor to America, but will be carried down to future generations as an epoch in the world's history that, as a means of education and works of art and science, shall surpass in grandeur and beauty anything man has ever attempted.

**5,000 Men.** The government could readily employ 5,000 men in this laudable enterprise four months each year, in the winter, from the first of November to the first of March, and instead of thereby depleting the treasury it would be adding to the real wealth of the nation, for improving the soil makes land worth more. In this instance it is not to make a profit in the sense of heaping up the dollars, but it operates as a double function: it will give employment to those who need it during the hard winter and at the same time give a mighty impulse to the progress of art and science and give the national mind that increase of richness that neither time nor foe can destroy. We believe in economy, but in affairs of public improvement we are as yet a young nation, and hence in these matters we must not be too close in our idea of economy.

The government could erect barracks for the accommodation of the workmen and furnish them rations at a given price. By paying these men $1.50 per day (eight hours constituting a day's work), and furnish them rations at army prices. The weather often being unpropitious during the winter, the wages we suggest we think about right. Or, what would be better for all parties interested, let the government hire these men and pay them $25.00 per month and board, or rations, furnished. This would keep 5,000 men provided with an honest living, keep them out of mischief and add additional attractions to our country. The entire cost could be paid annually from the illegal profits given for more than one government contract to favorite "contractors." The entire work could be placed under the control or supervision of some of the idle army officers, who draw *big pay* and do little work, and thus do away with expensive political jobbery.

**Idleness Cause of Crime.** It is an old saying that idleness begets crime, and if this affirmation is true then it becomes a sacred duty on the part of the government to adopt some measure to suppress idleness, since it is *incipient crime*. There is an old trite saying, that "the devil always finds work for idle hands to do." It was the idle *canille* of Paris that precipitated several bloody revolutions in France. National idleness is national death; and the greater the element of idleness is in a country the greater the danger threatening its life. We do not call to mind the author who said, "A hundred thousand idle men in the camp are more to be feared than the same number of an armed foe outside." The government should give employment to the idle in the manner we have already suggested. There are a great many men who are chronic idlers, and *will not* work if employment is offered them.

We refer to a class who will not work, yet they have not the visible means wherewith to pay their way. In all such cases idleness should be made a misdemeanor and be compelled to work. Ruskin very wisely says: "Since for every idle person some one else must be working, somewhere, to provide him with clothes and food, and doing, therefore, double the quantity of work that would be enough for his own needs; it is only a matter of pure justice to *compel the idle person* to work for his maintenance himself."

Brigham Young, one winter, when the times were threatening and work scarce among his people, gave employment to 300 men to build a stone fence around Salt Lake City, ostensibly to defend it against Indian depredations. When told that this wall would be no barrier to the Indians, he replied, "I am not half as much afraid of the Indians as I am of 300 idle men." Our government might wisely follow this example.

### A STEPPING STONE TO SUCCESS.

"Who is a good man?" *Horace* says: "He who respects the decrees of the Legislature, and bows to, yields obedience to, every positive law and every moral obligation."

> "Who then is good? Who carefully observes
> The Senate's wise decrees, nor ever swerves
> From the known rules of justice and the laws."

**Æsthetic Culture.** There is nothing that calls forth greater respect for a workingman than to meet with one who is high up in etiquette. It is not only required of the wealthier element to observe well the rules of good manners, but it is expected of them. For it is generally believed that æsthetic culture—rules of etiquette—are studies and accomplishments suited only for peoples who move in the so-called upper strata of society. This is erroneous. It is, however, necessary to possess accomplishments in this respect in order to attract to you cultured people, and here, we are inclined to think, is another rock on which many of our *wage-workers* wreck their best interest. Prof. DeHaven says: "It costs nothing to be polite under all circumstances." To meet with a reassuring reception among people who are cultured one must be their *peer*, or naturally there can be but little affinity. Emerson says: "If you have no brains, go to the merchant-tailor and leave your order." By this he means that where you lack in culture you will have to make up the deficiency in fine clothes.

To understand the rules and customs of good society is almost as essential to business success as a knowledge of your profession or trade. These rules are to society what our laws of state are to the people. To be a gentleman is not to be wealthy or famous, but to be *mannerly*. A millionaire may be a fool and an admiral a boor, while a shoemaker or a hod-carrier may be a gentleman. Formerly to be considered (recognized) a gentleman it was necessary to have a *title* or a *coat-of-arms*. But race caste is no longer the *sine quo non* for a gentleman, nor will education or wealth make a lady or gentleman if good manners are lacking.

Good manners are acquired by education and practice, and there is no better place to practice than at home with your wife and children. Be polite at home and you will not fail in good manners in society.

Manners and morals are almost synonymous and inseparable, and where they exist and are exercised no society can be bad. It is the duty of every man and woman, in order to succeed well, to cultivate good manners, not only for use in society, but in daily business. Rude manners are as harmful to the laborer as to the minister. True politeness is the outward sign of inner graces. Lord Chesterfield says: "Good sense and good nature suggest civility in general, but in good breeding there are a thousand little delicacies which are established only by custom." True politeness or civility is one of the great essentials to success. Good manners is a letter of recommendation among strangers everywhere. It is the business man's best "stock in trade."

Some people think there is no virtue or merit in being so particular in the observance of these trifling things in etiquette, such as a bow, the lifting of your hat, etc., but we should bear in mind that the aggregate of human life is made up of trifles.

If the merchant, the proprietor or salesman has his hat on and a cigar in his mouth when waiting on a lady customer and stands by while she opens and closes the heavy door she will scarcely trouble him much after one call. Little uncivil or rude words or actions are sometimes remembered when great acts are forgotten. The cultivation of good manners should be a part of the education of every person. Some one says: "A bow is a note drawn at sight. You are bound to acknowledge it at once and to the full amount."

Be careful in your conversation, avoid all profanity, vulgarity and slang. Be a good listener as well as a good talker. Be respectful and kind to the aged and infirm. Don't lose your temper in society; never gossip about an absent person; don't notice any error in language or actions of others present; never give advice unless it is asked for, and, above all things, *be polite at home* to your wife and children and even to the servants. It costs nothing to be polite. A volume on æsthetic culture should occupy a place in our "workingman's library."

> " Friend though to careless common sight,
> A kind word, like the widow's mite,
> Seems but a worthless thing ;
> In all the social marts of love,
> Its purchase power is worlds above
> The coffers of a king."

**Wrestling with that Intricate Subject.** It is truly a difficult matter to give work to all, even to the most needy. When it suits certain corporations to shut down they will do so. The only question with them is money. If it pays to shut down for a while this they will do ; the question of justice to their people is not taken into account. The only way to prevent calamities, such as are reported in mining districts frequently, is by a compulsory *labor bureau*, to whose good judgment such matters will have to be submitted. The subjoined editorial from one of our leading dailies will explain itself.

" It is too bad the coal miners are again thrown out of work, and people everywhere will pray that the suspension of all the collieries in the anthracite region will be of short duration. The miners do not make much money under the best of circumstances, and so when they are forced into idleness their situation becomes doubly bad, especially when suspensions come at the beginning of winter."

In the *North American Review* Cardinal Gibbons has a paper on the "Unhappy condition of the poor," in which he frequently uses the words "duty" and "owe" in speaking of the rich, and what their relations are to the poor. " Matthew Marshall," in the *New York Sun*, objects to the words "duty," "owe," etc., taking the ground that the *rich* owe the *poor* nothing, from the simple reason that the rich are what they are, and for no better reason "owe" nothing to the "poor" for the same reason that the "poor" are in need. The rich are willing to help the poor, but they want credit for being benevolent; that he gives, donates from his wealth, and that the poor are willing to acknowledge their dependent condition, and receive from the rich out of pure philanthropic motives.

Joseph R. Buchanan comes forward with a criticism and takes the ground that if the rich had been living under a more correct *regime* of government, in which every workingman would have received his just dues, then they would not be subjects of charity, for the exercise of which acts of benevolence the rich are lauded by those who do not reason, but jump at conclusions in a sort of *a priari* manner. "The poor have ye with you always" was spoken before there were any labor difficulties or disputes. To finish up this thought, we would say that we rather take the side with Mr. Buchanan; not that we are our brother's keeper, but we owe one another the necessities of existence, and every child born into this world has a just claim on society—to be educated and receive such guidance and help that will place it, at maturity, in line which leads to success.

### WORKINGMAN'S LIBRARY.

" From labor health, from health contentment springs ;
Contentment opes the source of every joy."

**Wealth of Mind.** The wage-earner, above every one else in society, should take a careful inventory semi-annually and carefully consider his resources and determine on how to invest his savings. Wealth is money saved, and while it behooves every one to, little by little, accumulate a competency, at the same time a *mental wealth* must be acquired as well, so that the wage-earner will not alone pass in society as a man of industrious habits and economic abilities, but *he*, more than others, should wisely utilize every moment in qualifying himself to be enabled to stand as a *peer* with his fellowmen in the possession of mental wealth, and this will lighten his soul. It makes him friendly and kind. Proper education carries a man out of a groveling state, and though he may have to perform the work of an underling, yet his learning brings true compensation to him, and by its wealth there will come a time when he can control circumstances so as to rise in position, which, if he neglects to lay up, little by little, mental wealth, he will fail and remain all his life a mere underling. ·If you work for a higher position in life you will in time make your point, but if you neglect your opportunities no one will elevate you to a place for which you are not qualified. The simple qualifications of reading, writing and spelling are no evidence of real intelligence. It is the quantity and quality of what a person knows and understands that builds up character. Of course these simple acquirements constitute limited *knowledge*, but are far from *education*. A silver dime is money, but $100,000 is wealth, though it is still money. Much learning is education. This you get from books, if properly selected and studied. All young people contemplating marriage, when of mature age, *should possess, as personal property*, some kind of a library as absolutely as a suit of clothing. For the most appropriate reading we would suggest the following books, recommending the *high school series*, and none but the *most modern text-books, physiology, natural philosophy, mental philosophy, chemistry, botany, astronomy, physical geography* and *geology, history* and *a good dictionary*. An expenditure of $15 will supply you with all these books and give you an excellent start in the proper direction, giving you a fair idea of the character of the world you live in and how to enjoy it. The young lady should add to these, for her special benefit, a work on food and how to cook it.

Correct habits and proper economy will soon enable you to procure this necessary life equipment, and if you can afterward add a work on anthopology, philosophy and ancient history, commercial law and bookkeeping, they will add to your usefulness. If you master the foregoing your desire for more may safely be governed by your own taste and judgment.

### REGULATION OF MULTI-MILLIONAIRES.

" Now leave the vain, low strife
　　That makes men mad, they tug for wealth and power,
　The passions and the cares that wither life,
　　And waste its little hour."

**Extra Taxation.** It is an inevitable tendency of people to accumulate great wealth. A comparatively few succeed, some by sharp dealing and some by chicanery, while a still less number become multi-millionaires by apparently honest means, who seem to have simply "luck" in whatever they engage. There is no reason in political philosophy why a man should not be taxed on what he possesses and even pay an extra tax on ownership of property when it far exceeds a reasonable competency. If, as it is affirmed, all property or possessions are taxable then why not enforce *pro rata taxation*? Moreover, there is no class more able to pay taxes than the wealthy. Syndicates, monopolies, trusts or corporations of whatever denomination should be required by law to pay taxes on all they possess. Money loaned or money in bank or vested in speculation should be subject to taxation.

Then there are those who have amassed large fortunes in manufacturing commodities under a highly protective tariff system from which the country at large derives little benefit and who, by such accumulations, are still adding to their fortunes daily. These should not entirely escape our attention. *Pro rata* taxation on all possessions, and then there should be an *extra tax* levied on accumulating wealth after a given point has been reached. This, no doubt, will regulate the multi-millionaire as an incongruous element, or such tendency in society may be regulated by law.

Excess of wealth is as great an evil as excess of poverty.

It breeds aristocracy and monarchy by placing too much power in the hands of a few individuals. A millionaire may be an independent man and a useful citizen; but when a man heaps millions on millions he becomes dangerous and much to be feared. Having more than he needs for himself for legitimate uses, he often uses his superfluous capital for illegal purposes. There should be a limit to a man's wealth, as there is in all else in nature. Now, to remedy this evil in overgorging in riches, has been a subject of thought with many a good statesman.

We have one idea to suggest on this subject which we think worthy of some consideration. It is *pro rata* taxation. Let every man be taxed on an equal taxation basis with the rest of mankind until his possessions amount to $100,000, then add one per cent. to each hundred thousand thereafter. Let this be the assessment on the wealthy in the larger first and second class cities. For third class cities, towns and rural districts let the tax be one per cent. after $30,000 is reached and one per cent. additional for every $30,000 more, namely, one per cent. on $30,000, two per cent. on $60,000, and so on *ad infinitum over* and *above* the usual taxes. This would be a tax levied irrespective of needs, simply on accumulation of wealth. After a man has obtained two millions he would not be so eager to amass more, as a tax of twenty per cent. or twenty-five per cent. would not leave him much margin in ordinary investments. This would, in a great measure, lock the wheels of monopoly. These multi-millionaires do a great deal of quiet "money-grinding" among the laboring classes.

### WHAT CONSTITUTES NATIONAL GREATNESS?

Greatness consists in knowing that you are right;
Then dare to defend it with all your might.

**The New Nation.** As a nation we are comparatively young and may, therefore, be called *the new nation.* No nation in the world's history had so many severe tests, and overcame them all, as *America*.

Foreign attacks were hard, but attacked by an internal foe was when the deepest sorrow came to men's hearts, and even now it requires the greater vigilance to guard against attacks from those among us than from foreign invasion.

We reason largely by the signs of the times and from past experience as to the future. The war prophet is ever foremost with his predictions. Some contend that a most disastrous *labor war* is even now darkening the horizon of our great country. There are doubtless many who leave nothing undone to bring on a war—a war that would be after their own heart—but it will never be.

We have confidence in the good sense of our people. A very large majority will join us in promulgating the principles of this volume. We have not only shown the various leading causes of the disturbances among us, but we have also formulated the treatment, or, in other language, we have suggested the *remedy* that will *head off* the difficulties and save us from any civil strife in the future.

There never was a time in this country when the *public press* was more united in the common sentiment of a *"government of the people,"* a "government for all the people," as at the present. In point we submit the following editorial, which we clipped at the time of reading it and neglected to credit it to the proper publication. We think, however, if we remember rightly, it was an editorial from one of our leading Republican dailies. Let this be as it may, it voices the sentiment of every editor of the land and every good citizen who calls himself an American. And so long as we can meet each other in the *open arena* of discussion and shake hands across the chasm of party strife when the battle is over, so long will there be no war in our national hearth and home. The following is an evidence of the grandest sentiment of true patriotism:

" The tributes paid to the memory of ex-President Hayes by the news-papers of all parties and all shades of opinion are creditable to the good sense of the American people. Other nations look with surprise at the intensity of our party strife and wonder how men can dwell together in peace and harmony who engage in such fierce debates and display toward each other so much political animosity. They do not take into account, however, the saving common sense of the American people. It was the lot of Mr. Hayes to encounter unjustly the fiercest resentment and the strongest political detraction of any man of his day, but he endured it all with a quiet dignity that won the respect of the great majority of the intelligent people of the country. And now that he is dead a nation mourns at his coffin and Grover Cleveland, the leader of the party that lost no opportunity to deride the ex-President, goes to his funeral as one of the mourners. A nation that can perform such an act of justice is safe from the demagogue."

## A FIGHT FOR LIFE.

We quote from Isaac H. Stearns, M. D., an idea regarding the constant conflict that arises between capital and labor, and that it is a common idea that life is a fight or struggle for existence, which should be understood is not a normal state ; co-ordination or harmonious relation is the true condition. He says :

**Conflict.** "It is most remarkable that so general an interest was taken in the prize-fights in New Orleans, and that the newspapers, in deference to the demand, published so full accounts of the brutal details of the several pugilistic exhibitions, and the reflection cannot be avoided that the civilized enlightenment of which we love to boast is still in the neighborhood of barbarism. That the prize-fight seems to so delight the public must be because it is a visible type of what is too common in the human heart.

"Our whole industrial system is founded on the principle of pugilism; our boys—and girls, too, for that matter—are largely taught that a successful career can only be won by a 'fight with the world.'

"And parents think their children can only do well by being left to 'fight' their way.

"Without question fighting is sometimes necessary, for individuals as well as nations, but it should be the last resort.

"These reflections, in their application to labor and capital, enforce themselves when we remember that within three

months of this writing there have been three civil wars in
as many separate states, instigated by labor organizations,
involving three widely different industries—mining, steel
manufacturing and railroading.

"These outward expressions indicate the constant spirit
and trend of our trade and commerce, for labor and capital
are alike organized for war.

"The questions involved in the relation of capital to labor
are far from being settled, and that things will be worse
before they are permanently better admits of little doubt.

"What our children and the world should be taught is,
that good citizens are not made by men and boys fighting
their way, or fighting the world, but by doing their duty
justly, sincerely and honestly in whatever calling or trust
that seems to open up before them and be satisfied with an
equitable remuneration for their services."

"Conquering may prove as lordly and complete in lifting
up as in laying low."

"We must spend our money in some way at some time, and it cannot at any time be spent without employing somebody. Every coin
spent in cultivating the ground, repairing buildings, making roads,
preventing danger by sea and land is so much absolute and direct gain
to the whole nation."—*Ruskin.*

> Let us meet upon the level, then,
>     While *laboring* patient here ;
> Let us meet and let us labor,
>     Though the labor be severe.
> Already in the dawning sky
>     The signs bid us prepare
> To gather up our working tools
>     And part upon *the square.*
>
> There is a time when all are *equal*—
>     We are going to it fast—
> When the man that rules a kingdom
>     And the man that pegs the last,
> When the prince that dons the purple
>     And the peasants linsey wear,
> All shall meet upon the *level*
>     And be measured on the *square.*

ANDREW CARNEGIE.
Fig. 1.

J. HOWARD.
Fig. 2.

W. H. BAILEY.
Fig. 3.

MRS. LEONORA M. BARRY.
Fig. 4.

Plate XVI—For sketches see page 222.

## THE PUBLIC PRESS—OPINIONS.

EDITORIALS—COMMENTS; EVOLUTION, PEOPLE AND JOURNAL-
ISM; CAMPAIGNS; EDUCATIONAL; MOULDING THE MIND;
IF THE PRESS IS SHAPING THE SENTIMENT OF THE PEO-
PLE, WHERE DOES THE RESPONSIBILITY REST? IF NOT,
ALL IS RIGHT, WHAT THEN? OTHER THOUGHTS AND
COMMENTS, ETC., ETC.

> "Some have too much, yet still they crave,
> They are but poor, though much they have;
> They poor, I rich; they beg, I give;
> They lack, I lend; they pine, I live."

**Growing Purity.** We speak the truth when we say that we are exceedingly glad (delighted) to state here what we know to be true regarding the *growing purity* of journalism. We have not in any manner courted the favor of any particular class or persons in writing this volume. We treated the subject of the *labor trouble*, capital, tariff, taxation, immigration, etc., from well established *data* and in keeping with our understanding, regardless of fear or favor; and now, as we are about to reach the end of our deliberations, we are not inclined to change tactics and break our motto, which we still hold to be our governing principle, as Polonius says in his address to his son, Larites:

> "This above all: to thine own self be true,
> And it must follow, as night the day,'
> Thou canst not then be false to any man."

It cannot be successfully shown that journalism is *not* very perceptibly growing in purity in the general moral tone, both in the secular work and more especially in politics. The editors are growing older and see things in a different light. For some time after the war politics was in a greater state of agitation than for many years, and there were many opportunities for a live newspaper. Then the professions were well filled; in fact, crowded, and this turned the attention of many a young man just home from

college to journalism. Sensational publications flourished
and some of the old and established newspapers unwillingly
gave way to sensational matter in order to keep together.
However, soon the people, and especially the educators,
brought about a grand reform in this particular and the
moral tone of the "public press" is on a much higher plane
than for many years and still moving upward. It has been
learned by quite a large number of journalists of this country that truth is much cheaper than false publications.
Some learned this fact by paying a high price for the lessons they learned. Moreover, there is nothing clever in a
lie; chivalry, patriotism, manhood, all, in fact, that makes
up a man is sacrificed in a newspaper simply, and for a few
dollars publish sensational articles, and often slanderous in
character. Often, and especially has this been the case
during hotly-contested political campaigns, and to such an
extent had this evil grown that the *press* lost much of its
influence among the people, so that in localities, to our certain knowledge, the papers were a dead letter in so far as
moulding the sentiment of the people was concerned.

It must be admitted that the *press* is a power in the land
for good or for evil. There never was a time since the discovery of the printing press when there was such a vast
number of publications, periodicals, dailies, weeklies, month-
lies, magazines, etc., as at the present and they are steadily
on the increase. This exemplifies two strong points in the
social movements of our people: first, that there is a great
desire for information, to keep up with the progress of the
times, and second, that there is going on a mental warfare,
contending for supremacy in the realm of the intellectual,
to which we had occasion to refer before in this volume.

It is becoming every day more apparent that the *public
press* is instrumental to a great degree in moulding or di-
recting the mind of the readers of current publications,
newspapers, magazines, etc., and hence it can scarcely be
otherwise than that the managing editors are beginning to
feel a responsibility not hitherto realized by them.

It may be still said, however, that there is much room for improvement in regard to the clean and high tone moral attitude of the ordinary newspaper. There are still many and able journalists who claim that the ordinary readers must have things dished up to them in the form of sensation, and the more speak-easy news the better will their paper be appreciated. Some base their success entirely on this feature being the most prominent in their publications; that the journalist, to be a success, must give to the people what they want, for some one will follow this course and make money, while those who take a high standard go to the wall. The dealer in spirituous drinks argues from the same point of view, that some one will suppress all moral sense and enter upon the traffic of liquors, for if he does not some one will, and why not make that money. This is not a tenable position, since all will have to settle moral actions with their own consciences; and, moreover, if our editors pander to the taste and idiosyncrasies of their readers, then, in that case, in place of being a leader of their readers, they are followers. Instead of leading the blind they themselves are led by the blind.

### COLONIAL DAYS.

"I only pointed out the paths that lead
  The panting youth to steep Parnassus' head,
  And showed the tuneful Muses from afar,
  Mixed in a solemn choir and dancing there."

**Colonists.** As in the earlier days of our nation, those who colonized and settled in the different parts of the country, lived in harmony together, worked for one common interest, developed the soil, built pleasant homes and many grew up families with an inheritance that done honorable service in the state as men of giant intellect, to whom we look back with pride; so may even now colonies form and settle on our western land, develop the country, keep close to mother earth, receive the strength, brain and sinew-building material into their blood from the first crops of the new-made farms, unworn soil, and grow to physical and mental greatness. The great men of our new states and territories will not be the great money magnates of the day, but those who now cultivate their new lands and create ways of communication, develop the country, as those of the earlier colonies, will rise to honor and fullness of enjoyment of the works of their own labor.

By colonizing the better element of our own people, who seek for homes in the west, and especially foreign immigrants, money will be saved and made. Colonization means success. Why spend your best days in cities and die prematurely for want of pure air? Colonize the immigrants; it is the best thing for them to do; it is the best thing the government can do for the country. By colonizing society can form at once. They can have schools, colleges, churches, public lecture halls, and in a few years all will be in a prosperous condition, with friends and neighbors altogether, enjoying an outlook that never can be realized in our large cities. Here lies the open sea through which many of our *wage-workers* of America may sail their little bark on to fortune, at least to a home and independence.

The greatest reward will come to those men who develop manufactories, start commercial enterprises, and the farmer who develops the resources of the country. The thousands of early pioneers will build up solid *fabrics* for future generations. They will leave histories and solid monuments of their life work. The Bentons, the Freemonts and the Carsons, aided by the honest farmer, intelligent teacher, wise doctor and skilled mechanic and the good pioneers' wives and mothers, will make the wilderness bloom like a rose garden.

> " Let us go forth and resolutely dare
> With sweat of brow to toil our little day,
> And if a tear fall on the task of care
> In memory of those spring hours passed away,
> Brush it not by !
> Our hearts to God ! to brother men
> And labor, blessing, prayer, and to these a sign ! "

## ACTS OF INJUSTICE.

" Some say that the age of chivalry is past. The age of chivalry is never past as long as there is a wrong unredressed on earth, and a man or woman left to say : I will redress that wrong or *spend my life in the attempt*."

**Hard to Overlook.** There is nothing so galling, so bitter and so hard to overlook as acts of injustice. The first effect it has on the mind is a feeling of resentment. The severest side of human nature is called forth. Revenge is one of its products. It is true that the better class, who love law and order, suppress feelings of revenge, but this is not always done. Injustice incites mob-law violence. No one who values self-interest, and his neighbors as well, would be guilty of acts of injustice. Retribution will come sooner or later. Hence the sentiment was fittingly spoken, "Woe be unto him through whom offense cometh." Moreover it never pays to be unjust. We quote the following editorial from one of our daily papers in exemplification of what we have stated :

" Tennessee has paid dear for the misplaced economy of its Legislature in insisting a year ago on convict labor because it was cheap. There is nothing so dear as injustice ; and farming out convict labor in convict camp is organized injustice both to free labor and to the convicts."

Injustice is like violence in personal encounter when directed with intent to do bodily harm. It places a person against whom it is intended in a position of self-defense. Those who act from the impulse of the moment, inaugurate great strife and go as far as to rebel, destroy property, shed blood and otherwise commit lawless acts. Acts of injustice, whether on the part of the State, or individuals, or corporations, may be within the perview of the law, and those who come under its lash cannot, therefore, find redress in law until the law is repealed and a more just law is enacted by the State. So long, then, as we have laws not strictly equitable may we expect strikes and insurrections. A free man with a highly individualized character and a keen feeling for justice, will not bear very long a condition which he feels is robbing him of what is dear to him in the enjoyment of life. It is true all people cannot be made to see alike, yet there is a sense of justice possessed by the general public which will render a just verdict, and this should not be ignored *too long* or trouble is not far off. Public sentiment may be changed, but this can only be done by educating the people to a point of correct understanding. To succeed in this all arguments must carry with them those self-evident truths which appeal at once to the man's sense of right, and laws enacted on this basis will stand and be respected by the nation. Moreover, unjust laws at last will only bring about contention and an unsettled state of affairs, liable to end in costly means of correction, if not in war.

Injustice never pays. Individuals in society who are disposed to be unjust toward their fellow-men will reap the fruit of their own acts and bring upon themselves often suffering and loss of money.

The same rules that will conduct an even and successful business in private life will also apply to the government of the great Republic and State.

**Get on the Right Side.** Man, through his perceptive faculties, at once recognizes the truth. He admits the truth without argument. He may not adopt it; his moral courage fails him. He may have to let go of some pet theory or belief (though not true), which is too much for his untrained moral nature. It is not that man does not perceive the truth, but he fails in surmounting obstacles that keep him from declaring himself on the side of truth. To conquer these requires vigilance, self-abnegation, deliberation and determination to *get on the right side*.

Everything in man's environment represents truth, facts; he himself is a fact. The genius that makes him what he is, is a fact. Truth is part of man, and nothing brings greater reassuring satisfaction to his mind than truth. Then get on the right side, if happiness is the goal. Subdue the grosser nature, divest yourself of all selfishness. As Wm. H. Hunt says, "He never knew a person yet who was unselfish but made life a success." Selfishness—selfish motives—disqualifies a person to receive the truth.

Under all conditions of life, *stand up* for the right.
Let come what will, *defend* your own with all your might.

## NINETEEN HUNDRED AND NINETY-NINE.

PERPETUATION OF THE NEW NATION; A NEW IDEA APPLIED;
ALL OF US ARE NEIGHBORS; HAND IN HAND WE KEEP
MARCHING ON; THE INTEREST OF ONE COMMON BROTH-
ERHOOD; AIR-MOTOR; GRAVITATION A MOTOR FORCE;
A HARMONY THAT BINDS, ETC., ETC.

> " He who can taste without allay
> The present pleasure of the day,
> Should with an easy, cheerful smile
> The bitterness of life beguile,—
> Should all of future care detest,
> *For nothing is completely blest.*"

A VISION AND STORY.

**A Steamboat Excursion.** During the winter of 1885 we made a lecturing tour through the southern states. We visited only the most prominent cities, delivering popular lectures, some sixty in number, on the *Principles of Scientific Living.* During our sojourn we made many acquaintances and not a few warm friends, learning much about the country and the customs and character of a people who, in due time, will become prominent in the building up of a New Nation, on principles of Reform, and eventually, in the years to come, furnish many of the ligatures which will bind together the filaments of our Union and make it a united family.

We tarried about a fortnight in the city of Mobile, Alabama. During our stay in this city we took great pleasure in visiting places of local and historic interest in and about the place.

One beautiful day in the month of April, when *here* already the full floodtide of summer had covered hill and dale with its magical charms, arrangements had been made by the municipal officers of the city to give the stranger visitors from the North in some way a public recognition. There were many visitors at the time, a large number of them came from the North to exchange the chilling blasts of their bleak hills for the balmy zephyrs of the South ; some to find a respite from threatening disease, and others simply seeking pleasure in new fields,—but all bent on enjoying the mild climate.

**Down to Deep Water.** An excursion down Mobile Bay to Deep Water was proposed—taking in Fort Morgan and Dauphin Island, a good feast of plump oysters, and a good time altogether. We embarked on a beautiful steamer early in the morning, when the fragrance of the orange groves scented the air, and the birds were singing sweetly in the magnolia branches. Though we were all strangers to each other, there was a sameness of thought and desire among us which made us feel at home and contented in each other's society

We had an excellent band of music on board, which added much to our enjoyment. We started early in the morning, while the dew yet glistened in tiny globules on flower and plant, and the feathered orchestra sang sweet carols in honor of the new-born day. Our early start gave us about three hours' time for rest and reverie at Fort Morgan.

As the day advanced the weather became warmer, and the sunlight glinting brightly on every dancing wavelet, and the cooling zephyrs that fanned our cheeks made the passage very enjoyable.

Our company was honored with the presence of a number of notable persons, among whom were Henry Ward Beecher, Carl Shurz, Judge Carter, of Cincinnati ; Mrs. Carson, of Dubuque, Iowa, and others. There were about 250 persons in the party, every one of them desirous of getting all the pleasure possible out of the day and the trip.

Some of us were looking for delicately-tinted sea shells, along the shore, while others enjoyed a bath in Neptune's kingdom.

For some reason, undetected and unmeant at the time, we became detached from the rest of our company, sauntering aimlessly down the beach. While thus strolling along we were attracted by an object in the distance which had

**Indian Mound.** the resemblance of an Indian Mound. The elevation, rising perhaps 130 feet above the level of the sea, was located but a short distance from the strand. We occupied but a short time in making the ascent on a reconnoitering jaunt, and being somewhat exhausted by our efforts, it required but little persuasion to induce us to take a rest. Timing ourselves, conscious of having three hours at our disposal before the boat returned, we sought the pleasant shade of a magnolia tree, and yielding to the soothing influence of nature's charms—we fell into a pleasant reverie. The sun poured down his hot rays —the shade was so inviting; the insects chirped so dreamily; the fragrant breezes in their fitful wanderings touched our heated brow so coquettishly like the gentle finger touches of angels, that we yielded to the charm of these voluptuary forces, and forgot the more sordid and vulgar influences and surroundings of humdrum life. We

**Humdrum Life.** had a dreamy consciousness of having wandered miles away from our companions. We half unconsciously changed our position and settled down on a mossy bed, leaned our back against a cypress tree, through whose (now hoary and tangled) branches the wild winds may have rioted for thousands of years.

The prospect before us was entrancing. The mellowed sunlight made broad lines of silver and gold among the emerald sheen of the foliage of surrounding trees.

All around us was still and silent except the whispering of the breeze that played amid the grass and the branches of overhanging trees. The unfathomable blue ether stretched overhead, the gossamer clouds, floating lazily over the wide expanse, brought to our mind an old-time song of which this is a part we never forgot :

> " If you and I were only ghosts
> Cut off from human cares and pains,
> To walk together day and night,
> Along the far sidereal plains."

**Silvery Vail.** The ocean seemed like the silvery vail covering the bride-face of an ethereal goddess. A calm, wonderful radiance came over the hills and plains and rested in magical splendor on the waters beyond. The windy clouds, now and then mingling like haunting ghosts among the lace-like pinions of fairer companions, crossing the blue sky, gave to the far-off woods and hills an ever changing picture of light and shadow and grotesque shapes, creating new landscapes in their restless flittings. Thus we lay as if in an enchanted castle, for which the horizon, bending down on every side, formed the tapestried walls. One white sail gleamed alone far out at sea like some silvery gull forsaken by its companions, while the white-capped waves danced and leaped in ceaseless antics to the shore. Far away the mountains stood silent and grim as Roman sentinels guarding sea and plain.

All these silent, subtle influences worked upon our senses with a syren's charm and brought us a respite in Young's "Tired nature's sweet restorer, balmy sleep."

It came opportunely; we coveted rest after many days of thought and labor to do good to our fellow-beings. We were as by one intoxicated breath wafted into *Dreamland*, losing sight of the stereotyped formulas of society and the stale formalities of every-day life, and we felt like soaring into the realms of *What is to come*, like Columbus seeking a new world.

**Lost Our Hold on the World.** We lost our hold on the *Present* and soared into the *Future*. We were intoxicated—not by the venal cup that robs the senses, but by the elixir brewed from the sunshine, the flowers, the bird songs and the ozone around us which, while it incites the senses, elevates the mind and ennobles the soul.

Whether we simply enjoyed the natural sequence of a day dream or the raptures of a trance we cannot tell, but one thing we know: While thus engaged we were forgetful of all ordinary surroundings and wandered in new realms we never trod before, entirely taken up with a new *regime*.

Days seemed to come and go as in a kaleidoscope, ever presenting new and beautiful features in the drama of life. Weeks, months and years lost their duration gliding on like the bubbles on a stream only to be followed by others until we drifted into the ages *to come*. We in our reverie, always burdened with the great desire to make the world better and brighter, looked anxiously ahead for changes that would

**The Year 1999.** realize our hopes. And while thus dreaming and gliding down the stream of Time, smoothly, but still rapidly losing sight of the calendar and the rythmic measure of the time, we struck a mile post marked 1999; we had drifted in our reverie or dream more than a hundred years ahead. Here we halted, almost bewildered by the changes we saw around us. However, we soon met with people and were saluted in a friendly manner. The cities and the rural districts seemed very different from what we were accustomed to, and on inquiry as to where we were and the peculiarity of this strange, yet beautiful, land we were told that it was simply a perpetuation of the "*New Nation*," which had its beginning in the "old;" which underwent a rapid change (metamorphosis) during the decline of the eighteenth century, and was now popularly known as the "*Dreamland*."

By an involuntary impulse, as it seemed to us, we wandered through the states in search of *datas* of interest, and to acquaint ourselves with the distinguishing principles of the "New Nation." The people seemed happy; had a fresh and healthy appearance. Everybody possessed a home of their own and this, doubtless, it was that gave all an apparent tone of independence, and yet with all there was a neighborly and brotherly feeling which pervaded their very being; readily discernable to eminate (impulses) from an honest heart. Hand in hand, as it seemed, all were marching together on life's high road of progress.

**An Old Scientist.** In our movements we met with an aged gentleman, who proved to be a well-known scientist, at the time in the employment of the general government. He was under orders, with his attendants of about twenty people fully equipped for an exploring expedition. His orders were to explore more fully the country lying southwest of Denver, with a view of ascertaining the possible resources of minerals ; he was also to extend his work into the great American Desert and by his knowledge of Chemistry report some practical method and the proximate cost (per acre) of converting the sand into rich soil. We did not learn the process, but inferred from his remarks that his first object was to sink artesian wells and by the use of air-motors pump the water and thus irrigate, and the first six months he would impregnate the water with salt to be followed with an alkali. He said that in three years he could have a fine producing farm and cheaper than to make a farm out of woodland. We had no doubt of his success, the only point is to know how and success must follow. *

**Hidden Treasures.** We learned the fact that many scientists were in constant employment of the government, whose special function or business was to explore and experiment in the different parts of the country, with a view of discovering hidden treasures as well as to discover unknown principles, thus find practical methods of developing the resources of the soil, and especially to make mining more practical, easy, safe and profitable.

We saw in practical operation, in mining districts, in the Rocky Mountains, immense electro-dynamos, the motivity of which was derived from vast air-motors and water-motors.

---

* When it once becomes a necessity that the *New Nation* will be too thickly settled, the inventive genius will find but little trouble in making the now worthless desert habitable and fertile. Skillfully constructed air-motors, pumping water into standpipe-reservoirs, and water-motors, electro-dynamos—burning the sand, the admixtures of cheap chemicals, such as salt, alkali, etc., with artificial rain producing means—will start soil-building, and nature will do the rest.

The deepest mines are lighted with electricity. Drills and other machinery used in the mines are run by the use of compressed air. Gold and other valuable metals are readily extracted from the earth and rock (caused to precipitate) in large quantities by heavy electric currents (a cheap process) being applied according to newly discovered principles. Gold is obtained from the bottom of rivers, flowing through gold-producing districts in California, by means of strong electric currents. Thus gold and silver and other valuable metals are obtained in an expeditious manner never known before. Truly the "New Nation" has grown far away from the "old"; we became restless, and almost over anxious to extend our observation into other departments, which we were not only permitted to do, but were invited to do so, the people being ready and willing at all times, in the most pleasing way, to explain and answer all inquiries.

**Air and Water-Motors.** One of the most ingeneous contrivances that attracted our attention in vogue in "Dreamland" is artesian wells. Air-motors are used to sink the well, and afterwards pump the water into large standpipe-reservoirs. Water-motors are run by the water from these reservoirs by means of which machines on a small scale are readily made available. Thus the farmer threshes his grain, cuts straw, grinds feed, and besides runs an electro-dynamo, lights and warms the house, which also serves for cooking purposes, runs sewing-machines, etc., all at a mere nominal expense, save the first investment. The waste water from the water-motor is utilized for watering the stock and irrigating purposes for the garden and the farm as it is needed. These contrivances are in extensive use throughout the western states, especially on the western prairies. Also similar motors are in use in running the machinery of many different kinds of manufactories in small towns, and street cars on the trolley order are in use between towns, and thus the whole country is connected by means of easy and rapid transit, the motive power of which is derived from air and water-motors, cheap, practicable and durable. The coaches are made of aluminum and papier-mache, hence have the advantage of lightness as well as strength.

**Another Notable Feature.** A noteworthy feature that struck us as being of great advantage to husbandry in this beautiful "Dreamland" is a portable fence in use, by which means pasture lots are made available at different seasons of the year and different parts of the farm without encumbering the land, as it was with the inartistic rail fence in the old nation. This is a great desideratum, as animals are not permitted to run at large, and yet health laws require that they should have the open air as much as possible. This fence is made of galvanized sheet-wire, the openings about four inches (square) apart and about five feet high. At a distance of a rod apart is an upright bar of iron, one-quarter by one and one-half inches, and an arm from each of these bars can be thrown out at a right angle and fastened in the ground with an iron peg. Thus any part of the land, on a larger or smaller scale, is made available for the temporary liberty to animals to pasture in the field, and also to keep them separated, if it is so desired. This fence is artistic and inexpensive and can readily be moved by rolling it upon a windlass, which is on two wheels, to which a horse is hitched, and in two hours a fence around a six or ten-acre lot is taken up and put down again.

**The Highway.** The public highway is smooth, lasting and artistic; macadamized with a cheap material made by mixing the proper equivalents of earth, sand, lime, cement and asphaltum, which readily become as solid as rock. The highways thus made extended all over "Dreamland," like walks in a park. There are no heavy vehicles, for reason there is no heavy freight to be moved. Tricycles and bicycles are extensively in use, both by the old and the young. Carriages drawn by horses are still in vogue, but ordinary driving does not effect the roads in the least.

The race-course for speeding horses has reached a high state of perfection. We were shown a fine trotter, owned by a lady of Detroit, Michigan, who had a record of one minute and a half, six and three-quarters seconds. Horseback riding is still fine sport. Heavy road wagons have gone out of use, for there is no heavy freight to be moved. The leading motor force is air, water and electricity. The highways are like garden walks, beset on either side with evergreen and flowering plants, and there are walks for pedestrians. The whole country has the appearance of one grand garden scene.

**Garden Homes.** In "Dreamland" it seems, from the grandeur and beauty of the rural environment, that every husbandman makes the art of landscape gardening a special study. The fields are beautifully laid out. Farms are worked with more method and care. The science of the chemistry of the soil is a study, and applied with a thoroughness that as the soil exhausts in the phosphates is soon reclaimed by proper fertilizers, and thus the average yield is far greater under the management of the *New Nation* than the "old" was capable of. A beautiful *garden home* is appreciated more than all other wealth, exemplifying the fact that people of the "New Nation" have got at least some distance away from the grosser, heavier weights of former times.

The architectural science of dwellings, barns and the commonest outhouses have the appearance of the master's hand, rule, method, design and evident studiousness, combining ancient and modern principles of embellishment, reflecting on every hand the *beautiful;* showing a higher mental condition of the inhabitants of "Dreamland" than ever before attained by man. The *era* of the *intellectual rule,* so long in nature's gestating womb of evolution, is here fully inaugurated.

**Amazingly Wonderful.** The most abundant element in man's environment has hitherto been utilized, the least of all, by man in compelling it to work for him. We refer to atmosphere or wind. As a source of motivity the air has had a good long rest, but not so now, for in the *New Nation* it has been harnessed in such a skillful manner that the wind is made to do work in many departments of the industrial art, that the expensive and grosser methods in use in the old nation are entirely obsolete.

The main points that will be of great interest to scientists we will take up again further on and explain some of the more intricate parts which made air available as a motor force. In our rambles through "Dreamland" we learned much, and only hope that we may some time meet each other there, should any of us be so fortunate as to be permitted to make a trip to that country.

**Among Scientists.** There are just as many possible things as there are impossibles, but there are possible things enough to keep us in a state of wonderment all the time, for nature is, doubtless, unlimited in mysteries, and every time a new discovery is made it does not exhaust or contract the realm of undiscovered principles, but simply serves as a stepping-stone to enable mankind to make other discoveries.

Furthermore, it is a sentiment or belief among scientists that scientific discovery does not only imply progress in physics, but it also gives an impetus to mental, moral and social progress. The moral and social go hand in hand with science. The moral and social condition of society, in the *New Nation*, is just as far in advance of the old as the system of government, and the science of machinery, wants of the people, supply and demand ; the wonderful harmony of society is advanced so that no one can be found in all "Dreamland" who longs to go back to the *regime* of the "old nation."

**The President.** We are amazed to learn what great changes have taken place in the affairs of the general government. The president is elected for

THE OLD HOMESTEAD

*eight years*, and by the popular vote. The electoral college is entirely abandoned. Perfect freedom of speech prevails all over "Dreamland." The "Printing Press" is revered as the great exponent of the sentiment of the people, and to the honor of the "Press," be it said, that the moral plane to which the "Press" has reached, in the *New Nation*, to such a high order, that in all the world's history there never was a time when the "Press" had such power, and it may be amazing to think that the tendency is still to a loftier plane. It seems especially amazing when we contemplate the comparison, that only a little over a hundred years ago, in the old nation, the moral status of journalism had almost fallen into utter disregard of leading mankind to a loftier plane of moral practice.

**No Cyclones.** To our surprise throughout all "Dreamland" there are no social cyclones, no "lockouts," or "strikes," and none are expected or predicted. The croakers and civil war prophets died with the "old nation." There are no trusts or "corners" in commerce, no monopolies, no combines ; great corporations and all monstrosities in the entire social systems gradually faded out of existence as the new system of government came into power. Wage-earners share in the profits of capital, and the ownership of their own labor and its profits is undisputed. Every state has adopted a legal system of *compulsory arbitration.* There are few labor disputes. *The Labor Bureau* adjusts in an equitable way wages and settles all matters that are not running smoothly of themselves. Labor riots, bread riots, strikes, lockouts, insurrections, etc., all these things and *curious* circumstances are related by the older people in the form of stories, and as historic events of a people having lived in the eighteenth century when (as they believe) people were yet in a semi-civilized state.

**State Elections and Tariff.** The tariff question is entirely under the control of a national *Customs Bureau*, the chairman of which is a member of the cabinet. The tariff question is, therefore,

out of politics.   During political campaigns customs duty
is not broached at all by the speakers.

The different states elect their governors for the term
of three years.   Legislative enactments are comparatively
few.   The Legislature assembles every two years only, and
both the members of the State Legislature and members of
Congress receive their regular pay throughout the term
for which they are elected whether in session or not.

This we saw was a good feature in the system of the government of the *New Nation*, which, doubtless, has the effect
of keeping many a legislator, as well as members of Congress, from trying to make money by crooked turns, for the
commonwealth is willing to pay officers of the law, especially
the law makers, *well* for their service.

A protective tariff is in vogue, which gives to the wage-
earners, as well as the people in general, *that* protection of
home interests to that extent and end that the markets of
commodities of every description are strictly regulated by
supply and demand.   There seems to exist an equity in dealing among the people that bartering and competition are in a
manner so closely allied to the "golden rule" that courts of
arbitration are sought rather than the courts of the law.
The law cases, where the disputes rise to that pitch requiring
or forcing trial by court, are as a rule very few, proving the
highly advanced state of society in the "New Nation."

**No Sex in Politics.** We were pleased to learn that
universal suffrage is in full work-
ing order in "Dreamland."   Woman is recognized as a
citizen in the fullest sense of the term.   She is not looked
upon as a helpmate alone, but as a co-partner in the family,
state and business.   There is no sex in politics.   Woman
brings a sort of redeeming quality of character with her,
that it has a purifying effect on politics, that campaigns
are conducted on a purer and higher moral basis than ever
known under the management of the "old government."   A
woman is Secretary of State, and, of course, a member of
the Cabinet.

**Civic Education.** The educational system in vogue in the "*old nation*" is continued, in as far as we could learn, only perfected. The University Extension system of educating the citizen is in working perfection. There are *public lecture halls*, built for that purpose, in every voting precinct. The general government is thoroughly secularized.

We are informed regarding the different religious denominations that there exists the fullest liberty and the enjoyment of the rights of conscience, each according to *inalienable* laws, fully guaranteed to all believers in the "*New Nation*" as was the case in the old nation. There exists astonishing harmony and neighborly feeling among the people. This state of affairs is accounted for on the ground of the thoroughly *secular* government. The total non-recognition of (religious) denominational differences (and yet all legislation gives support to all alike) is, doubtless, the basis of all successful government where the church has been divorced from the state.

The public school system is about the same as under the "*Old Nation*," only the teachers are given four months' vacation and their pay goes on the same as if school was keeping, and this seems to us the right and just thing to do. This enables our teacher to attend the Normal College for personal improvement. *The Sabbath day is universally observed as a day of rest.*

**Many New Points.** The marriage and divorce laws are uniform throughout the Union. There exists nowhere in the states of the "*New Nation*" capital punishment. Capital crime is rarely perpetrated, as also crime of any sort is far less than in the old nation. Trials by jury in all criminal cases have been abrogated for many years, but are tried by judges of the law. State's prisons are changed largely into reformatory institutions rather than places of punishment. Insanity and disease have decreased in ratio in the "*New Nation*," largely by reason of greater attention being given to the observance of the rules of health and sanitary laws than ever before, hence, as we learned the facts, institutions for the indigent are few in the land.

The eight-hour system is in vogue everywhere in the "*New Nation*," and people enjoy themselves, both [1] by the extension of means of education, and [2] by improved social organizations. Of secret societies there are few, and organizations having for their object, as in the *old nation*, self-preservation and protection in personal interest against *organized capital*, gradually became metamorphosed into social institutions for self-improvement in acquiring personal accomplishments, fitting personal qualities for continuing in the *New Nation*. The capitalist and the wealthy readily foresaw that pauperism would not pay ; that such a condition as an element appended to society was evidence of a wrong system of government, and they joined the great phalanx of political reform, that it is better for all, and the capitalist in particular, to dwell in a land where every man is a gentleman and every woman a lady.

**Foreign Nations.** But little attention is given to foreign countries. The *New Nation* is at peace with all the nations of the earth.[*] The government, through its immigrant bureau, has full management of immigration. England, France, Germany and many other foreign countries have assumed systems of government Republican in form.

Imperial rule has passed into oblivion. In the oriental east Jerusalem has grown into a great metropolis and scientists are at work in reclaiming the soil, and the system of government of "*Dreamland*," under which the "*New Nation*" *of America* succeeds so admirably, is copied almost in its entirety by them.

**But to the Story.** As was before said, progress in physical science means also progress in governmental, moral and social science. The people of

---

[*] There is no standing army, no state police, or state guards. There is no need for these institutions.

the *New Nation* are comparatively happy. Nearly every-body worked and has work. For many reasons the people do not work very hard. Local communities (colonies) are everywhere self-sustaining. Colossal machinery is no longer in demand. Gigantic corporations are no longer a necessity to combine capital enough to start the great machinery to manufacture what could not be produced on a small scale. There is no further use for these ponderous works. Commodities needful can, in the *era* of the "*New Nation*," be produced in a much smaller way. The monstrous coal-beds became nearly exhausted in running engines, some to the extent of over 10,000 horse-power. The very element, most abundant in the environment of man, hitherto not made to *work* (atmosphere), familiar though with it, unbroken still, wild, but so tame, is applied as a source of motivity in "Dreamland."

**Light-Weight Vehicles.** Light-weight vehicles are propelled by *gravity*, in a manner applied so that the weight of any one riding produces all the force that is necessary, and occasionally rising on your feet gives the reproducing spring a chance to regain the expended force. Other vehicles of various size are propelled by storage electricity, easily regulated and guided. We saw an ingeneous contrivance, running at great speed, simply by a reversible fan standing up over the head of the rider as an air-motor.

We are told that improvements in many departments are still going on. Air-motors, altogether of a different order from anything known before, are in use. Compressed air is in use, in this wonderful land, extensively. Standpipe-reservoirs and water-motors are applied in producing electricity. Electro-motors, water, air and the wind, one way and another, do the work, whenever machinery can be made possible thus to lighten labor.

Railroad trains, street cars, mills, shops and many forms of manufactories and machines used in husbandry, are run by air-motor force, the principles of which *were, for ages,* hidden in the secret recesses of the human brain ; doubtless electricity, atmosphere, water and *gravity-motor* or gravitation, will be the coming *motor-forces* of the world. We were shown many forms, or ways, by which air-motors and wind-fans made air available in the industrial arts. The machinery, generally speaking, is not complicated and easily managed.

We remember, in the "old nation," one hot summer, we spent our vacation on the northern lakes, at Ishpeming and Calumet, compressed air was conducted far down into deep copper mines, which run their drills, and the same air thus used gave the miners *fresh* air to *breathe*. Several of these mines were lighted by electric incandescent light.

**Pneumatic Service.** There is in extensive use a pneumatic-tube mail service between all the larger cities by means of which small packages of mail matter reaches its destination in a few minutes. This is a great improvement over any other known means of interstate communication, save that of the telegraph, which, of course, was available only so far as brief messages would answer the purpose. There exists a perfect net-work of pneumatic service all through the United States, reaching all cities of 5,000 inhabitants and upward. Packages weighing as much as three pounds can be sent with perfect safety and with almost electric speed.

**The Great Falls.** In our reverie through *"Dreamland"* we were shown the wonders of Niagara Falls and its utility. We saw immense electric plants in operation that lighted the city of Buffalo. The falls are lighted. The effect of the scenery by night far exceeds the scene by daylight. There is an electric light-house service on the lake, from Buffalo to Detroit, so vessels sail by night with as much safety as in the day time. Immense factories, within fifty miles of the falls, receive their power as well as their light from the water-power afforded by the Niagara. This power is merely nominal in cost, or else the atmospheric motors would be the source of power even here.

**Model Factories.** Factories everywhere over the state are constructed so as to combine health, comfort and art. Ventilation, warming and reading rooms receive special consideration; sun-lighted bath-rooms, lunch and toilet rooms nicely furnished; every convenience that would add to the enjoyment of the *wage-earners* while performing their task of eight hours' labor. Everywhere sanitary rules are the first of all considerations in constructing factories. Even great machine shops have an aspect which give you the impression that refinement predominates. The working people have a professional air about them which at once impresses you with the idea that labor is receiving its just reward and the former line of *demarkation*, which separated (socially) employer from the employed, is almost entirely obliterated.

**Floating Palace.** We wandered through "Dreamland" with much interest.

There are none very rich and none very poor. People are interested in each other's welfare and give help to the unfortunate. Men and women (it seems) are putting forth every effort in matters of reform and improvement. The sciences are made practical and applied so as to *lighten labor*, lifting all physical weight from the brain that the *intellectual* faculties of man may the better work in unison with the physical brain and hand down to man ways and means by which he can rise to eminence and loftier thoughts and aspirations. The "New Nation" practically demonstrates that as man *rises* intellectually the farther he gets away from the physical, ponderous environment.

**Navigation.** The entire system of navigation in use in "Dreamland" so widely differs from the old methods that accidents are few and the trip by passenger ships is readily made in from three to four days between New York and Liverpool. The ships are constructed of *papier-mache*, aluminum, maleable glass, iron rods and bolts, so that they are entirely fire-proof; double hulls propelled by compressed air. Wind-motors to compress the air, and this, then, is elaborated to run the propelling screws, of which there are three. These ships are 600 to 700 feet long, built in sections, and the hulls are so constructed as to serve for storage of air. The passenger capacity is not more than 500, and only one cabin service.

We were shown that these vessels float in a depth of from 5 to 8 feet of water and cross two waves, which overcomes the heaving and plunging of the vessel, and, having two hulls, obviates also extreme rocking. By the new motor one single item, of carrying many hundred tons of coal, is overcome, and is a great improvement over the "old" and ponderous ships.

*Railroads* and also telegraphs, that are connected with running of trains, are entirely in the hands or management of the government.

*Railroads* are so constructed that there is scarcely a possibility for an accident to occur. There is a passenger road, entirely separated from the freight road. A double track, beside the track for freight trains. No switches connect with the freight road; all switches work with automatic springs, besides every switch is guarded by a sentinel, who is relieved every six hours.

The rails are made of the best of steel—continuous and charged with electricity. This serves as a magnet. The wheels of the coaches are made of *papier-mache*, with a *steel tire;* thus the body of the wheel being a non-conductor of electricity the steel tire is attracted to the rail by the electricity with which the rail is charged, making it thus almost impossible to derail a train, and the greater the speed the greater is the magnetic attraction. Extra rails are placed on either side of the regular track, so if the train does leave the track the rails outside will possibly prevent its going farther. The body of the coach is built of light material, aluminum and *papier-mache.* The entire coach above the wheels does not weigh over a ton and each coach accommodates seventy-five to one hundred passengers. There are coaches for summer use and coaches adapted for winter.

The coaches are warmed and lighted by electricity, generated by the motion of the train. The propelling motor force is derived from air and electric-motor. Each trunk line runs two special fast express trains each way daily between all large cities. Those running between New York and Chicago make the trip in twelve hours. Then there are accommodation trains. There is no dust, making travelling in "*Dreamland*" really a pleasure and absolutely safe and in quick time.

In our rambling visit to the "*New Nation*" we seemed unconscious, still our memory and understanding served us well, and by some unknown law, while in a dream or trance, we passed from the realizing point of existence, in the drama of life, to the vanishing distance of the dissolving view, all of which was so vividly portrayed on our mental *ken*, where all was *real* but *new*.

The bird in the tree against which we were reclining was still discoursing his little song and we realized that we were no longer in "Dreamland."

We felt a deep regret that our vision of the "*New Nation*" could not be materialized and continued there forever.

Those of us who have reached the age of *silvery hair*, and who are beginning to look through the leafless branches of what was once in the green tree, may know that, as we are in the closing scene of the last act, that the curtain must soon drop, and now shall we importune the gods that we may be permitted to return in spirit and look in upon the "*New Nation*" a hundred years hence and enjoy ourselves, even with a people who are most prosperous and happy?

> " If solid happiness we prize,
>     Within our breast this jewel lies,
>   And they are fools who roam :
>     The world has nothing to bestow :
>   From our ownselves our joys must flow,
>     And that dear hut, our home."

# BIOGRAPHICAL SKETCHES.

### Plate I.
### I. H. Stearns, M. D.

The Stearns family came to America with Gov. Winthrop, June, 1820. Was born at Mansfield, Mass., June 14, 1825. His boyhood days were spent with his parents on the farm and in attending the common school. While yet quite a youth he mastered civil engineering; was the first to sink artesian wells in the South. Meanwhile all available time was devoted to the study of medicine, in which profession he attained eminence, especially as a surgeon. Was surgeon of the famous 22d Mass. V. I. Was a member of the Mass. Legislature in 1868. For many years was surgeon in charge of the Soldiers' Home in Togus, Maine, and at Milwaukee, Wis. Also U. S. Examining Surgeon for Pensions and Health Commissioner of that city. Is Chaplain of Lynn Post. No. 5, G. A. R., Dept. of Mass. Has been a zealous worker for humanity, contributing both to medical and journalistic literature. Wrote the history of his native state, and ranks to-day with our most noted self-made men.

Dr. Stearns raised a happy family of one son and eight daughters, who are married and doing well. May the years be kind to him, that he may safely land in the harbor of perpetual happiness.

### Plate II.
### Edward Evans.

Born Sept. 14, 1830, Ontario, Canada. His father was of Welsh and Irish descent; his mother was of Irish and German, a combination of the best blood, and doubtless accounts for that never-failing energy Mr. Evans has manifested all through life. At the years of majority he took the side of reform. Helped to overthrow the Tory government. In 1861 he settled in Tonawanda, N. Y. Became an ardent supporter of the Union cause. In 1880 cast his vote for Gen. Garfield, the last in line of that party, being unwilling to support a party, directly or indirectly, that would sanction Monopolies, Trusts and other combinations of Capital against Labor. He also boldly proclaimed his absolute opposition to the liquor traffic. He was unanimously nominated on the Reform ticket, and in 1885 received 308,904 votes for the New York Legislature. In 1889 he wrote that well-known and popular "Address to the American People," calling in conference all good citizens who were opposed to class legislation, and all who favored a government where the rich and poor have equal chances under the law to acquire a competency, to meet and enter upon establishing a National Reform party. The progress of the new movement is well known. Mr. Evans is an historic man of the age, widely known in National Reform and philanthropic movements. He is a wealthy man, is president of Evans, McLaren & Co., bankers. Has employed thousands of workmen in his lumber and timber trade for over forty years. Never had a "strike" to contend with. He was always ready to share with his people, and, with all his liberality and philanthropic work, he gradually became a millionaire, for the "Bread cast upon the waters will return again after many days" verified in the life of our friend and humanitarian.

## Plate III.
## A. Wilford Hall, Ph.D., LL. D.

Was born August 18, 1819, near Bath, Steuben County, N. Y. His father distinguished himself at the battle of Lundy's Lane under General Scott in the war of 1812. His boyhood days were spent on the farm and much of that time he was driver-boy on the Erie Canal. He early emigrated to Ohio, where, by his own energy, he rose gradually to eminence. Science and philosophy were his choice. His first work of note is entitled "Problem of Human Life," which reached a sale of over 100,000 copies. His monthly publication, entitled "The Scientific Arena," has reached a circulation of over 700,000. As a scientist Prof. Hall stands as a peer with such men as Tyndall, Spencer, Hurley, Helmholz and others of like reputation. His new discourse on "Sound" and others of nature's hidden principles of the elements will give the hero of our imperfect sketch a place in the world's history, as well as a place in the hearts of mankind, as a humanitarian and philanthropist of greatness that makes us proud of the human race. The wage-workers of America have a zealous co-worker in Prof. Hall in all that is right and demands reform for the progress and welfare of mankind—a man who rose from a farmer's boy to a sage in the highest attainments in science and philosophy.

## Plate IV.
## Fig. 1.—John Wanamaker.

Ex-Postmaster General; his administration was a brilliant success. He conducts a great general store in Philadelphia, Pa.; employs over 5,000 people and shares profits with them. He is a true philanthropist, an able business man and statesman, and, if nominated, will be our next President.

## Fig 2.—Frances E. Willard.

Has passed the half-century post in good condition; is mistress of the platform; has lectured and written in the interest of the wage-workers of America more than any other woman, devoting the greater part of her life to reform and the elevation of mankind.

## Fig. 3.—Hon. Daniel Hand.

Is a self made man: is widely known in the South as a generous and successful business man and philanthropist. He donated $1,000,000 for the education of negro children.

**Fig. 4.—Richard M. Hunt.** The architect of the World's fair at Chicago, Ill.

**Plate V.**
**C. G. Conn.** Has passed over on the shady side of life, yet in a good condition, and hence has many useful years before him. He rose in the world by his own endeavor, gradually built up a world-wide reputation as a man of honor and a genius in his line. He has also acquired a good fortune, and being endowed with a congenial disposition he is qualified to enjoy it. Mr. Conn never had to contend with strikes, for he is kind to his people, shares profits, and takes as much pleasure to see his employees get on well in the world as himself. He does not look out for cheaper labor, but is satisfied and glad to keep his old hands, though they may cost him more. He has the largest band instrument factory in the world. He makes the best instruments that are made. His trade extends to all parts of the world wherever band music is heard. Mr. Conn is widely known, and through his inventions and improvements *band music* is as far superior to that of fifty years ago as the electric light over the farmer's tallow dip. He is a humanitarian as well as a philanthropist. His factories are at Elkheart, Ind., and Worcester, Mass.

**Plate VI.**
**Fig. 1.—Ben Tillett.** A well-known labor leader.

**Fig. 2.—Isaiah V. Williamson.** Donated all his wealth to *found* an Industrial Training School for Boys, Philadelphia, Pa.

**Fig. 3.—J. H. Stead.** Editor of *Pall Mall Gazette.*

**Fig. 4.—Florence Nightingale.** England's philanthropist.

**Plate VII.**
**Frank P. Sargent.** Grand Master of the Brotherhood of Locomotive Firemen; a man eminent; widely known; the child of nature and the man of the hour; is of the people and labors for the welfare of his fellow workmen.

**Plate VIII.**
**Fig. 1.—Helen H. Gardener.** Is a lady of middle age and already has shaken the social world. Her life is devoted to reform; the establishment of laws that will give all peoples an equal chance for "life, liberty and the pursuit of happiness." Her last book, entitled *"Pray You, Sir, Is This Your Daughter?"* and *"Is This Your Son, My Lord?"* published by the *Arena Publishing Co., Boston, Mass.* The sale of these books *has been unprecedented.*

**Fig. 2.—Hamlin Garland.** *"A Son of the Prairie."* He delineates its life faithfully, powerfully.—*San Francisco Chronicle.* " Is fresh, vigorous and original ; leaped into fame ; promises as much as any cotemporary American writer."—*Toronto Globe.* He shows the apparent hopeless position of the wage-earners of to-day a way out.

His works are published by the Arena Publishing Co., Boston, Mass.

**Fig. 3.—Rev. Minot J. Savage.** Is yet in the prime of life and all the space we have at our command is simply to say that the hero of our sketch has reached popularity with such as Beecher, Theo. Parker, Lyman Abbott, and in point of reform and help of the wage-earners' cause, as well as a correct reconciliation of *Capital* to Labor, law and order and good American government, he stands to-day unequalled. His writings are extensive, national, humane and philanthropic ; a character grand, great, honorable and cosmopolitan.

**Fig. 4.—B. O. Flower.** Is a man yet in the prime of life, of unbounded energy and a worker for humanity. Editor of "*The Arena,*" a popular monthly magazine devoted to literature, science and reform. He is author of many works. Notable among them is his "Civilization Inferno," "Studies in the Social Cellar," etc.; should be read by everybody. Published by the *Arena Publishing Co*, *Boston, Mass.*

**Plate IX.**
**Fig. 1.—Christ Evans.** Secretary of American Federation of Labor.

**Fig. 2.—Hon. Joseph N. Dolph.** Senator, of Portland, Oregon. He worked his way up from the farm to law and Congress.

**Fig. 3.—Mrs. Potter Palmer.** Ladies' Board of Managers World's Fair. Is eminently a superior woman ; a true reformer; a leader in whatever channel she moves.

**Fig. 4.—Rev. Lyman Abbott, D. D., Ph.D.** A famous preacher and author.

**Plate X. Gen. Russell N. Alger.** Ex-Commander of G. A. R.

**Plate XI.**
**Fig. 1.—G. M. Pullman.** President Palace Car Company.

**Fig. 2.—P. M. Arthur.** Grand Master Brotherhood of Locomotive Engineers.

**Fig. 3.—Mrs. Margaret Gibson.** Is Factory Inspector of New York.

**Fig. 4.—John P. Haines.** President of the American Society for the Prevention of Cruelty to Animals.

**Plate XII.**
**General James B. Weaver.** Presidential candidate of the People's Party, 1892.

**Plate XIII.**
**Hon. Walter Q. Gresham.** Secretary of State under President Grover Cleveland's Administration. His second term.

**Plate XIV.**
**Hon. William B. Allison.** Senator from Iowa. Eminent, proficient and philanthropic. He is the most popular among the people who know him best.

**Plate XV.**
**Hon. John Griffin Carlisle.** Secretary of the Treasury under Grover Cleveland's second term as President of the U. S. of A.

**Plate XVI.**
**Fig. 1.—Andrew Carnegie.** The wealthiest iron manufacturer in America, and perhaps in the world. He rose from a poor boy, whose father was a potter, in Scotland. He first attained telegraphy, then to an iron manufacturer. He never had any trouble with his people until he allowed his factories to pass under the management of unprincipled capitalists.

**Fig. 2.—Joseph Howard.** Celebrated journalist and philanthropist.

**Fig. 3.—W. H. Bailey.** Executive Board, K. of L.

**Fig. 4.—Mrs. Leonora M. Barry.** Organizer of Woman's Branch of the Knights of Labor. President and ex-member of Executive Board of K. of L.

---

# TABLE OF CONTENTS.

## THE WAGE-WORKERS OF AMERICA.